MORGUE
DRAWER
NEXT DOOR

MORGUE DRAWER NEXT DOOR

Jutta Profijt

TRANSLATED BY Erik J. Macki

amazon crossing

Morgue Drawer Next Door by Jutta Profijt was first published in 2009 by
Deutscher Taschenbuch Verlag GmbH & Co. KG in Munich, Germany,
as *Im Kühlfach nebenan*.

Translated from the German by Erik J. Macki.
First published in English in 2012 by AmazonCrossing.

Published by AmazonCrossing
P.O. Box 400818
Las Vegas, NV 89140

ISBN-13: 9781611090406
ISBN-10: 1611090407
Library of Congress Control Number: 2012934470

PROLOGUE

I'm going to start this account with an incident that occurred before the plot of this book even began. My editor explained this is typical for a prologue, and she jabbered something about structure, dynamics, the arc of suspense, and loads of literary lingo like that. The woman totally geeks out about her field of expertise, and I guess a prologue won't hurt me, so I'll just go along with it so I can have some peace and quiet around here. That's how you deal with women.

OK, so this is about an incident that I had absolutely no clue about back when it occurred. And even if I had, I couldn't have cared less. But at the time, of course, I couldn't have known that my life would be veering back into crash-dummy mode.

The incident I'm talking about was a fire. That's not so unusual, you may be thinking, but there you're wrong. Because, first, this fire broke out in a convent originally built in the Middle Ages; second, it happened in the annex where the nuns ran their homeless shelter; and, third, the fire resulted in my getting to know Marlene. But I'll get to her later.

So on the aforementioned evening there were no homeless people sleeping in the annex because a new heating system was being installed. The nuns' old gas furnace, which served up tropical temperatures to one corner of the annex but a barely tepid breeze to another—and stuffy air everywhere—was going to be replaced with some modern, energy-efficient equipment. New heating pipes, installed at low cost along the surface of the wall, led to window alcoves where radiators were going to be installed.

The fire broke out around three in the morning. It destroyed the annex, but that was no great loss to the history of art and architecture since it had been built in the nineteen fifties and looked that way, too—hideous as hell.

Actually, no one should have been in there at all during construction since the bums were being temporarily requartered. Nonetheless, after their blaze-snuffing operation, the fire department found a charred corpse in the smoking ruins. And a second person was seriously injured when she was caught standing with a bucket of water in front of the decrepit exterior door. A gas explosion blasted it off its hinges, striking the amateur firewoman with both the aforementioned door and the fireball that followed.

The charred corpse found its way into Morgue Drawer Number Five at the Institute for Forensic Medicine at the University of Cologne, while the critically burned woman arrived at the same hospital where Martin had been admitted after his stabbing. And that's how everything began.

ONE

I've always hated hospitals, and I still hate them even now, and I hated this one in particular. Not that I wasn't grateful to the people who saved Martin, since I was responsible for his near murder. But the same equipment that helped save Martin's life—namely the medical facility's ultramodern, electronic apparatuses—was making my life hell.

For those who don't know me yet, I should probably clarify who you're dealing with. My name is Pascha Lerchenberg. I used to be a gifted car thief who was murdered in the deep freeze of February this past year at the tender age of twenty-four. My soul departed my body but didn't find that tunnel with the light, and I've been moldering around here ever since. With Martin.

Martin Gänsewein is the forensic pathologist who autopsied my remains. Or dissected, if you prefer that term. Either way it means he disemboweled me, the way a hunter does a wild sow, to examine everything up close, and then he stuffed my organs back into my abdominal cavity and sewed me shut with crude sutures. In the course of investigating my murder, Martin got stabbed, but the doctors were able to revive him, unlike me, and that's why he was here in the hospital, almost ready to be discharged, when Marlene came into my life.

"Martin!" I shouted with relief.

At last he had emerged from the hospital room where he had been spending most of his time. Even though the doctors had been telling him for a week that he should stand up more often, maybe take a walk alone through the hospital grounds, Martin preferred the intimacy of his hospital room. Not because he was averse to appearing in public in his fleecy pajamas wrapped in his terrycloth robe with his genuine-wool, moose-pattern slippers. No, he utterly lacks self-awareness, when it comes to fashion at least, and he has no sense of embarrassment. The real reason Martin preferred the hospital room was because the remote alarm in there that triggers a code blue was highly sensitive and went off if there were any strong electromagnetic waves. And electromagnetic waves are what I am made of. So I had to be careful about the comments I made or emotional outbursts I had in his room—when I could risk entering at all. And that was fine with Martin.

I had divided my time over the previous few weeks between the hospital and Martin's workplace, the Institute for Forensic Medicine. Neither thrilled me. Martin's hospital room was depressing and technologically hazardous, whereas the Institute for Forensic Medicine was boring, since I couldn't communicate with anyone there. That didn't stop me from trying to communicate with Martin's hot colleague, Katrin, whispering hormonally motivated compliments down her knocker knoll, but she wasn't picking up my transmissions at all. Martin was and remains the only person I can communicate with.

"So when are we going home?" I asked.

"Monday," he replied tersely.

"And when are you going back to work?"

"Tuesday, if everything goes well. Or Wednesday."

That was good news, and it appeased me, so I left Martin alone and whooshed through the corridors toward the pediatric ward. Fidgetylipp the Clown was scheduled to appear there at eleven o'clock. He came every week to cheer up the short shots. Whenever the weather was nice and he could perform on the lawn in front of the building, he would bring his rabbit with him too, although last week it had bitten his finger. I was curious to see whether his future Russian hat of a pet had been forgiven its sin or been braised, seasoned, and chased down with dumplings by a clown who had less of a sense of fun at home than on stage.

The shortest way to the pediatric ward is past the hospital chapel, which is how I ended up being totally broadsided by the plumes of incense. Actually, I've washed my hands of chapels, churches, and the Good Lord himself since being stiffed by the Dude with a capital D. He might have at least gotten in touch at some point since my demise! But in point of fact he has not, so his existence seems even less likely to me now than it already had for the majority of my short life.

But I do like incense. It reminds me of Christmas with my Gran, who, unlike my parents, didn't used to just give me socks, scratchy wool sweaters, or pointy-headed physics books but also R2-D2 action figures and James Bond cars. The kind with the moving parts. Plus, she liked me and I liked her, and in our family that was pretty frigging far-out. So I lingered for a second. I still had some time before eleven o'clock, so I followed my childhood memory and floated into the chapel. A statue of the hospital's patron saint was adorned with flowers; today must be her saint's day. Hence the incense. I was enjoying the Catholic version of a doobie and sliding into the sentimentality of early childhood when it hit me.

I was not alone.

One glance around was enough to establish that no one was sitting in the six wooden pews. The chapel had no confessional or other dark corners where someone could have been hiding. And yet someone was there. And that someone was praying.

"Hail Mary, full of grace . . ."

I shivered, much like the candle flames that were flickering in the draft and casting eerie shadows on the walls.

". . . our Lord is with thee. Blessed art thou among women . . ."

Hmm. That's actually not the worst pickup line.

". . . and blessed is the fruit of thy womb."

Loom? What, are they selling underpants in here or something? I snickered. The prayer ended abruptly.

". . . ?"

Yeah, yeah, I know . . . My editor says that a few periods and a question mark don't properly contribute to the reader's understanding too. Incidentally, an editor is sort of like a German teacher who marks up all the mistakes in your essay in red. So with a book, the editor is allowed to put big circles around mistakes, carefully write comments in the margins, and delete four-letter words. Or pick a petty fight about direct speech that doesn't contain any speech, just a question mark. But I refused to cave on this point because the waves I got were exactly like what I wrote above. No words, not even a clear "huh?"—just a solitary, frazzled, speechless question. Now the perfect punctuational device to articulate my *own* emotional befuddlement would have been a mob of exclamation points, but these have fallen victim to the red pen of my inexorable editor as well.

How to express the chaos I felt in my skull? Since my death I hadn't met a single other soul still hanging out here in the sublunary realms. No idea where all the souls are, but they're not here, at any rate. Two or three times I've crossed paths with a soul that was just leaving its earthly husk. My first encounter of this type was with Martin's soul when he was almost stabbed to death. Luckily, I was able to persuade Martin the Ghost to stay with Martin the Body, and then the paramedics arrived and started doing CPR like crazy, thereby luring his little soul to return to its rightful place. And here in the hospital I'd encountered two souls that were just making their getaway. Where to? No clue. They were in a pretty frigging big rush and just whooshed past me. So this unexpected encounter in the chapel hit me like a head-on collision.

"Hi, I'm Pascha."

Now, during livelier times I would never have been the first to introduce myself. If you want to be cool, and everyone except Martin does, you shut it, shoot fierce glares out of your headlights, and let others come to you first. But when you're a ghost—or, for the scientists out there, an "electromagnetic anomaly" (as Martin is in the habit of saying)—then you can't give people fierce glares, and your remaining options for communicating with other people are extremely limited. So I felt out of practice. And soft. And lonely. Which is why the uncool verbal bootlicking just kind of slipped out of me. Way embarrassing. Had I had a tongue, I'd have bitten it now—because no one should be *that* uncool, even as a ghost.

"I'm Sister Marlene of the Charitable Sisters of Saint Mary Magdalene."

I had to sort out all this sister drivel first before I got who was hovering there in front of me: this cookie was a nun! I couldn't fathom my bad luck. Or was it some lame-ass trick staged by the Good Lord, to whom I'd been politely praying for proof of his Almighty Existence and conveying my preference for a pretty female to work with instead of Martin. If possible, one with a hot chassis, big hooters, and tons of power under the hood. And the Joker sends me a penguin?

"Has the Good Lord sent you?" I asked with an accordingly low level of enthusiasm.

"The Lord guides all our steps," was her cryptic response.

Oh, right. That was their ploy. Never pin anything down. Why is there poverty and misery in the world? The Lord works in mysterious ways. How can God allow wars? The Lord works in mysterious ways. Why is Pascha hanging around on earth as a ghost while all the other souls are off enjoying themselves somewhere else? In paradise, for example? Or in heaven? (Not necessarily the same thing, by the way.) Once again, God's ways are mysterious.

"What is upsetting you so?" asked the sister of the Sisters of the Saintly Sister as she slowly took form before my mind's eye: around fifty, short, pretty fat. More meat than heat. Still, she blinked at me with friendly, dark-brown eyes behind old-fashioned eyeglass rims.

"Nothing," I grumbled.

"You've been hoping for company—but not mine," she said.

Really uncool when a chick can see into your attic. The whole world knows what can be found in any guy's head;

ultimately all of us—except for Martin, of course—are thinking about only one thing. But anytime you actually get caught, then there's high drama.

I didn't respond.

"Well, I'm sorry I'm not the one you were expecting."

Huh? No dressing-down about impure thoughts? No outrage over the fixation on big hooters, sexy chassis, and so on? Ugh, that was even worse. People who are fabric-softener soft and gentle, people who radiate compassion really get on my nerves. God, that unctuous, Botox-y smile with the rapt expression used to make me puke when I was on earth, but then I used to pretty much steer clear of anything in a priest's collar or habit. But here? I tried to make a discreet retreat toward the door and the kids' clown.

"Did you just—die here?" the nun asked.

"Nah. I've been dead for a couple of weeks."

I could feel her trying to integrate this information into her worldview, but it fit as well as an air dam on a low-floor articulated bus. She was obviously more recently deceased than I. I could relate to her confusion. In the beginning I'd found the whole situation fairly opaque.

"Are there other . . . ?"

"I've seen a couple of souls fly by so far, at their moment of death," I said. I felt dizzy, like whiplash or something, recalling Martin's soul suddenly rising over his body. "But none that stuck around. And I've got to admit, I wasn't counting on running into another one. And certainly not a nun."

"Why 'certainly not a nun'?"

Could this Sister Marlene really not grasp anything, or was she just acting like a dumbass? I mean, wasn't it obvious?

But fine. It's not like I was in a major rush, so I explained my own worldview to her.

"Nuns are kind of supposed to get a first-class express ticket to heaven, like priests and popes, right?"

She didn't say anything.

Then a thought occurred to me. "Or did you do something naughty? Something totally disgusting?"

"No."

Again no outrage, no passion, just a well-meaning no. Ugh. Was this Holy Roller operating on the horsepower of a folding scooter or what?

"I've got it!" I said. "You killed yourself. Suicide is a big no-no for you, uh, habit types, right?"

"I died in a fire," she explained in a friendly and relaxed tone.

"Did you set it yourself? Closet smoker?"

"It broke out in a construction site at our convent. In the annex under my room. I could smell the smoke coming into my open window, so I went downstairs to see what was happening in the annex, and . . . well, I never made it out."

"Why not? What happened?"

"The door closed."

"Closed? You mean behind you?"

"Yes. And locked."

"You went into a burning room and locked the door behind you?"

"Someone else locked the door."

I was speechless. The friendly nun was so calm, pouring out her soul (!) about someone trapping her in a burning room. Could it have been one of her sister nuns . . . ?

"No," she said emphatically, interrupting my train of thought. "The annex has no door connecting directly to the convent, so you have to go outdoors to enter it. Which means *anyone* could have closed the door behind me."

"Anyone who happened to be sneaking around there at night and had the key," I said.

"The key was in a little box next to the door because the new heating system was going to be delivered the next day. And the construction workers usually come while we're at matins."

A whole series of questions shot through my electron cloud, but there was no way I could ask them all at the same time, so I pulled out the one that seemed the most obvious at the moment. "And what are you doing here now in the hospital?"

"Sister Martha also noticed the fire. She tried to extinguish it and was severely burned. She's here, in the ICU."

"Oh."

My dismay was genuine and oceanically deep. I've always been terrified of burning to death. It was a true phobia, originating from a news broadcast in the late nineteen eighties that showed graphic images of a burning building. I must have been three or four at the time and should have been in bed long before that, but I couldn't sleep and snuck into the living room to find my parents sitting in front of the tube. The images of burned and burning victims shocked me so much that I started to cry.

"Oh, my poor boy!" my mother said, pulling me up onto her lap.

"If you don't pipe down and go to sleep, that's how you're going to end up too," my father said.

I didn't sleep that night, or the next twelve nights, but I didn't dare bug my parents anymore. Ever since then, my relationships with open flames and with my father have been unequivocally strained.

"Is she going to make it?" I asked.

"It's not looking good."

Suddenly Sister Marlene didn't sound that calm anymore.

"She has burns over seventy percent of her body. So it would probably be better if the Lord called her home . . ."

Marlene broke off, probably because it had just clicked for her what I also spontaneously thought: where *was* this Lord who, in Marlene's worldview, should be calling *her* home as well? The bastard still hadn't put in an appearance in her case, so why would he be attending to dear Martha?

"He probably set everything up so that I can stay with Martha until her fate is decided," Marlene declared with conviction. "Whatever happens to me or Martha, it's God's will."

Well, duh. Let the sanctimonious nun go ahead and believe whatever floats her boat. As long as she doesn't try to convert me.

"What's the status of the investigation?" I asked to bypass all the holy talk and get back onto solid ground.

"Investigation?" she echoed, a little distracted and rather indifferent.

"Yes, investigation. What was the cause of the fire? Was it negligence on site or arson? And who closed the door behind you? Any evidence? Forensics? Suspects? Maybe Sister Martha saw something when she was trying to extinguish the fire?"

"The earthly conviction and punishment of a poor, misguided soul is no longer relevant to me. In the end, heavenly justice will prevail."

If I'd still possessed a hand and a forehead, I'd have smacked the former against the latter. This much pigheadedness in the face of an obvious murder, possible arson, and a half-charred witness got me boiling like engine coolant at a desert rally.

"First of all, the thing about heavenly justice, given the unproven existence of the Judge, is that it's a little doubtful; second, your sisters who are still at the convent might be in danger as long as somebody is lurking around looking for satisfaction through pyromasturbation."

Marlene didn't react, though she was clearly troubled.

"I'll repeat my question: what do you know about the status of the investigation?"

"Nothing."

This time she sounded unambiguously sheepish. *Good.* "Then let's find out if your sister knows anything."

At first Marlene wanted to object, but she shut her trap, beaming a quick prayer at the saint's statue in the chapel as we zoomed off together. Along the way we passed over the head of the clown, who had arrived without his furry sidekick after all. I refrained from joking about his braised buddy, though this was hard for me.

"Have you been here before?" I asked as we arrived at the ICU.

Marlene said no.

"Well, you've got to be careful," I tried to explain to her. "Keep your thoughts together as well as you can, and don't look at the equipment close up, and above all: stay absolutely cool. Showing any emotion is strictly prohibited."

I wasn't getting the impression she was listening to me attentively. To the contrary. She was jittery like a virgin before the momentous night and could hardly wait for me to finish my admonitions and then whooshed at unholy speed through the crack in the door and directly into her sister's room.

I hurried to catch up.

"That's her," Marlene whispered, trembling.

This is how the Egyptian mummies must have looked when they were very freshly wrapped. My old anxieties vis-à-vis fire victims hit me like a gravel truck on a down slope, but I fought them back with a vengeance. After all, in my condition there's absolutely no reason to fear anything that affects physical well-being. Or, more simply: I can't singe the hair on my balls anymore because they've been rotting for a few weeks now, along with the rest of my former physical glory, about two meters underground inside a shiny black casket.

"Oh dear, my poor little Martha," Marlene whispered.

"Careful . . ." I tried to warn her, but by then it was already too late.

The alarms on the equipment monitoring the vital functions of poor little Martha all started piercing, beeping, and buzzing at the same time. The EKG, EEG, blood pressure, and pulse all seemed to be going crazy. It took exactly three and a half seconds for the orderly to arrive, another twenty seconds for the nurse, and only slightly longer for a doctor to enter the room. They all bent over the patient, madly checking the white bandages, then staring first at the equipment and back to the mummy. Finally they shot puzzled looks at each other. Except for the doctor, of course. He didn't look questioning so much as accusing.

"What did you do?" he barked at the pimply orderly.

"Nothing," he said, defending himself. "The alarm went off when no one was in the room."

Of course that was bullshit, but there was no way for the poor mummy warden to know that. I cleared Marlene out of the room and took up position with her outside the window, peering into Martha's room so that we could follow the events inside.

"Did we do that?" Marlene asked.

We? Ha! Hadn't I warned her in advance? I for one had not caused interference with any of the equipment, I was very sure about that. During the weeks Martin had spent in the ICU, my observance of absolute radio silence had become second nature. Well, OK. There had been a couple of slip-ups. For example, the time when Martin finally woke up from anesthesia and reported back among the living with the, for him, totally atypical words "fuck off." At the time I really couldn't control myself and got pretty mad. The code-blue alarms that I triggered summoned all the staff nurses and three doctors to his room. After that I got more careful, but two more unplanned incidents occurred nonetheless. After my most recent ghost alarm—as the resolute nurse unknowingly but aptly termed the unfounded scares—the hospital had swapped out all of Martin's monitoring machines for new equipment.

At least today it wasn't my fault.

"You seriously have to hold back like when you're . . ." *Not supposed to come yet,* is what I wanted to say, but I had not only a woman in front of me but also a nun. How was she supposed to know what I meant by that?

"Just keep all of your thoughts and emotions to yourself," I said finally, hoping that she got it.

"But how can I communicate with Martha, then?" she asked, confused.

Hell, the dreaded moment of truth.

"You might not be able to. At all," I said. "I'm only able to communicate with one single person. His name is Martin, and he's in room seventy-three."

Marlene didn't say anything, obviously concerned.

"Were you able to communicate with anyone before Martha came to the hospital?" I asked.

"No."

"Have you tried to at all?"

No clear answer from Marlene. She was staring through the window at the doctor and the two nurses, who had calmed down in the meantime but were still gaping at the equipment. All the readings had gone back to normal.

"I wasn't worrying about the fate of those left behind," Marlene whispered. "I was busy finding my way to heaven."

Cool, huh. So much for charity, the community of nuns, and all that holy mumbo jumbo. When it really comes down to it, even a fat little nun wants to be the first in line at the gates of heaven. Of course it had been just the same with me, but when I was alive I was a career criminal, not some God-fearing monk. No one expected me to somehow behave properly—and I didn't either.

"What do we do now?" Marlene asked.

OK, I'll admit it: I felt sorry for the nun. I already mentioned how I'd gone soft. Plus, I was bored to death, and it's a hellishly frightening kind of torture when you can't even die to escape the boredom. But here was the ultimate change of pace. A murder case. With a completely spiritualized nun (nice wording, eh?) and a chance to finally think about something other than blood tests, heparin injections, and Martin's fleecy pajamas. So I did not abandon Marlene and her bad conscience but instead laid my arm over her shoulders, figuratively speaking, and said: "Come on. I'll introduce you to Martin."

Martin was in one of the sitting areas at the end of the hallway down from his room. He didn't have either his pajamas or his bathrobe on. He had slid his scraggy legs into some track pants that, based on their color, must have last been in style in the late eighties or early nineties. They were turquoise blue with purple piping. The likewise much-shrunken upper torso of the former chubbo was enveloped in a cardigan that my Gran would have called a *Wöbche* in her heavy Cologne dialect. No one knows what that term actually means, but items of clothing described with it look the way the word sounds: somehow warm, somehow fluffy, and beyond dorky. At least the color was a fairly subdued dark red, which in itself was all right. But together with those pants, of course, it was a psychedelic puke pill.

"This man is our only hope," I said, funereally.

Marlene cringed but pulled herself together quickly. "He looks very nice."

"Nice" is one way to say it, I thought, and had to grin. There is no more scathing way to judge a man. "Mother-in-law's favorite" is another way of saying it, as is "understanding." Real men are different. Which should make clear what Martin is not.

"And the woman at his side is Birgit," I added with emphatic coolness.

Birgit was looking effervescent as always. Outside this bedpan bunker, in the real world, springtime had settled in, and Birgit was wearing a light-blue linen suit with a white blouse. The fabric of the blouse was embroidered with an openwork design that would have made any other woman look dumpy, but not her. To the contrary. All the tiny holes let just a touch of lace shimmer through, softly rounded and perky in the right spots with . . .

"Manners!" the nun said, interrupting my ruminations.

Just what I needed. A has-been nun trying to censor the most intimate thoughts inside *my* head.

"That's none of your business," I snapped.

Marlene didn't say anything. In a disapproving way. Which took all the fun out of slowly penetrating the blouse's delicate pattern. I sighed and withdrew to the ceiling light.

Martin and Birgit were holding hands and cooing. I had seen my fill of that the past few weeks. OK, in a shared hospital room it's not exactly easy to organize a truly intimate visiting hour, but some chump change would surely have kept each of his three previous roommates busy for a while in the cafeteria. But that idea never occurred to Martin. Other men don't even need a bed; a broom closet is plenty for them to get more closely acquainted with someone. Martin, by contrast, had been holding hands for five weeks. With sweaty palms, knowing him. Yet Birgit persistently returned to this palace of pestilence to rest her beautiful and undoubtedly strong hands in his clammy mitts. The woman was a saint. A veritable Mother Teresa. But a damned hot Mother Teresa.

"Hi, Martin. Allow me to introduce you to Sister Marlene of the Chewable Sisters of Saint Mary Magdalene," I announced.

"What?" Martin thought, startled.

"Just a moment!" Marlene yelled.

I giggled. I hadn't even cut the joke on purpose, but its effect had the striking force of an armored Hummer. Martin stammered out an incoherent answer to Birgit's question about what they'd served him for breakfast today, while Marlene projected a surging wave of politically correct outrage.

"Your insults are of relatively little importance to me personally," said Marlene, "but dragging the order through the mud with your comments is going too far. Even for me."

"I thought we'd agreed that you would leave me alone whenever Birgit's here," Martin mentally snarled at me.

"Should I get us a slice of cake and some hot chocolate from the cafeteria?" Birgit asked.

Martin didn't like the cafeteria because it was too noisy. And he didn't drink coffee because caffeine increases your blood pressure and damages your stomach and has myriad other toxic effects from which, unfathomably, the rest of humanity has been dying wretched deaths for centuries.

"That would be really great," he said, and Birgit walked off in hip-swaying steps.

I made a second attempt at introductions, this time in an appropriately boring register.

"What does that mean?" Martin asked. "Where is this Sister Marlene?"

Something awful dawned on me.

"Can't you hear her?" I asked.

Martin shook his head.

"And you, Marlene? Can you hear Martin's thoughts?"

"Thoughts? No, I can hear him only when he speaks."

"She's here with me," I said.

Martin grew pale. He clenched his trembling hands together.

"She was murdered. One of her convent sisters is in the ICU with the worst possible burns. Martin, we've got to help her."

"She's . . . ?" he started, but his voice failed him.

"A ghost like me, yeah."

Martin took on the coloration of an albino salamander. "Pascha, I don't want to know about other ghosts. I don't actually even want to know about you. Why hasn't your soul finally found peace now that we've solved your murder?"

"We might pose that question to our lovely expert here," I replied with irritation and quickly conveyed the question to Marlene.

Martin and I had argued over this topic now more than once. But I didn't know the answer myself. Naturally, at the time I also thought I would find my way through the tunnel into the light as soon as we caught my murderer. My dear departed soul was going to find peace, and I'd be out of here, off to paradise, and everyone was going to be happy and content. The hope of this was the only thing that persuaded Martin to help me at all during my investigation. We were totally bummed when we realized—even though Martin had solved both my murder and the other deaths related to it—that nothing had changed in my stuck-between-worlds condition. I was still hanging around here.

"That's not something I know anything about," Marlene said.

"That's not something she knows anything about," I said to Martin.

We were in for a fun time if I was going to have to interpret every word between these two.

"Surely the police have opened an investigation already," Martin parried.

"We should look into it," I suggested. My faith in the cops was not as rock solid as Martin's, even though I had to admit Martin's detective buddy Gregor wasn't a bad guy.

First, I passed on what I knew so far to Martin. He was acting like he was on drugs. He wasn't listening properly at all, and he kept glancing back down the corridor, hoping Birgit would finally come back. Which she did, right on cue.

"Apple torte or chocolate cake?" she asked with a sweet smile.

Martin of course chose the fruit.

"Say, have you heard about a fire at the convent of the Charitable Sisters of Saint Mary Magdalene?" Martin asked with forced casualness. Casualness is something that stands in the most starkly conceivable contrast to Martin's fabric-softener-soft nature; his deliberately casual body language was therefore more reminiscent of a bunny rabbit being lifted by its ears trying to squirm out of the grip.

"Yes, isn't it awful?" said Birgit. "One nun died and another is severely injured. Who does something like that?"

"Who does what?" Martin asked.

"Sets a fire in a convent."

Marlene reacted with wordless dismay.

Martin looked more relieved. "So they know it was arson? And the police have opened an investigation?" And mentally to me he added: "There you go. No need for me to get involved."

"Well, they're not entirely certain it was arson. It may have been an accident. They were doing some renovation work on the heating system at the convent."

"And what about the victims? Do they know why the one nun died?"

"She was looking for the source of the fire. She must have lost her bearings while she was doing that. In any case, she passed out from smoke inhalation and then burned to death."

"She walked into the fire without a fire extinguisher or water or anything like that?" Martin asked.

"Normally a fire extinguisher is mounted on the wall in the annex because that room is apparently used as a homeless shelter. But because of the renovation they think it wasn't there," Birgit said, clearly quoting newspaper coverage of the fire.

"Oh my goodness!" Marlene said suddenly. "I just remembered something. When I entered the annex, someone disappeared through the door on the other side of the room."

I had a sketchy memory after I was murdered too, actually. I relayed the information to Martin, but he kept quiet.

"I ran after them, but the door was locked. Then I groped back along the wall to the door I'd come through, but it was locked too. Then I passed out."

"Ask Birgit about a pair of locked doors," I prompted Martin.

But before he could open his mouth, Birgit—following up on his earlier question—asked Martin: "Why do you ask? Why are you so interested in the case?"

"The nun who was injured but survived is in the ICU here," he said nervously.

Martin always feels anxious when he has to justify information he's received from me because he can't explain what his source is. Even now that it's been several weeks, he hasn't gotten used to just telling a harmless little white lie. You'd think he'd have learned by now, in a hospital, of all places. You get forced into all kinds of white lies in a hospital. Just say you heard it in the hallway, because in hospitals people talk about anything you can possibly imagine. First and foremost about diseases, of course. Makes sense. The most popular game is Cholesterol Canasta, where the plague patients, vivisection victims, and ambulant biohazard bags try to one-up each other with their hellish blood panels and urine tests. For a long time the undisputed winner was a two-hundred-and-fifty-kilo diabetic with renal insufficiency, fatty liver disease, and food poisoning. The only infection he didn't have was HIV, and he said he was proud of that because AIDS was something "only for queers and losers." Martin had tried to bring him up to date on the statistics, but they bounced off the fatso like water off hot grease (what an appropriate simile, as my editor put it).

Birgit's eyes—because despite my minor thematic digression here, we are still in the middle of the two turtledoves' conversation about the fire at Marlene's convent—dwelled a bit longer and more intently on Martin than should have been necessary to notice the piece of apple torte stuck in the corner of his mouth. Birgit is not stupid. Not in the least.

In fact, she's not only a fox but smart as one too, even though she works at a bank. She was very clearly running through the fact that there were about seven hundred bedpan warmers in this hospital and that Martin had not expressed the least interest in any of them before. So why was he suddenly focused on a scorched nun? But Birgit ranks among those who know when it's better to shut up. So she put on a serious and thoughtful face, suddenly smiled, bent forward, and kissed the crumb from the corner of Martin's mouth.

"Let's not talk about that sad story. Let's think about where we should go out to eat next week to celebrate your getting out of the hospital instead," Birgit suggested. She punched Martin gently in his stomach. "After all, you've got to work on getting some meat back on these ribs."

I would probably have stayed with their conversation, hoping for some fornication fodder, if Marlene hadn't suddenly whooshed off. So although I was torn, I chased after my new kindred spirit back to the hospital chapel.

"Whoever set that fire also locked the door behind me," Marlene murmured. "Did they lock the other door as well? And did they unlock them again afterward so no one would notice?"

"Whatever they did, their plan was successful," I said, adding some fuel to the carburetor to jump-start her interest. "The cops may be looking for an arsonist, but definitely not a murderer. And what they're not looking for they won't find."

Marlene communed for a while with whatever celestial powers remained hidden from me, then came to a decision that made my day: "I can't let it rest. After all, my sisters are in danger as long as the murderer is on the loose."

"That's something I would totally raise a can of beer to," I agreed, "if we had that sort of thing here."

"Well, we could pray together instead," Marlene suggested.

I whooshed off so fast I left the chapel candles flickering in my wake.

TWO

So we didn't spend the night together, Marlene and me. Yes, even disembodied spirits have to spend the night somewhere, although sleep is ruled out due to a lack of the physical prerequisites. We don't release sleeping hormones, and we don't have eyelids to close. We're always awake. Which is beyond crappy. Shortly after my death, when my body was still in Morgue Drawer Four, I used to hover all night next to my mortal shell. But after my funeral, this refuge was taken from me, and my morgue drawer was reoccupied. Ever since then, I've tried all different kinds of abodes. The conference room in the Institute for Forensic Medicine, which has a TV set that Martin would leave on for me. Martin's apartment, either with or without a tube on. The nocturnal streets of the city. Dance clubs, Russian tochkas, and movie theaters. But I've never yet spent a night in a church. Or a hospital chapel. And I was not planning on starting now. Apart from the fact that a church offers no entertainment, the chapel was Marlene's refuge and therefore taboo for me.

Instead I spent the night in the emergency room at Cologne's central trauma center. There's always something interesting happening in the ER, especially on weekends. So my entertainment was taken care of. Plus, there was always the chance that I might encounter a recently deceased person's lingering spirit to talk to. Apart from Marlene. But no other ghosts tonight, as usual.

The next morning I shuffled back to the hospital to see Martin. It was Sunday, and so two things were clear to me. First: Marlene would probably be spending the majority of the day in the chapel, and second: Gregor would show up to see Martin after his visit to the gym. Gregor is Martin's best friend and—considerably more importantly for Marlene and me at the moment—a genuine, true-blue cop. The truest bluest of any *Kriminalhauptkommissar, Kriminaloberkommissar,* or whatever other kind of *Kommissar* in town I've ever heard of.

Gregor came as usual at half past ten, and I left them to their welcoming routine of inquiries regarding health (Gregor), work (Martin), food (Gregor), the latest conquest (Martin), and Birgit (Gregor).

Instead, I zoomed over to fetch Marlene in the chapel.

"Leni, wake up! The cop is here!"

". . . full of grace . . ."

"OK, you're awake, please pardon the interruption, but you still need to come over with me right now!"

". . . art thou among women . . ."

"Hey, the Good Lord already knows that prayer from yesterday, remember? Come on!"

". . . pray for us sinners . . ."

I sent her an electromagnetic squall of indignation.

". . . now and at the hour of our death."

"Amen," I yelled, annoyed. "The hour of your death was a couple of days back, and apparently your intercessor is on vacation, so why don't you treat yourself to a break and focus on the investigation for a while."

"Don't be so impatient," Marlene sighed, but finally she followed me out of her candle-flickering prayer cubby through the fluorescent-flickering passageways to Martin's favorite sitting nook, the same place he'd perched yesterday with Birgit, pigging out on apple torte.

"Hello, Martin. We're here," I said, greeting him with exaggerated formality. I didn't want him to refuse to help us because I'd snuck up on him again.

"So tomorrow's the day?" Gregor was just asking. "Should I pick you up?"

"Aw, yeah!" I hooted. "With handcuffs, squad car, and flashing lights."

"No, thanks," Martin politely answered. "Birgit promised to drive me home."

Gregor made his slightly sarcastic grin, which I like on him. At least he's a guy who occasionally gives off outwardly visible signs of a testosterone-guided mindset among all these modern milquetoasts.

"Say," Martin began cautiously. "What's the story about that convent fire?"

Oh God: the Coca-Cola Holiday Caravan with its twenty-seven thousand Christmas lights and speaker-amped jingle-bell soundtrack would have been less conspicuous than Martin's idea of subtle questioning.

"Why are you interested in that?" Gregor countered in his cop's voice, suddenly suspicious.

"Oh, just that . . ."

The ensuing silence was awful. To appreciate this, you need to know what happened after Martin was stabbed a few weeks ago. Martin Gänsewein, yes, my own little gosling, had been suspected of murder. To get him out of the whole shemozzle I had to avail myself of an ingenious trick. You can read all about it in *Morgue Drawer Four*, incidentally. (And yes, my editor says it's OK to work in a little self-promotion.)

Martin was saved and the real murderer was apprehended, but because of this trick, both Gregor and Martin's cute colleague Katrin had become aware of my existence. So, on the one hand, Gregor and Katrin understood the reason for Martin's weird behavior during the two weeks before the knifing, but on the other hand, it's not like anyone could officially let on what really happened. You just can't write up a report about a cop closing a case with critical help from the Beyond—or an Institute for Forensic Medicine with haunted morgue drawers. Therefore, Gregor and Katrin both agreed to absolute secrecy, and they'd stuck to it ever since.

So with his detective expression on his face, Gregor now scrutinized Martin and repeated his question: "So why are you interested in the fire?"

Martin was stuck in a catch-22. He'd sworn to himself he would never, ever speak again to anyone about my existence—not to mention Marlene's existence. On the other hand, he knew full well that Marlene and I wouldn't leave him alone until he helped us.

"The sister who was burned in the fire is in the ICU here," Martin offered.

Gregor wasn't going to let it go as easily as Birgit. "So what?"

"The other nun burned to death because she was *locked* in the annex."

"Wrong," Gregor replied. "She didn't make it back to the door."

"The door was locked," Martin replied stubbornly.

"No, it wasn't," said Gregor.

"Was the key found?" interjected Marlene.

I repeated the question, and Martin repeated it out loud for Gregor.

"Yes," Gregor said. "In the little box outside the annex door, right where it belonged."

"But it should have been in the door lock," Martin said, to our specifications.

"Says who?"

Martin didn't say anything. He looked as unhappy as if the doctor had just told him he had only two and a half hours to live and had to spend two of those holding perfectly still inside the MRI scanner for one important, final exam.

Then his overcast expression brightened slightly. "Imagine that you wake up overnight because there's a fire. You rush to the annex, pull the key out of its box, open the door, and go in to put the fire out. How likely is it that you'd still have the wherewithal to stick the key back into its little box on the wall?"

Sometimes Martin was really bright. No, actually he's always pretty bright—although his mental capabilities are sensitive to disruption in the presence of ghosts.

Gregor hesitated. "The nuns weren't entirely sure whether the door to the annex had really been locked that evening."

Birgit's arrival saved Martin from the further inquiries—and further skepticism—that Gregor surely had ready in the pipeline. The three of them, with Martin now wearing proper, creased trousers, made their way out to the hospital grounds to enjoy the spring sunshine. Marlene receded back to her chapel, and I decided to keep an eye on things in the ICU in case the poor, burnt mummy cared to make any comments.

Of course the mummy didn't say anything. I made a gentle attempt at communication, which despite my truly galactic caution, triggered another mass alarm of all the monitoring equipment, so I sidelined myself back out in front of the window in the hallway. I couldn't wait for Martin to finally be discharged from the hospital.

Around six I looked for Marlene to talk with her about how to proceed. I found her—surprise!—in the chapel.

"Marlene, we need to sit down and really go through the case systematically. Who might have an interest in harming the convent?"

"Our Father who art in heaven . . ."

"That's nice of you, but I'm not old enough to be your father, nor, as we both very well know, am I in heaven."

". . . hallowed be thy name . . ."

"You can just call me Pascha."

". . . thy kingdom come . . ."

"You wouldn't care for the mess in my pad, Leni. Seriously."

". . . thy will be done . . ."

"Well for once that's a very good idea, so stop with the droning and let's make a plan!"

She took no notice of me at all until after she had reeled off the whole homily, puffed out a couple of intercessions (even for Pascha, that lost soul), and sworn total allegiance to both her good Lord and his holy Church.

"What did you want to know?" she finally asked, quite jovially.

"Who wants to harm your convent?" I repeated, quite graciously.

"Why would anyone want to harm our convent?"

I sighed. "You tell me. What we know already is that someone has tried. We just don't know who, and we don't know why. To find that out we've got to start the investigation. If you have any idea who would have a motive, that would do a lot to help us get started."

I felt like a special education teacher, frankly.

Marlene seemed to be thinking intently. "I can't think of anyone."

"OK, that's not going to work," I explained. "Think about it—with your feet firmly on the ground for once. Who might the hourly pealing of your church bell be pissing off? What bra-burner has been feeling fu—uh, messed around with by you and your sisters' unemancipated humility? Things like that."

"Our bell doesn't chime, and why should a feminist feel we're messing around with her? Really, that's laughable."

I honestly did not feel like laughing; instead I was slowly but surely approaching the point of full-blown exasperation.

"But I think I do know what you mean," Marlene said at last.

I didn't breathe a sigh of relief just yet, out of an abundance of caution, but instead suspiciously awaited whatever was going to come next.

"Well, I've heard some talk about our support services for the needy being a bit of a, well, thorn in the side of a few people."

I was waiting for a more detailed explanation, but instead she mumbled a few intercessions for those people whose hearts were hardened and whom the Good Lord should please bless with his love that they too might love their neighbors. If things continued at this speed, we were still going to be sitting here at Christmas without a single lead and our electrons frazzled from endless prayer. I waited for another moment, but when it got too stupid for me I made a decision.

"If you can't think of anything else, then let's just go take a look at the scene."

The doctors arrived for rounds. Sitting up in bed, Martin got to air out the top of his fleecy pajamas for the last time so the doctors could make sure his stab wound was healing properly, and then he got a friendly handshake and became a free man. He pulled up his creased trousers, which had gotten much too big for him, and slipped on his warm sweater, which I had no doubt he would immediately start sweating like a pig in, and packed his stuff into his bag. He signed the discharge forms, all the nurses gave him a friendly good-bye, and he took the elevator down to the lobby. Marlene and I stayed hot on his heels—finally he was bringing on some actual locomotion. After weeks in this home for the hampered, I was jonesing for a change of scenery. Birgit was waiting for him at the exit. She took his bag, gave him a kiss on the cheek, and pressed a hat into his hand.

The temperature was only slightly cooler outdoors than indoors. Birgit was wearing a summer dress with a linen jacket, but it was warm enough that she had still put down the top to her hella hot BMW convertible—though she was obviously very concerned about the warmth of Martin's ears.

"We've got to head to the convent and ask around a little in that neighborhood," I said, forcing my way back into Martin's mind.

He pretended not to notice me at all.

"Tell Birgit that she's more than welcome to come along if she'll drive us over there."

"Should I take you home directly, or would you like to get some gelato?" Birgit said, breaking into our mental conversation.

When chicks ask a question like that, it's obvious that they are actually the ones who want the gelato, ice cream, or whatever. Martin naturally didn't get this at all, but then he also has practically no experience with living women. So I could already see his wrong answer headed right for me when Marlene abruptly chimed in: "There's a gelato café a hundred meters away from the convent."

I repeated this quickly to Martin. "Got that?" I said, adding: "You *want* to eat gelato!"

Martin suggested this great old gelato place, and Birgit gladly agreed to drive there. But we had to make our way through half of Cologne with Marlene providing directions through me—an exhausting game of Telephone made worse by the fact that Marlene had never had a driver's license. She knew the city only as a pedestrian or bus rider and kept trying to steer us the wrong way down one-way streets or pedestrian walkways. Fairly often she'd say "turn left here," and I'd translate "turn right here," and she'd start griping until she caught on that the pedestrian stairs or bike path to the left might pose a problem for Birgit's Beemer. Finally, though, we managed to guide Birgit, who was the only one unaware of our unique, three-headed navigational system, to the convent.

In the event that you may have noticed I'm not disclosing the exact location and neighborhood of the convent, you're right. Because if there's one thing I cannot stand, it's disaster tourists who go gawking at the suffering of other people, maybe even taking movies of especially dramatic scenes with their digital voyeur lenses and later getting wet panties telling their family and friends how up close to it they had been. Disgusting. Of course my nighttime excursions to the emergency room were something entirely different: I was hoping to meet people like myself there.

Now, my editor is insisting I give the convent's neighborhood a name, so I'm going to invent one and call it "Mariental." That's a totally common German place name, so it's impossible for people to figure out where it actually is. And I picked something neutral-sounding on purpose, even though a city like Cologne with such silly-sounding real neighborhood names as Zollstock ("Yardstick") or Bilderstöckchen ("Little Wayside Shrine") would apparently accept just about anything. But for people who aren't from here, and that includes my editor, it's just easier this way.

So we drove to Mariental and settled in on the patio of a gelato café overlooking the convent grounds. Although I don't really have any idea about churches, convents, and other places made of old rocks, Leni's prayer pit was basically a fossil. The convent was built of the ubiquitous sandstone that even the Romans used in their construction projects whenever they weren't boozing themselves into comas, mincing up barbarians, or fornicating with male slaves. The ruins were slightly elevated, set atop a mini hill. To the right, left, and rear was woods, and the neighborhood that the gelato café was part of sort of thrust through the forest like a thick slice of pie whose tip almost touched the convent.

To the left of the convent was the aforementioned annex, and it was the only ugly thing around. The view from the café centered on the main entrance to the convent's church, which was flanked by two turrets. To the right and left, attached directly to the church, were four immense, two-story convent buildings that, as Marlene explained to me, were arranged in a quadrangle, forming a cloister in the middle.

"Oh, it's so beautiful here," Birgit whispered. "How do you know about this place?"

The question was not entirely unjustified, because Mariental was not really the bright center of the universe, and gelato cafés in front of architecturally stunning backdrops are not among the places Martin usually spent his life. He preferred sojourning in the autopsy room, the university library, or other temples of the bloody and bloodless sciences. He occasionally made forays to flea markets, where he pursued his only personal passion: collecting old city maps.

"This is the convent of the Charitable Sisters of Saint Mary Magdalene," Martin mumbled. "Where they had that fire. You remember . . ."

"Oh." Birgit looked sad. "I wonder how that poor nun is doing."

Martin shrugged and shook his head.

"*Buongiorno, signora, signore.* What can I get for you?" said the smug *Colognese* with his olive-oil curls, who pronounced Italian in a Rhinelander's accent except with a heavily rolled Mediterranean *r*.

"I'd like a banana split, but only with chocolate," Birgit said with her sweetest smile, transforming the unctuous waiter into a tail-wagging puppy dog.

"Do you have chamomile tea?" Martin asked.

The puppy dog vanished. A raised eyebrow at Martin's hat was the only reply.

"Any other tea?"

"Black." Encapsulated within this one word was the totality of possible contempt for males who aren't man enough to drink coffee. Not to mention the hat worn on a warm day.

"Cocoa?"

"*Sì*."

Martin nodded, and Giuseppe, Luigi, or whatever his *mamma* may have named him, nodded and hurried off. Birgit smiled lovingly at Martin, and I wondered again how this wonderful woman could have ended up with such a colossal hormonal defect. I mean, she could definitely have any man she wanted with a normal testosterone level and functioning erectile tissue. But instead she was sitting here with Martin. I've been racking my mind about this for weeks, and I just cannot get my virtual brain around it.

When the waiter returned with gelato and cocoa, I urged Martin to ask him about the convent. We weren't here to have fun, after all.

"Isn't that the convent that recently had the fire?" Martin then politely asked.

"*Sì*, oh, what a tragedy," the waiter lamented theatrically, making the sign of the cross. "Such a cruel fate for those two sisters in our Lord Jesus Christ. One nun is dead, and another was severely burned. *Una tragedia!*" He rolled his eyes toward heaven and signed the cross again.

"People are saying it was arson," Martin said softly.

"Those—people were simply careless," the waiter replied with bottomless contempt in his face and voice. He made a gesture as if he were smoking. "Fall asleep drunk with a cigarette and—boom."

"You mean . . ." Martin said, adding an artificial pause.

"Yes, the vagrants," the waiter said, waving his arms around wildly.

Marlene's outrage swept over me like a wave. "He always greeted me so warmly whenever I walked by here," she whispered to me.

"They're always here—*sempre*—pissing into the planters," he said, pointing at the two large, Mediterranean-looking bushes to the left and right of the entrance. "They pester the guests when they're sitting along there," he continued, pointing at the old stone wall that separated the square the café was on from the convent's little hill, "waiting for the nuns to open up the shelter at night. I don't understand the nuns. They're supposed to be praying for those poor souls, that's their sacred duty. But instead they usher them all over here and make life hard for us. Let me ask you: what's the point? The neighborhood association here has raised it with the city administration before, but the bureaucrats at city hall are happy that the vagrants are hanging out over here and not on Cathedral Square downtown. After this disaster, hopefully the people responsible in their air-conditioned offices are now thinking about it differently."

"Neighborhood association?" Marlene asked, irritated. "I've never heard a thing about that."

The puppy dog turned back into a waiter. He buzzed off in a huff, Birgit's smile evaporating in the wake of his harsh words.

"Wow, what a good neighbor *he* is," she said indignantly. "Do you think he had something to do with the arson?"

Martin shrugged. "I'm sorry to have burdened you with it. I didn't mean to spoil your gelato."

"No problem." Birgit was already smiling again. "Something much worse would have to happen to spoil my gelato. I'm just so happy you're finally out of the hospital." She rested her hand on Martin's knee. "Aren't you happy too?"

"Of course." He attempted a timid smile.

"We're happy too," I explained to him as Marlene kept trying to digest the IED of hatred that the gelato-serving sourpuss had served up. "All right, let's move up a gear here. This neighborhood association is something you're going to have to—"

"Stop!" Martin thought vehemently. "I do not want to hear anything more from you today. I would like to enjoy my first day out of the hospital with Birgit. I'll tend to you again tomorrow."

"I've been waiting longer and more often at your bedside than Birgit has. Now the time has come for you to return the favor some," I grumbled.

"You were waiting at my bedside because you had no idea what else to do when facing such utter boredom," Martin retorted. "We're done now. You've got today off."

"By all means," I said, insulted. "If you can reconcile your conscience with letting down the victims of this horrendous fire just like that . . . Marlene, say something!"

Martin winced noticeably but didn't cave. "Sister Marlene, I'm sorry, but I've got to take care of myself a little bit today."

He thought his apology only because he couldn't say anything out loud to Marlene because of Birgit. I didn't bother to convey his twaddle to her.

"First thing tomorrow morning, seven thirty. Until then there will be radio silence," he demanded again and then turned his full attention to Birgit.

"Well, Marlene, now you see how hard things are when you're dead."

Her feelings were still fluttering back and forth between dismay and anger. And surprise that she had never really given a thought before to the immediate vicinity of the convent.

"Since our cocoa cadet here doesn't care to help us, today we're just going to have to go see how we make out on our own. I think we should take a little tour through your convent."

Marlene composed herself, thought for a moment, and nodded. "But only on condition that you stay with me and don't go running off on your own through the convent."

My goodness, why do women in general and nuns in particular have to be so difficult? Was she afraid I was going to go peeking up the skirts of her sisters when they were on the can? Nothing could interest me less. Although . . . who knows? Maybe there were G-string aficionados among the penguins . . . Well, finding that out would be easy enough at some point. But for an initial tour under Marlene's oversight I was certain I could control myself. So I agreed.

Of course the first thing Marlene did was whoosh right into the church to pray in front of the wooden likeness of her convent's saint. This time no Hail Mary, although the saint's name was Mary. Her full name was Mary Magdalene. Wasn't she the patron saint of prostitutes or something? That made her OK by me.

Marlene finished her prayer relatively chop-chop and gave me a church tour on fast-forward: the chancel, which is the sanctuary with the choir behind it (where for the first time it became clear to me that this kind of choir has nothing to do with a yodeling troupe but is a part of a building); two flanking transepts; a confessional; and an organ loft. An old nun was scurrying around bent over in squeaky crepe-soled shoes, replacing burned-down candle stubs and setting two bouquets of flowers in bulbous vases.

"Magdalena!" Marlene yelled. "Can you hear me?"

The old woman turned around, lowered her head, and made the sign of the cross.

"She can hear you!" I exclaimed.

The old woman folded her hands in front of her chest and then walked on, unperturbed.

"No, she bows her head only before the Lord," Marlene said, disappointed.

The old woman kept scurrying around, bending over, and crossing herself anytime she passed the altar. I was slowly getting creeped out by all the saintliness, so I urged Marlene to show me the rest of the convent.

We whizzed down a seemingly endless corridor on the ground floor that had various doors leading off of it, but only to the right. On the left you could see through little windows out into the cloister.

"Along here are various rooms that used to be used as workshops," Marlene explained. "A chandlery, embroidery and sewing workshops, and so forth. Today they serve as storage rooms, housekeeping rooms, laundry rooms, ironing rooms . . ."

I followed along, not interrupting.

"Right over here are the rooms where the sisters sleep," Marlene said as she zipped down a stairwell without slowing, "and everything in the wing on the other side of the church is the mirror image of the rooms on this side."

"How many bedrooms are there?" I asked.

Marlene hesitated. "Forty-eight."

"And how many of them are occupied?"

"The order has fifteen members."

I didn't ask if this number included Marlene and the mummy.

"And the other rooms are just empty?"

"Um . . ."

The question had apparently irritated her.

Marlene quickly regained her composure and moved on. "The north wing," she said, pointing to the opposite side, "houses the novitiate. They need more space. You are never to go over there, Pascha. Promise me."

"What's the novitiate?" I asked. Before I swore another oath to the outer edge of the universe, I wanted to know what I was forgoing.

"The novitiate is for women who are new to the order and haven't professed their Final Vows yet. That's where they're quartered."

"Young women?" I inquired.

"Not necessarily. But promise me you'll never go over there without me."

Good Lord, that sounded pretty serious. What was up with that? Was I going to miss out on something interesting? But Marlene had mentioned only more nuns' rooms, not a fitness center or sauna. So I promised.

We left the stairwell and headed out into the cloister. A surprise was in store for me here. A covered walkway attached to the four surrounding convent buildings ran all the way around a square courtyard, and between regularly spaced columns the walkway was open to the garden in the middle. The columns looked pretty crumbly, and each was surrounded by scaffolding that continued upward to the rain gutter. Many of the columns were also being reinforced with heavy iron bars.

The courtyard garden looked like it had been meticulously groomed by the most avant-garde horticulturalist the suburbs had to offer. There was a large area covered with fine gravel in the middle, but otherwise the rest of the space was covered with raised beds containing every conceivable kind of greenery. However, I cannot tell you what was growing there. As far as flora and fauna go I know just about zilch. Cannabis—the only vegetative matter that I can reliably identify as such—wasn't growing there, in any case. Would've surprised me too.

A couple of nuns were bent over, tiptoeing over the beds and digging, raking, planting, and whatever other things that are presumably done in a garden. The nuns were all in full uniform with long skirts and veils and therefore looked like giant moles. Especially the one wearing the yellow rubber gloves. Some of them had tied gardening aprons over their black caftans. The only type of attire that would have been more impractical would have been pants with their legs sewn together. But if these girls thought the Good Lord would be more pleased with their black habits than with the latest in leopard-print jeans, well then by all means.

Along the cloister-side foundations of all four of the surrounding buildings construction workers were busy exposing and sealing the walls. At the back of the church there was scaffolding on which a few trapeze artists were performing gymnastic feats. The hellish noise that the legions of workers were making upset the image of peaceful convent life considerably.

"This way leads to the common areas," Marlene explained, whooshing through the nearest door.

Inside on the ground floor was a huge kitchen where multiple nuns were preparing the midday meal. All the goings-on reminded me of a youth hostel where German schoolkids on their annual class trips encounter the appetizing world of commercial-kitchen fare. Mushy spaghetti overcooked until it disintegrates in some nondescript sauce that no matter its ingredients is always called Bolognese. With reddish or orangey goo served in tiny glass bowls that you're supposed to spread onto a slice of insulating foam, falsely advertised as bread. And with meat that I, as a butcher's son, immediately recognized in all its repulsiveness for what it was: loose leftovers of muscles, tendons, or fat scraped off the bones mixed with spices, glued and pressed together with a binding material to dupe gullible starvelings to believe they're eating schnitzel.

However, the likes of that was nowhere to be seen in this antediluvian convent kitchen, which was even older than the oldest hostel kitchen. Next to the tub of vegetables was a smaller bowl of real meat. Well, diced into goulash-sized squares, but real meat nevertheless. Point to the nuns.

Next to the kitchen was the dining hall with the obligatory vases of flowers on the long, worn tables. A large crucifix was the only wall decoration. If you can call that a decoration. Personally, my appetite would vanish completely if Jesus were gawking at my plate with his eyes bloodshot and his hands stapled onto a cross. Right next door was what Marlene called the gatehouse. The gatehouse was a large, covered passage closed off to the outside by a decrepit gate that was hanging crooked on its hinges. During the renovation work this passage was being used as a warehouse for construction materials.

"On the opposite side, the arrangement is similar to this, except for the kitchen," Marlene explained. "The administrative offices are housed over there as well."

I looked across the cloister to the windows of the building on the opposite side and was impressed by the size of the whole complex. From outside everything seemed much smaller.

During our whirlwind tour we had seen only a few sisters, but I could sense Marlene's longing to rejoin them. Fortunately she refrained from any whining, instead suffering quietly. But that kind of made me sad. Gone soft—as I've already said.

"Now we're coming to the most beautiful part."

I followed Marlene to the wing opposite the church, which she entered through a large, central portal. We crossed a small vestibule and then found ourselves in a huge hall whose ceiling was a full two stories high. So far everything I had seen of the convent had been functional. No pomp and splendor, no room larger than it needed to be for its purpose. That didn't apply over here anymore.

"What is this?" I asked, stunned. Then I noticed the row of bunk beds down the long wall, which reminded me of a hostel again. "The new dormitory for the b—uh, homeless?"

"The beds actually came from a youth hostel that had bought stylish, comfortable wood beds when they remodeled. They donated these beds to us because our old cots were even older."

"And the gym?"

"It's not a gym. It used to be the library," Marlene explained with a hint of wistfulness.

A lending library, I thought, because its size reminded me of the public library where my mother used to schlep me to read Erich Kästner's pre-Disney-fied yawners about Emil, Lottie, Lisa, and the like. I'd check out the books, set them down someplace in my room, and return them after the due date. Secretly, of course, I would instead read those old Jerry Cotton paperbacks you used to be able to pick up at the grocery store, about a G-man in New York who drove a red Jag XK150. My editor didn't think I needed to broadcast this to the whole world, but I love Jerry—to this day.

"There were periods in the past when our order was quite wealthy and influential. Times when the nobility might come to the convent to seek shelter from the cruel world. There were many women who came to the order when they were widowed, and some brought all their possessions with them. We owe this wing of the convent, along with the library and the adjoining rooms, to a sister like that. Some of the books are many hundreds of years old and very, very valuable."

I'm pretty sure she didn't mean they had first editions of *Asterix and Obelix* or something, but Bibles. The sort of thing one actually used to read in a convent.

"Where did the books end up, then?"

Marlene sighed. "They were sold off, a long time ago."

"Then you guys are rich!"

"Oh, no," Marlene protested. "Quite the opposite. Just look around. Look closely."

I did her the favor. The walls of the library were pervaded by long, wide cracks. A lot of them extended from floor to ceiling. The windows were single-glazed and didn't shut properly, as I discovered when I flew closer to them. I went outside the building and looked at the whole complex from there. The roof's best days were behind it; some of the dormer and garret windows looked as if the next storm would suck them up into the sky. All of the windows were old. The outer wall of the library was being held up by exposed timber beams. The hallways, as I recalled, had linoleum flooring that easily more than five generations of penguins must have waddled over.

"See?" Marlene said. "Our order has only two convents left: the motherhouse in Belgium and this wonderful site. One year ago, the mother superior decided that we should sell off this convent. We couldn't afford the upkeep anymore. She found a buyer who didn't offer a lot of money but who at least wanted to free us from the burden of the convent and its ridiculous maintenance costs."

"How does the new heating system in the bum asylum fit into the story?" I asked.

Before answering, Marlene sent me a mental reprimand for *bum asylum*. "Well, the situation suddenly changed. We got some help from heaven."

"An angel appeared with a suitcase full of gold, incense, and carrots," I presumed.

She ignored my interruption. "We received a bequest."

"Ah-ha," I replied. "The Good Lord took out some rich dude so you could bag his dough."

Marlene continued undeterred. "This money allowed us to start on the most important of the conservation measures."

"This kind of redistribution of wealth is of course easier for the Lord of Life and Death than for a mere mortal, who would land in the clink for it."

She didn't take the bait. "And then we had some more good luck: the construction work is being done for us at a special price by a general contractor here in Cologne, Siegfried Baumeister."

"What's in it for him?" I immediately asked, since do-gooders are totally suspicious to me.

"Knowing he's done something good," Marlene answered.

"Bullshit."

"Lots of people donate money for a good cause," she said. "Many donate money for victims of earthquakes or floods, and others donate money for people who are hungry or sick and can't pay for medicine."

"Fine, then," I relented. "But those examples are about people, not buildings."

"Well, there's a church that has been under construction in Barcelona for more than eighty years, funded solely from donations."

In this area she surely knew more than I, and presumably she was right as well, so I didn't pursue the topic any further.

"Nice digs, in any case, if you ignore the structural problems," I said optimistically. "So now show me the annex where . . ."

"Where I burned to death," she added softly. "This way."

The advantage when you are a ghost is that the cops' crime-scene barriers don't prevent you from touring a scene. So we buzzed into the annex, which was permeated with a revolting stench of fire, soot, and wet plaster. The worst damage in a fire is usually caused by the water that puts it out, actually, which, to make matters worse, had come much too late in this case.

The long room was empty except for the remains of the collapsed roof and a pile of charred wood in the middle; the two doorways and shattered windows were provisionally boarded up with planks of wood. The floor was made of old flagstone showing its cracks and fissures. The walls were bare and blackened by smoke, but the new heating pipes still ran along the soggy plaster to the three window alcoves. Apart from these pipes, there was no sign the space had just been under renovation. Charity or not, the order had obviously not spent an excessive amount of money renovating the annex. But since this was a homeless shelter and not a five-star hotel, I overlooked this graciously.

The place where Marlene's body had been found was marked with chalk. We hovered over it for a moment, but Marlene clearly felt uncomfortable.

"Are you sad to be dead?" I asked her.

The question just kind of slipped out of me, though I knew the answer.

"I think so, yes," she mumbled. "I had an important job and was happy doing it. And you?"

Job? She missed her life because she had something important to do? Not because she was just having fun? Having pillow fights at night with her sisters or downing greasy pork roasts? Not because of an awesome TV show or over-the-top concert DVDs? And those were just the small pleasures in life—which I would have thought convent-compatible. To say nothing of other pleasures. No, Leni missed her life because now she couldn't do her job anymore.

I kept my trap shut. I'd actually been asking myself this very question again and again for weeks, but I don't know the answer. Sucky, huh? Actually, you might think I missed my life—and mine wasn't the least bit cloistered, either. Pinching the freshest rides, boozing with my best buddies, making it with the hottest chicks. But happy isn't what I was. I wasted tons of time in front of the boob tube and making it with myself. I can still hang out in front of the boob tube, but getting hammered doesn't work anymore. And definitely not screwing.

Before I slid all the way into a sentimental spiritual rehash, I deftly changed the subject. "So what should we do for the rest of the day?"

"I'll stay at the convent. It's almost time for terce, and I'd like to join my sisters in prayer."

Ugh, great. Martin didn't want to have anything more to do with me today, and my dear Marlene, who was under the same forced radio silence as I was, still wanted to pray with her sisters. Whatever she was hiding behind, doing her "terce" apparently had little to do with what I thought it meant. I'd rather be bored all by myself. I said good-bye and made up my mind to do a little checking on the neighbors in the vicinity of the convent who might be lacking Christian tolerance. Even if I didn't come up with anything, I wanted to at least try to do something meaningful. After all, important jobs were something you could still do even if you were dead.

THREE

I wandered, if that's what you'd call pleasantly wafting around through the streets of the neighborhood in the shadow of the convent. Figuratively speaking, of course, because the old convent obviously doesn't cast that many shadows. Still, Mariental consists of four streets that run up toward the convent and three cross streets that connect the others. Martin, the collector of old city maps, would undoubtedly have taken great pleasure in interpreting the details of the city planning here. Even I, who was more used to assessing localities by their potential escape routes, also appreciated how this area was laid out. If I had to steal a car here, the way out wouldn't have been a problem. I'd take one of the four streets heading away from the convent, and then I'd take the ring road they all led to. And bye-bye— getaways don't get any easier. But I wasn't here to scope out swanky wheels, so I pulled myself together. Which was hard for me because there were tons of hot rides around here.

The area reeked of rich people. People who earn their living procuring luxury items can tell that kind of thing at first glance. The buildings were old, not seedy-old but ritzy-old. That is, renovated at great cost. Façades relieved of centuries of grime, roofs rehung with shiny new ceramic tiles, windows not only replaced with double- or triple-glazed panes set in stylish tropical-hardwood frames but also equipped with inconspicuous little wires that run to a little keypad next to the front door, which is probably not where these people should also be mounting the rack for all their keys.

A lot of the buildings were just plain big and swanky—"impressive," as Martin would presumably say. I whizzed through one living room just to see what kind of impression a pricey pad gives you from the inside. The seating accommodations looked like the designer had been in violation of the Controlled Substances Act before taking his pencil in hand. Not comfortable, but lots of artistic value. The TV sets were all hanging on the walls and as flat as freshly pressed hundred-euro bills. The culinary facilities—including a fully automatic espresso machine with integrated bean grinder, coffee-cup pre-warmer, and milk frother for a morning latte (or, as we say in German, *Espressobohnenmühlenmilch-schäumerkaffeetassenvorglühvollautomat*)—had probably cost more money than I earned, even in good years. In short: moola lived here.

My treat for this sunny afternoon, however, was a foray through the garages and parking lots gradually filling up as more and more banks, brokerages, or other bullshit boutiques hit quitting time. Everything that ever rolled off an assembly line to scorch the autobahn was represented. Mommies picking up their broods from horseback riding or music lessons tended toward Winnebago-sized SUVs that they could not see over the roof rails of, despite their four-inch heels. Daddies preferred things lower, faster, and pricier.

There was no model I couldn't have cracked.

I used to be the best.

Now I was dead.

Life really sucks sometimes.

Mariental is not exactly a happening place, so I was not planning on spending the evening or night here. I was just deciding whether to head back to the emergency room or to go to the movies when I noticed an increase in pedestrian traffic. Bipeds who have two or three motor vehicles per household, each of which cost more than thirty thousand euros to acquire, rarely walk. So the situation made me suspicious. I watched the procession, which more and more people kept joining. They were walking toward the convent. Ah-ha, they must be having some kind of devotion, mass, service, or whatever they want to call it, that the nuns offer for the evening edification of the neighborhood.

I was all ready to turn away and check what movie was playing at the movie theater when I took a double-take. The pedestrians weren't on their way to the church but to one of the buildings on the square directly across from it instead. A trapezoid-shaped corner house whose narrow side faced the convent's hill. The Gröbendahls—that was the name by the doorbell—were thus the immediate neighbors of the annex-turned-homeless shelter. They lived literally within spitting distance of the wall that the bums sat around on, waiting for the gate to open. And the Gröbendahls were being paid a visit by about thirty neighbors, and not one of them was carrying a bouquet of flowers, a bottle of wine, or a present.

Interesting. I mingled among the guests as they entered.

Apart from the folding chairs, the living room held no surprises. Dudes and dames in spendy duds entered, greeted Susanne, the lady of the house, and the other arrogant douche bags in attendance with an air kiss here and an air kiss there, whirling up the aromas of expensive toilet water (seriously, that's what it's called), aftershave, perfume, and fragrance into a class 2 hazmat disaster, then sat down. The men crossed their legs casually while leaning back; the women pressed their gold-buckled pumps chastely together. Susanne Gröbendahl finished her job as doorwoman and shifted to hostess mode, pushing a little tea cart with rattling bottles and glasses into the room.

"Red wine? White wine? Richard will be right back with the beer. Please do help yourselves."

Fashionable snacks that looked like inflated pretzel sticks strewn with something bearing a striking resemblance to pine needles were passed around in large glass vases. Bright-red lips closed in over the swollen sticks as one or another of the guys shifted around nervously on his folding chair, crossing his other leg, taking off his sweater, and laying it over his lap. It took amazingly little time for the air to turn hot and stuffy. Like in a brothel—only without that certain extra scent. I was hoping that was about to change, however, because the lady of the house dragged a newly arrived, well-tanned prick with her out of the living room and into a side room sparsely furnished with floor-to-ceiling built-in cabinets, an ironing board, and a stationary bike. The door clicked shut behind them.

I eagerly anticipated seeing how people screw on a stationary bike and thought I might learn a thing or two here before the event got underway. And right off the bat the tan guy tried to grope her and suction-cup his lips onto hers, but she resisted. Yeah, well, some women believe that a bit of fidgeting makes them more interesting. Maybe. But a chick is better off not overdoing it.

And this one here was overdoing it.

"Rolf, it's over, you've got to get that through your head," she barked at him.

Ooh, bitch alert! But if she didn't want a quickie, why then had she dragged him in here between the ironing board and the bike? Despite the rejection, Rolf, with his impeccable tanning-bed tan and expensive jacket over an open shirt over designer jeans over high-end leather shoes, grinned and leaned back on the bike, folding his arms across his chest, and asked the same question that was also haunting me.

"Well, why'd you drag me in here, then, sweetie?"

Susi Sweetie was getting visibly pissed off. "What were you thinking? I'm the president of the neighborhood association. Your solo operations have not been sanctioned by a majority vote, nor do they serve our cause. Quite the opposite!"

Rolf kept on grinning. "The majority of the people attending actually do want to get rid of the bums but won't do anything about it. You're just like them. You're scared stiff it'll make you unpopular. Which is why you're so fantastically well-suited to playing hostess for the meetings but unfortunately a bad choice for president. So I took matters into my own hands."

Susi was seething now. "I forbid you to—"

"What?" Rolf asked with a smirk. "What do you want to forbid me from doing?" He laughed out loud. "Forget it, sweetie. You and the other kindergarteners keep playing nice-nice; I'll do what I think is right."

He grabbed her by the shoulders, forced a kiss onto her mouth, and left the house. I wasn't sure if I should follow him or stay and listen to the meeting of the neighborhood association, but I decided to stick with Susi for now.

Richard, the cuckold, stuck his sparsely haired, pale head through the door. "Is anything wrong, Susanne? Can we get started now?"

The broad—whose obvious agitation could have come either from pleasure or pain, I couldn't tell, unfortunately—took a pit stop in the bathroom, where she freshened her hair and lipstick. Then the meeting finally got going.

"We've got to do something" was the most common utterance of the evening, followed closely by "We don't have to put up with it." The only tangible result, apart from fourteen empty bottles and a red wine stain on the expensive wool rug, was the decision to ask the local chapter of the Child Protection League for assistance. After all, they agreed, children are the ones most threatened by the presence of vagrants and junkies. Susanne promised to take care of it the next day, right after her appointment at the nail salon.

In the end I envied Rolf, who had spared himself the kindergartener drama.

———•———

"Can we finally get going with our investigation?" I asked Martin at seven thirty the next morning. I had no clue why he bothered setting his alarm clock, since he didn't need to be at work today, but that's just how he is. Orderly and meticulous. Which in itself would sufficiently characterize the potential for conflict in our relationship.

I lifted the expression "potential for conflict" from a TV show for wannabe shrinks. There's this crappy new "format" that's been springing up on TV like foot fungi at the public pool. A preschool girl tells her own parents how to raise their wayward spawn; a bean counter informs astonished families in debt that they can't be spending more money than they have anymore; and lately there's been this buxom blonde giving couples relationship advice. Totally unnecessary, in my opinion. There are only three basic rules whose compliance is sufficient for an effective relationship. If the chick wants to prattle on and on, shut your ear flaps and let her prattle. If she wants to screw, give it to her. If she doesn't want to, find a new chick. It's actually quite simple.

Thanks to the tube, I now knew I had the opportunity to entirely resituate my relationship with Martin. According to the buxom blonde, we'd have to respond much more openly to each other and share our wishes and needs with each other while also accepting to some extent that we will never be able to understand the other fully. What we still lack in understanding must be balanced with tolerance.

I had nothing better to do, so I was willing to try it out.

"I've got an appointment with the doctor at eight," Martin explained, still totally bleary-eyed.

"With the doctor? You just got out of the hospital."

"But the hospital isn't allowed to issue me the doctor's note that I will need for the institute to pay me for my time off sick."

"Very logical," I replied. But the hot shrink on TV also said people shouldn't fight over things that are outside the control of either partner, so I kept my opinion to myself regarding doctors' fee procurement procedures under the German health care system. "But after that we can get going."

"First I'll drive to the institute to submit the sick leave form and thank my colleagues for the flowers, chocolate, books, and wishes for a speedy recovery."

"You can mail in the sick leave form like everyone else, and you'll be seeing your colleagues again soon enough," I objected.

"And then I have to go to the library . . ."

Martin had since arrived in the bathroom. He ordered me back out curtly and closed the door behind him. I'm not some perv who watches how unwashed men put the plumbing to use, so the ejection was unnecessary. I didn't tell this to Martin, however, because in such situations my blonde psych guru recommends sticking to the main topic of conversation and not switching to secondary areas of conflict—i.e., the unnecessary emotional cruelty of the ejection. So I stayed on topic and communicated very clearly.

"I want to see you in Mariental by no later than ten o'clock," I yelled through the closed bathroom door. Obviously I can't scream, but the intensity of the exchange of thoughts is something that I can very much modulate.

Martin tore open the door and stared at a point where I was not located. But he couldn't know that, of course. "I'll be at the gelato café at eleven o'clock. Until then I want some peace and quiet."

He slammed the door shut again.

"OK, see you at eleven, then," I thought, at normal intensity.

I was proud of myself. I had made a concession. That is a sign of inner greatness, the psycholady said. Martin's defensive attitude would collapse and the crisis would be resolved.

"Give in to win" was the catchphrase that she had whispered into the camera with a beaming smile. The way she said it made me wistful for my erectile tissue.

I didn't even have to go looking for Marlene; I found her right away. In the church, of course.

"Have you found out anything new?" I asked as a greeting.

"The Lord be with you," Marlene answered.

I wasn't sure if that was part of a prayer or her cloistral way of saying "hey, dude," so out of caution I didn't say anything in reply.

"They're thinking about tearing down the annex," said Marlene.

"Who? What for?"

"The mother superior spoke with Mr. Baumeister. He considers the structural integrity of the annex to be compromised, and renovating it would be too expensive."

"Uh-huh."

"In addition, we've now received the bid to replace the convent's roof. It's going to be much more expensive than we had originally hoped. Even with the bequest, it's doubtful we can keep the convent in the long run."

Well, these questions were certainly important for Marlene and her sisters, but they had nothing to do with our investigation, so I didn't go into it.

"Is there any news about the night of the fire?" I clarified, repeating my question from before. "Or about the . . ." *Mummy*, I wanted to say, but I managed to bite my tongue. ". . . uh, your sister in the hospital?"

"No. We're praying for her."

Terrific. Fortunately, in addition to the nuns, there were still medical professionals trying to help her in a more tangible way. And there was me, who wanted to get to the bottom of the case.

"It's almost eleven," I realized. "Time to meet up with Martin. Are you coming?"

Marlene said one more short prayer for Martin, asking for success in his efforts, and then she followed me into the sunshine, which was slowly burning off the fog.

"The president of the neighborhood association is a woman named Susanne Gröbendahl," I told Martin as he arrived in front of the gelato café at eleven o'clock on the dot.

Despite the summer temperatures, he'd again dressed as if an arctic cold snap were imminent. Of course without his beloved duffle coat that, despite multiple dry-cleanings, would not fully let go the almost two liters of blood that Martin had lost when he was stabbed in it. So now he was wearing a long wool coat instead. On a day when it was warmer outside than in. At least he'd ditched the cap.

"She lives over there in the corner house."

"Is Sister Marlene with you too?" Martin asked.

"Yes," Marlene and I responded in unison, although Martin could hear only me, obviously.

"What kind of experience have you had with this neighborhood organization, Sister?" Martin politely asked.

"None at all," Marlene said. "I didn't even know that this group existed."

"Are you personally familiar with Ms. Gröbendahl?"

"No. She's never attended a devotional or mass."

"Are these events open to the public?" Martin asked.

"Our hourly prayers are open to everyone, and masses on Sundays and feast days are public in any case since we have a priest come out for those from downtown."

"Perhaps Ms. Gröbendahl is Protestant," Martin mused.

Yes, and perhaps she just doesn't give a shit about all the sanctimonious drivel and prefers screwing her UV-irradiated neighbors.

A minute or two later, Martin's finger was pressing the Gröbendahl doorbell. It didn't take long for Susi Sweetie to open the door.

"Yes?" she asked, no doubt surprised at the sight of a gentleman in a wool coat.

"Good day, Ms. Gröbendahl. My name is Martin Gänsewein."

Marlene twitched at his unfortunate last name. It literally means "goose wine," apparently some medieval joke referring not to wine but to water. It actually suits Martin pretty well. Regrettably, however, Martin couldn't sense Marlene's amusement.

"I'm here about the fire in the annex to the convent," Martin continued.

"That has nothing to do with me," Susi said quickly.

"We're looking for witnesses," Martin explained without blushing. He'd already picked up a fair amount from me.

"I didn't see anything."

"Obviously not—the fire broke out overnight," Martin said with a halfhearted smile. "However, it would be of material importance if you could provide some general information about events regarding the homeless shelter. May I come in?"

"You're with the police?" Ms. Gröbendahl asked.

"I report to the Cologne District Attorney's Office," Martin said.

That was not entirely a lie, because it is the responsibility of the DA to order autopsies, and it is the duty of the forensic pathologist to carry out these orders.

Fortunately, Ms. Gröbendahl didn't ask for ID, and instead she stepped aside holding the door open for him.

The red-wine stain had disappeared from the wool carpet. The devil only knows how she managed that. In my apartment stains never disappeared. Just more and more new ones showed up. I saw no other evidence of the meeting the night before, either.

Martin asked a few courteous questions about general events, but the gentlewoman was already letting loose on the bums.

"Those men have been hanging out around here all day, right in front of our house." She made a vague gesture toward the convent's wall. "They leave shards of glass behind, and I've even found syringes. They also relieve themselves on the wall and leave their garbage everywhere."

"They have to clean up their garbage before they're allowed into the shelter," Marlene interjected.

I relayed the information to Martin, who then spoke it.

Ms. Gröbendahl tucked a strand of hair behind her ear. "Well, when the nuns open the door at night, they hand out a garbage bag and broom so the bums can get rid of their filth at that point. But all that crud is lying around here all day long."

"Have you recently noticed other people taking an interest in the shelter?" Martin asked.

"No."

"What was the business with Rolf?" I whispered for Martin to ask.

He dutifully referred the question to Ms. Gröbendahl.

She expectedly froze, blushed, frantically tucked strands of hair behind both ears, and cleared her throat several times. "What does that have to do with anything?"

Martin helplessly shuffled his feet where he was standing, buying time to answer.

"Who is Rolf?" Marlene and Martin mentally asked at the same time.

I was enjoying the total confusion of all concerned.

"The stud muffin she keeps on the side," I said with great satisfaction.

Martin turned bright red; Marlene asked what a stud muffin was.

"Ask her why she was so mad at him yesterday," I ordered Martin.

"What business of mine is Ms. Gröbendahl's personal life?" Martin softly asked while giving Susi Sweetie a weak "Um, well, you see . . ."

Ms. Gröbendahl looked at him expectantly.

"It's not personal," I interjected.

Martin stepped toward the door as if he wanted to leave.

"Ask her!" I yelled. "It has to do with the fire."

Ms. Gröbendahl still looked taken aback, but she followed him to the door as well.

"How do you know that?" Marlene asked.

"I've been here before," I explained. "Yesterday. He practically admitted to setting the fire."

Martin stopped again.

Ms. Gröbendahl waited, becoming increasingly uncertain.

"What are your thoughts on Rolf's . . . action?" Martin asked, making a new attempt.

"I didn't have anything to do with it," Ms. Gröbendahl asserted loudly as she incessantly kept tucking strands of hair behind her ears.

"But you knew about it," Martin said, pressing without knowing exactly what it was all about.

She stared at him aghast. "Only afterward."

"But you didn't go to the police," Martin said.

"To the police?" she asked.

I was getting worried that her outer ears would wear down over the course of the conversation and she'd end up looking like van Gogh, post–razor blade.

"Covering up for an offender is itself a crime," said Martin.

"A crime?" Ms. Gröbendahl asked in a tone that sounded suspiciously like a case of incipient hysteria.

"I'm getting the impression something's off here," Marlene announced.

"Did he threaten you if you turned him in?" Martin asked.

"Not yesterday," I noted as a matter of courtesy.

"What would I be turning him in for?" Susi asked, now fully distraught. "The whole thing was in the paper."

Martin stared at her silently, Marlene's electromagnetic waves were forming one giant question mark, and even I didn't get at all what the lady of the house was talking about. But I tried to hide that as well as I could. Ms. Gröbendahl stood up, took a folder off a shelf, opened it, and laid it open on the table for Martin to read.

RESIDENTS OPPOSED TO HOMELESS SHELTER was the headline next to a photo of "Rolf von Berg, member of the Mariental Neighborhood Association," according to the caption. The three of us hung over the article reading the interview in which the handsome Rolf bemoaned misunderstood Christian charity, social parasites, and the shunting of an inner city problem to a nice residential area.

"He hadn't discussed the interview with you?" asked Martin, who could read fast and think quick. He was the first one to figure out what was going on.

"No." The hair-tucking drill dropped back to a normal pace. "And that interview has spurred a lot of outraged mail."

She flipped a few pages further. "Here, read these."

Seven letters to the editor were about the interview with "that arrogant bastard" who displays a "disgraceful contempt for his fellow human beings" and "understands as much about Christian charity as does a dog about flying." It continued in that style. Only one letter supported the demand to prohibit the shelter, and that was penned by the Cologne district chair of a political party called Germania Ahead.

"Is it plausible to you that Mr. von Berg could have committed the arson?" Martin asked.

Susanne Gröbendahl considered the question. For a long time. Then she shook her head. "Although he is indeed an arrogant bastard, I don't think he's capable of that."

I got the impression that Susi was firmly convinced of her own statement.

After leaving Ms. Gröbendahl's house, Martin was exhausted and wanted to go home, and Marlene, shaken

MORGUE DRAWER NEXT DOOR

by the attitude of the convent's neighbors toward helping the homeless, wanted to pray. I was able to convince both to devote another half an hour to debriefing. We went to the gelato café where the waiter with the overly greasy hair was at first surprised to see the odd patron from yesterday and then disappointed that he had not brought the pretty blonde with him again. He glanced wistfully several times at the door before he finally decided to ask what he could bring to Martin's table.

"A cappuccino, please."

Wow, Martin drinking caffeine? Progress!

"*Sì, subito,*" said the waiter, zipping away to fill the order. Wow again.

"Maybe the gelato café set the fire," Marlene said. "Or the allotment gardeners nearby. Or this Germania Ahead party."

"Marlene," I said. "Now you're exaggerating."

"Just tell him what I said," Marlene pleaded.

"You're swinging from one extreme to the other," I said, trying to reassure her. "Yesterday you couldn't imagine anyone . . ."

"Tell him," she scolded. Her tone reminded me of the slowly rising level of hysteria that we had just experienced with Susi Sweetie. I guess this is the universal form of over-reaction women always have.

"Marlene now suspects the gelato café owner, the allotment gardeners, and Germania Ahead," I rattled off.

Martin put his hand to his forehead.

"Apparently people aren't interested in neighborly love," Marlene continued, unable to let it go. "We are doing something good for all of humanity by helping the poor and

65

outcast, but this engenders hatred rather than gratitude. I cannot fathom that they've even started a neighborhood association just to oppose the shelter. Only meters from our church dedicated to Saint Mary Magdalene. These people are Pharisees."

"Marlene . . ."

"Tell him!"

"Come on," I said. "Your righteous anger really is a little over the top, don't you think?"

"TELL HIM!"

I did her the favor so she'd stop tearing apart my electromagnetic waves with her roaring. But her rage did not subside. Instead, now Martin was broadcasting unambiguously irritated signals as well.

Great! I hadn't imagined the end to my loneliness like this at all. For weeks it had been my most desperate wish to have someone else to communicate with. To not be dependent on Martin alone. To have contact with another soul, or even another living human being. And then my wish was granted—only to leave me stuck between two first-class neurotics.

"Quiet!" I roared into the gabble swirling around me. It was abruptly quiet.

The waiter returned with Martin's cappuccino. As soon as he left, Martin projected a question for Marlene at me:

"Marlene, why should the allotment gardeners have something against you and your sisters?"

Allotment gardens, if you didn't know, are these small parcels of out-of-the-way land that urban gardeners who don't have enough yard space at home can rent to plant with vegetables, flowers, trees, or even set up swings and slides for their kids. Sometimes they're spacious enough to include little pavilions or summerhouses the owners can stay in during the warm parts of the year. And there's usually some kind of common clubhouse or rec hall all the gardeners share. There are tons of them all over Cologne.

"The allotment gardens abut the convent property," Marlene began. Her soul wasn't exactly back at peace, but at least she wasn't having conniptions anymore and could formulate coherent thoughts again. "The allotment gardeners have the same concerns as the convent's other neighbors. A lot of homeless people prefer spending warm nights outdoors on the benches in the allotment garden area rather than indoors in the shelter. Occasionally some of the summerhouses in the allotment gardens have been broken into by the homeless, who like to sleep in them."

"How do you know that?" I asked. "And why didn't you mention that before?"

"The allotment gardeners' club wrote us a letter. They asked us to get through to the men who were sleeping in their summerhouses. So we reminded our guests that they shouldn't be going into the allotment garden area at all."

"And?" I asked.

"Well, what do you suppose?" Her tone wasn't bitchy anymore. More resigned. "These people know they're undesirable; they don't need us to tell them that. But sometimes the shelter fills up, or the night is so pleasant that they prefer sleeping in the garden area anyway."

I brought Martin up to speed.

"Where are the allotment gardens located?" he asked.

Marlene said the gardens were located in the woods to the right of the convent, directly accessible via unpaved paths.

I passed all of this on to Martin. He nodded obediently, jotting "Mariental allotment gardeners," "Caffè-Gelateria Venezia," and "Germania Ahead" on a piece of paper. He drank the rest of his cappuccino and shuffled over to his trash can on wheels passing for a car.

"I'm going to need an afternoon nap," he mumbled and disappeared.

"Oh no, I've almost missed terce!" Marlene cried as she too instantly disappeared.

I didn't need either a nap or prayers; I just wanted a little entertainment. Was that too much to ask?

FOUR

Three dead-boring hours later when I was on my way to Martin's place, I passed by a newsstand and was broadsided by the headline: FIRE SET BY CONVENT'S NUNS? Unfortunately, the papers were folded so you could read only the headline and nothing else. I zoomed into Martin's apartment. In the front hallway there was a strange tingling in the air that was somehow unpleasant. Martin was sitting in the living room in his favorite armchair with a book on his knees. He seemed quite engrossed in it.

"I'm getting strange vibrations here," I said.

He jumped in terror, stopped a moment, and then smiled. "Really?"

"Yeah. But much more importantly: you've got to go pick up a newspaper. At the newsstand downstairs."

He buried himself back in his book. "Today I don't need any bomb attacks, financial crises, or other disasters."

"It's about the convent," I said. "The newspaper is saying the nuns set the fire themselves."

Now I had his attention. "Why would they have done that?" he asked.

"That's exactly what I want to know, which is why I'm waiting for you to buy a paper."

He pushed himself up from his armchair with a bit of difficulty, pulled on his coat (the outside temperature today was still room temperature), slipped his wallet into his pocket, and returned minutes later with the newspaper. He laid it out on the table so we could both read it.

The article said that it had definitely been arson. Evidently some old wooden benches from the shelter that the construction workers had been using for seating and some insulation material they were storing on-site had been soaked with an accelerant. The police suspected that this material was ignited with a blowtorch that the heating contractors had left behind, and the old gas furnace that they were supposed to replace with the new equipment subsequently exploded. In any case, the initial ignition could have taken no more than half an hour due to the substantial heat generated by the blowtorch. And since the fire broke out at night—or nine hours after the contractors' quitting time—the article claimed the police were ruling out contractor error. The new twist: the investigation was now focusing on the nuns, first because they were the only ones with access to the annex, and second, because they had recently taken out a new fire insurance policy. Plus, since the CSI unit had ID'd the accelerant as oil used for the eternal flame in the convent church's sanctuary lamp, there was a mounting body of circumstantial evidence—including, first and foremost, the convent's well-known financial straits—to support the suspicion. Blah blah blah.

Before Martin could shape his surging indignation into words, the doorbell rang. Martin pressed the buzzer, and just moments later Birgit stormed in—with a newspaper under her arm.

"This is really too much!" she yelled. "Now they're saying the poor nuns did it themselves."

"I was just reading that as well," Martin said.

"Can you imagine? In all seriousness?" Birgit asked.

Martin reflected, because he is a meticulous and deliberate person and thinks things over before he speaks. He weighed the strength of the evidence, reminded himself what he knew about the convent and the nuns, and compared this information with the report by Marlene about the night she was killed in the fire. Or at least the night her earthly life ceased, to be precise.

"No," Martin replied.

Which earned him a kiss from Birgit.

"The fact that you're not cynical but have faith in the goodness of people is another thing I like about you," she whispered in his ear. Which was exactly the location where I had settled while Martin was thinking, so I watched as Birgit's soft, red, bee-stung lips moved in very close to me. It felt like grenades were going off all around me, but, as I was painfully aware, the feeling was not reciprocal. Too bad.

"Oh, uh, thank you very much," Martin stammered back, hazarding a quick kiss to those sensual lips.

I sighed with envy.

"Hey, are the sparks really flying between us, or is there some kind of electrical gadget squeaking in here?" Birgit asked.

Martin reflexively turned toward a little plastic thing stuck into the outlet next to his front door.

"It could be coming from this device over there, although it said on the box that humans can't hear it," he mumbled.

"What is it?"

"An ultrasound device to keep mosquitoes away."

Birgit gave a puzzled stare first at the gizmo and then at Martin. "It's the end of April. There aren't any mosquitoes out yet."

Martin shrugged.

So that was what had just been bugging me when I came in! I knew exactly what Martin was trying to keep away—me! What an incredibly dirty trick. Fortunately, the ultrasound mosquito deterrent apparently doesn't work that well on disembodied spirits, although it continued to tingle a little.

"Well, the suspicion falling on the convent is some tricky business," Martin said as a distraction.

It worked. Birgit turned away from the bug-slash-ghost zapper and looked at Martin thoughtfully. "Is Gregor on this case?"

I could feel Martin cursing himself. Now he'd gotten Birgit on track and she still wanted to involve Gregor, who had already noticed in the hospital that Martin was strangely interested in this convent case. Martin didn't want to talk with Gregor about it under any circumstances.

"I don't know," Martin stammered.

"Well, then ask him," Birgit suggested.

"What am I supposed to tell him?" Martin asked. "We don't have anything to show him. Just a feeling that the nuns are not so audacious that they would set fire to their own convent."

"You're right," said Birgit. "I just think this smear campaign is so appalling . . ."

Martin ran his hand over Birgit's flowing blonde hair and hugged her. "You have a good heart."

"And an empty stomach," she replied, laughing. "Let's go get something to eat. After all, you still need to get your strength back too."

I waited for them to decide on a destination, and then I started making my way lickety-split to the convent. We ghosts have to overcome distances too. We can't just beam around. No idea why not. Anyway, I hit the accelerator to tell Marlene about the plan that I had just come up with.

I found her, of course, praying. Not just her, but the other nuns too. They were all sitting in the church, singing an unmemorable, nearly monotone melody without any discernible beat in their thin, quivering voices. It sounded like it had come from another time. It probably did too.

"To Thee, before the close of day,

"Creator of the world, we pray

"That with Thy wonted favor, Thou-wow-wow

"Wouldst be our Guard and Keeper now."

Musically not a hit, but somehow it affected me. If I had known that song the time my father had sent me to bed unconsoled in my fear of fire, I might have grown up to be something else. Oh, man, this is so awkward. I am really turning into a candy-ass. Totally embarrassing.

Before the sister act could take enough of a breath to start the second verse, I called for Marlene.

"Shh, we're singing the compline."

"Well, your sisters and you have got a totally different problem that's going to put an end to your singing once and for all if we don't do something," I hissed back at her.

"Banish the dreams that te-e-e-errify,

"And night's fantastic company,

"Kee-e-e-ep us from Satan's tyranny,

"Defend us from unchastity."

"I'm pretty sure chastity isn't exactly what we should be focusing on right now, Leni, so let the choir do their warbling on their own and come on. The police suspect you nuns of setting the fire yourselves. Which means you're not going to get one cent covered by the insurance company, and they'll drop your policy faster than a rapper drops a hot sixteen."

"WHAT?"

Finally I had her attention. I updated my Charitable Sister on the newspaper article while the other chorus girls kept yodeling "Thou, Holy Gho-o-o-ost, our Advocate . . ."

"I can't believe it," she stammered, interrupting my thought.

"I know, but I've got a plan. We'll need Martin for it, and he'll need you to give him some information about the bum—uh, shelter. So are you coming now?"

She joined me, and we zoomed together out to Martin's favorite joint, Veggie Paradise. Personally, I do not know how a chef can reconcile his professional training with the processing of only withered leaves, spices, and other scrub into fodder. But I guess as long as there are people who will save a cow but kill a carrot, there will also be chefs who will take the cash out of such people's pockets with a cold smile only to spend it on a hamburger or T-bone after work.

Because my life unfortunately no longer required the ingestion of nutrients, it no longer mattered to me how Martin preferred putting the paunch back on his pudgy physique, because at least I didn't have to eat across from him. The dining selection at Veggie Paradise would have

been a fail for me, anyway. The sight of the whole-grain cut-
lets topped with roasted vegetables on Martin's plate would
have sooner moved something out of my stomach than in.
Birgit at least was eating lasagna: the tomato sauce makes it
so you can't really see what chicken feed is hiding between
the layers of noodles.

"Martin, we've got a plan," I yelled.

He choked, which I blamed on the vegetarian patty. A
certified-organic emetic, delicately spiced.

"Tonight you're going to need to spend the night in the
bum shack and keep your ear flaps open among the nuns
and other bums."

Now he was really retching.

"What's the matter?" Birgit asked with a worried expression as she patted him lightly on the back. "Aren't you feeling well?"

"Everything's fine," Martin wheezed.

"That's a good idea," Marlene commended me. "Sister
Maria manages the dormitory, and she's always delighted
whenever she gets to chat with someone."

Marlene, Martha, Magdalene, Maria . . . What, this order
accepts only women with names beginning in *M*? But since
it looked like Martin wasn't going to choke his way into the
hereafter just yet, I didn't want to digress from the topic.

"You should go put on something suitable and get going,
otherwise everyone will already be sacked out when you get
there."

"But what kinds of questions am I supposed to ask?"
Martin thought.

"We'll worry about that later," I decided. "But what will
we tell Birgit?"

Easy: the truth. Birgit was thrilled with Martin's idea and his commitment. She accompanied him home, helped him choose a bum costume, which was pretty difficult because he didn't even have a pair of jeans, to say nothing of tattered jeans. She tousled his hair, which she took obvious pleasure in, and dropped him off close to the convent in her fly convertible. She gave him another long kiss that caused Martin's blood pressure to spike alarmingly, and then turned around and drove off.

"So?" Martin asked.

"Listen in on the other bums and see if any of them have noticed anything unusual recently. Maybe one of them got kicked out and—"

"We don't kick anyone out," Marlene interjected.

"Not even if he's smoking hash, snorting blow, or pissing in the corner?" I asked.

"You have a very peculiar imagination," Marlene said, piqued. "These people have no money for cocaine, and they're happy to be able to use a clean toilet. Sitting down."

I didn't inquire whether the nuns checked that, but even though I suppressed it quickly, this flash of a thought still reached Marlene, who shot another reprimanding wave back at me. For cripes' sake, I'd gotten more feedback on my comportment over the past two days than I did in my last four years of school combined. Including that class camping trip when I got caught in the girls' shower room. What was that chick's name again with those giant bazooms?

"PASCHA!"

Marlene was getting the hang of projecting her outrage with the intensity of a galactic neuron storm.

"All right, just go in, we're right here with you."

Martin followed the signs guiding him around the convent to the temporary shelter in the library. He was impressed at the sight of the giant room, stopping in the doorway for a moment to take it in.

"Good evening, the Lord be with you," the nun said, giving him a friendly welcome.

Wowza! This woman was temptation incarnate. Her skin was as fair and smooth as the velvety peel of a ripe apricot, her eyes a vivid blue, her lips (minus lipstick) rose red, and her dark eyelashes silky and long. Her body was easy to make out despite the sack of a habit she had on, prompting the question whether the Good Lord had called this beautiful creature into his service for semipersonal reasons. She looked like a creature straight out of a fairy tale—Snow White gathering her unwashed dwarves around.

"Uh, yes, yes, hello," Martin said, not particularly eloquently.

"Would you like to sleep here tonight?"

He nodded silently.

"If you are able and would like to make a small donation to support us, that would be lovely. There's a piggy bank over there."

Shrewd entrepreneurs, I thought, and—surprise!—Marlene rebuked me yet again.

"Very few people want to depend on charity permanently," she schooled me. "It's good for their dignity and self-esteem if they can pay a little something. Most of them make an effort to give at least fifty cents."

Meanwhile, Martin had shuffled over to the fat, pink, grinning piggy bank and pulled his wallet out of his jacket pocket. Snow White saw the movement out of the corner of her eye and then looked closer. Presumably it was not with particular frequency that she encountered a guest who pulls out a bulging billfold and slides a bill into the pig.

"It's great that you're providing shelter even during the rebuilding phase," Martin said, making small talk.

Snow White smiled kindly. "Yes, although we're going to have to make do with this 'transitional' solution for quite a while."

"Terrible, about the fire," Martin said.

"Yes." Snow White's blue eyes welled up. "Sister Marlene died in the fire, and Sister Martha was severely burned and is in the hospital." She made the sign of the cross. "We miss them both very much. We've been praying for them every day."

"That's good," Martin whispered. As a forensic patholo-gist, he had a small bit of experience dealing with survi-vors. "How did the fire end up starting in the middle of the night?"

"The police are saying it was arson." She crossed herself again. "I can't imagine who would want to do something like this to us."

"Did you perhaps have some trouble with one of your, uh, guests? Did you have to turn someone away because . . ."

"That does happen from time to time . . ."

"See?" I said to Marlene. "Told you so!"

". . . but not recently. Occasionally if someone arrives here quite drunk, then we send him away. Or call the police, who put him in the drunk tank. Oh—excuse me, won't you?"

Snow White left Martin standing there to go help an elderly man who could hardly walk climb up into the top bed of a bunk bed.

"Why doesn't he sleep on the bottom?" Martin asked the guy standing next to him.

"If the guy above you wets the bed . . ."

Martin frantically scanned all of the beds. The top bunks were all occupied.

"Kidding!" the guy said, who was tall as a tree, had dreadlocks, and was wearing two winter coats. He grinned cheerfully down at Martin. "Most of them associate an unobstructed view above them with freedom. Self-determination. I mean, how do you imagine your own bed? As a double-decker?"

Martin shook his head.

"I'm Marley," said the Rasta man. "Fiercely loyal customer."

"Martin."

"New?"

Denial would have been more or less futile. Martin nodded.

"Lucky they've still got beds. 'Cause of the fire, I mean. There were even a couple of people who died," Marley whispered. "Pretty shitty. Though I didn't know the nuns who got caught in it. They didn't work here anyway."

The thought briefly occurred to me that Marlene hadn't actually told me what her job at the convent was. No doubt she was picking up my thoughts, but she wasn't volunteering anything. By all means, don't put yourself out, lady. Maybe she was on toilet duty. I wouldn't go broadcasting that to the whole world, either.

"Didn't you notice anything when the fire broke out?" Martin asked. "Since you're a regular guest here, I mean."

Marley shook his head, dreadlocks wagging. "Nah, I was sleeping. I sleep really well here. Maybe it's a little metaphysical, but I don't sleep as well anywhere else as I do here."

"Did the . . ." Martin wanted to say *crime scene investigators,* but thought better of it. "Did the cops ask any of the guys here any questions?"

Marley nodded. "Sure. But they didn't turn up anything. No one sneaks around here at night. Everyone's happy just to spend a night in a comfy bed."

"Uh-huh." Martin picked out a bed and laid his jacket on it. "What else should I ask?" he wanted to know from me.

"Ask Maria who was on door duty that night," Marlene suggested.

"What's door duty?" I asked.

"Since we don't have a doorwoman, every day one sister is assigned to open the door when someone rings the bell. It's more practical that way than if everyone were to run over—or if no one did. And that sister also locks all the doors at night."

I relayed the information to Martin, who then asked Snow White about it.

"Sister Martha," she answered.

"Shoot!" said Marlene.

I was speechless.

"She may have seen something or someone, but obviously we can't ask her now," Marlene lamented. "But that reminds me: didn't Martha ring the bell?"

"Ring the bell?" I asked. "To make enough ruckus so your wings would already be waiting for you at the Pearly Gates?"

"To warn everyone about the fire," Marlene replied, ignoring my remark.

"Wouldn't it have perhaps made a bit more sense to call the fire department?"

"Of course," Marlene replied. "Only we nuns don't carry cell phones around with us. Certainly not in my nightgown. The only phone in the convent is in the mother superior's office. The bell would have alerted the sisters; they would have noticed the fire and then called the fire department."

This was sounding like when you line up a bunch of dominoes and then tip the first one and watch the others fall. So first the bell, then the mother superior's phone, and finally the fire department. Medieval.

I raised the question of the bell with Martin, and he asked Snow White.

"Its rope had been cut," Snow White whispered. "And because the tower staircase isn't accessible from outside, it's extremely mysterious how the rope could be cut. But since we only rarely ring the bell, no one knew about the cut rope."

"And the oil for the sanctuary lamp is normally kept in the sacristy," Marlene added. "There is no way for anyone to get in there without a key."

I passed this along to Martin.

"I came here to gather evidence to exonerate the nuns," he whispered to me in his thoughts. "Not to find even more evidence that the nuns set the fire themselves."

"Then talk with the other guests and ask them if they noticed anything unusual the night of the fire."

Martin made the rounds, slinking from bum to bum and reciting his lines. Most of them explained they were asleep and woke up only when the fire department arrived with their sirens howling. A few of them couldn't call it quits with their answers and tried to unload their whole life stories on Martin. He listened to the first one for a solid ten minutes, but with each additional candidate he got more practice clearing out when they started rambling on about their personal dramas. Backstabbing friends, job stress, divorce, back rent, and—presto—homelessness. Somehow the stories all resembled each other, and I was struck by the idea that my own story would have probably turned out about the same eventually. I pushed the thought far from my mind. I'd had a good job. I was the best car thief in the whole city of Cologne. And experts are always in demand, in any field . . .

Suddenly Marlene zinged me—a reminder that I should pay better attention—so I concentrated on Martin again.

The wizened old man who had practically burned through Martin with his piercing gaze was going on and on in a hoarse whisper. He was almost impossible to make out under the mountain of clothes and blankets over him. He was lying on one of the upper bunks, so he looked down at Martin.

"What do you mean by 'conspicuous'?" Martin asked.

"He was darting from shadow to shadow and kept looking around. His eyes glowed red."

"Red?" Martin asked. He managed to keep any doubt from his voice, but I sensed that he didn't think this piece of information was very credible.

"He was limping," the wrinkly witness continued. "And whenever he took a step with his left foot, a loud sliding noise shot up from the cobblestones."

"So he walked across the square over to the convent?" Martin asked. Clever to put that together, because the square was the only place around here paved in cobblestones.

The head under the mound of blankets nodded vigorously.

"Could you see which street he came from?" Martin asked.

A strange crackling sound was coming from the bed. The hobo-goblin laughed. "He didn't come from any street. He came from below."

"From below?"

"From the dark bowels of the earth. A fissure opened, a cloud of sulfuric steam hissed up, and when the fog cleared, he was just standing there, looking me right in the face."

"With his eyes glowing red," Martin said. His shoulders slumped. "Thank you. You've been a huge help."

"Bah!" The old man crawled deeper under the covers. "You won't get him."

Martin questioned two more men, one of whom acted as if he had not heard him, while the other tried to get him to marry his sister.

"I've had enough," Martin thought to me. "I'm going to sleep."

Marlene invited him to say the evening prayer together with her.

I didn't say anything.

"Tell him," Marlene ordered me.

"And then what?" I asked. "Then I've got to relay all the sanctimonious drivel between you and Martin?"

"There's no harm in that," Marlene replied.

"I'm not in the mood."

"Ask him if he wants to say the evening prayer with me."

"No."

"Ask him."

This game went back and forth about five more times until I gave in. Otherwise Marlene would have spent the whole night busting my balls. This stubborn wannabe saint was on crusade with no regard for casualties, and my interest in listening to the clatter for hours upon hours was exactly zero. So I decided it'd be better to ask Martin to belt out a quick hallelujah and be done with it.

Martin responded hesitantly to her invitation. A huge amount of doubt and uncertainty was swirling around in his thoughts. Made sense. He was a scientist who spent his working life dissecting corpses. He'd never wondered about the eternal life of the soul, because if there was such a thing then his soul was shut out long ago when he started slicing up stiffs. My emergence had trashed his whole philosophy of life. Since then he'd been rattled. Now he was wondering if it would be beneficial for the future of his soul to revive his childhood faith in a higher power.

"See, he doesn't want to," I quickly said.

"I'd love to," Martin said.

I had the impression he said that only to contradict me, but now that I had vultures gnawing at both the earthly and spiritual ends of my existence, I relented.

"OK, but pray fast so it'll be over soon," I said.

"To thee before the close of day," Marlene droned.

"Hey, you didn't mention singing," I protested.

"It's a very simple melody," said Marlene. "Even you can handle it."

I didn't ask what she meant with her catty "even you" comment, and instead I droned the phrase at a pitch that seemed reasonable to me.

"Creator of the world, we pray."

We managed all three verses, and inside Martin's brain-case I felt calm set in. A comforting calm. Which is what droning off a couple of sanctimonious articles of faith was good for! It took only a few minutes, and then my Little Goose was out like a baby in a car seat. I stayed with him as a precaution.

Martin awoke with a jerk just before three o'clock. No wonder—he'd just taken a big, unwashed foot in a holey sock to the stomach.

"Urgghh," he groaned, quietly, because even in a situation like this Martin is rather reticent.

The guy who had climbed down from the top bunk and into Martin's bunk slid on his shoes and jacket and headed for the door. On the inside of the door was the familiar emergency exit bar that you just need to lean on and the door pops open. The guy disappeared through it into the dark night.

"You've got to follow him!" I yelled at Martin, who was still curled up under his covers feeling sorry for himself.

"Why should I?" he asked. "He's probably just got to go. And why can't you do it yourself?"

"Dude, I can't stop him if he gets up to no good," I replied. "And anyway, you're here for investigative purposes, so kindly go and *investigate*."

Martin plopped out of the bed, pulled on his shoes and jacket in the dim light, and followed the bum out into the night. Into the cold night. It was freezing. It was a clear night, and the sky was filled with stars. The waning moon was still bright enough to make out the ghostly outline of the man, who was walking single-mindedly and quickly, but still like a zombie, along the convent's wall toward the main entrance and the cobblestone square outside.

Like a zombie—that was it. This guy was a sleepwalker! He was trudging along like he was on remote control. Martin followed him to the front corner, past the main entrance to the church, around the next corner, down the long side of the building, and around the last corner for the home stretch back to the front door of the former-library-now-temporary-homeless-shelter. The distance between the two men was a good twenty meters by now because Martin's footing was slow and unsteady in the darkness. The sleepwalker pulled the door open, stepped back into the library, and let the door fall shut behind him.

Martin stumbled the rest of the way and pulled on the door, but it wouldn't open. He pulled harder.

"This can't be true," he mumbled, pulling even harder. "It opened fine just a minute ago."

I flashed through the door into the virtual sawmill where a chorus of fluttering soft palates was performing a hideous concert of snores. The sleepwalker had just lain back down in his bed and was sleeping quietly and peacefully.

Snow White wasn't around.

Marlene either.

"Do something," Martin ordered me.

"Like what?" I asked.

"Anything," Martin stammered. He was shivering.

I raced in search of Marlene, but I couldn't find her. Maybe she was at the hospital with her mummified sister or on her way up Mount Brocken to take in a moonlight performance of *Faust* for all I knew. Whenever you need a woman . . .

Still, I did notice that the church door was open a crack. Geez, those convent girls don't lock their prayer pit up even at night. Admittedly they didn't keep any major treasures in there ripe for the picking, but trusting in God that much while an arsonist was on the loose targeting convents was still pretty much borderline insanity. For Martin, who was freezing his ass off, the open church was definitely going to be good news.

He was able to hide his enthusiasm pretty well, though.

"What am I supposed do in the church?" he asked.

"Sleep," I replied. "Better than hanging around out here."

"I'd rather drive home," he said.

"Great," I replied. "Let me call you a cab."

Of course he didn't have his cell phone on him, and there actually wasn't a single cabstand anywhere in sleepy Mariental. So he gave in.

Martin gathered up all the tattered cushions that were scattered along the pews. Then he unhooked the curtain of the confessional, lay down on the pillows, and covered himself with the curtain. I'm pretty sure that the surroundings were the only thing shielding me from Martin's malediction.

I watched over Martin, who quickly started snoring, until the church got too boring for me, and then I whooshed off again. This was about the time that the fire had been set. If you took one of the gravel access roads to the back of the convent, you could avoid the residential streets in Mariental altogether. There was also an unpaved road that ran behind the allotment gardens and another that ran along the edge of the woods set back a few meters behind the outermost buildings of the convent. I checked both out. The road past the allotment gardens was pitch black. Since as a ghost I was unfortunately not equipped with night vision capabilities, I turned around and took the other road. In the pale light of streetlights I flew leisurely toward the first couple of buildings. If a car were driving here in the middle of the night, someone would be more likely to notice it than on the road behind the allotment gardens. Right now the whole area felt dead, in any case.

I stopped and was heading back to Martin when I noticed a much bigger spot of light next to me. It wasn't the dim light of a streetlight. It was light coming out of a penthouse. Lit up like the anniversary sale at a lamp shop. At half past three in the morning. I cautiously approached the windows.

Tanned neighborhood activist Rolf von Berg was setting a fat bottle back on a bar cart and carrying a half-full glass to a big leather armchair. He sank back into the cushions and sloshed the liquid around in his glass, its color reminiscent of weak tea. However, it didn't seem to me that Rolfi, here, who looked like he'd been pulling out his hair for seven hours straight, was spending his night with lemon tea. I invited myself in and gave him some company.

What was keeping him from sleeping? I wondered. A guilty conscience maybe? Or had he just gotten back from another round of firing pistons with Susi Sweetie? Whatever it was, something was keeping him up through the dark of night. And if he had just gotten up out of a strange bed, maybe he hadn't gotten his tailgate up, because something had cut the power to his smug grin.

I took it all to be yet more evidence that even the coolest penthouse bachelor pad isn't enough to guarantee happiness. Although in this case the pad was pretty cool. I sometimes used to dream about having this kind of place. Not as suburban, of course. No, more authentic. But I had always wanted to live in an old warehouse, like this one. With a huge freight elevator that could transport whatever fly ride I was driving at the time right into my bedroom. Kind of like that private eye in Vegas on TV, except he drove his car into his crib at ground level. My elevator would be a whole notch cooler. And of course I wouldn't have any furniture, except a bed and a long couch, a supersized flat screen, steam shower, and Jacuzzi—otherwise, industrial austerity. I decided to take a look around on the lower floors. Maybe there were lofts more to my taste than Rolfi's yuppie living room.

In fact, the other lofts offered any and all possible arrangements and designs—because they were all completely empty. Here in the middle of one of Cologne's hippest areas to live, front-row seating with a view of the beautiful old convent and its grounds. Weird, right? But perhaps loft living was going out of style. I did another pass through the building and peeped in again on Rolf, but since he still wasn't writing out a confession, I took off to keep Martin company in his own personal homeless shelter.

FIVE

Martin's attempts the next morning to speak to the sleep-walker about his nighttime excursion failed miserably.

"I was asleep the whole night," the guy explained, whose name we still hadn't figured out.

So for simplicity's sake I'll just call him the Zombie.

"I followed you when you left the room, around three in the morning."

"Why would I get out of my warm bed in the middle of the night?"

"You walked once around the convent."

The Zombie stared at Martin strangely, wondering if he had hay or chewing tobacco between his ears.

Snow White was taking him a bit more seriously.

"Why is this important?" she asked.

"If he was sleepwalking the night of the fire as well, he may have seen the arsonist."

"Then I'd best call the police," Snow White said, suddenly even paler than normal. "You should stay here in any case so they can take your statement."

Martin's shoulders slumped. He hadn't counted on this. I could read in his thoughts that he was hoping to bail on this regular sawmill here as quickly as possible to go have breakfast with Birgit.

It took half an hour for an officer to show up at the convent. All of the bums except Martin and the Zombie had ditched the shelter in a hurry. None of them wanted to have anything to do with the cops. One of the detectives took down the Zombie's personal information, and the other took care of Martin.

"Let me see your ID, then."

Martin fumbled for his wallet—and turned pale. "It's gone."

He searched the bed, his pants pockets, the floor under the bed, the route he had walked overnight outside, and the church. Nothing.

"Do thefts occur frequently here?" he asked Snow White.

"Sometimes," she said, blushing. She is so sweet!

"So your photo ID was stolen?" the officer asked.

"Yeah. And my debit card, credit card, phone card, work badge, and my university library card. And I had about a hundred twenty euros in cash in the wallet."

The officer and Snow White stared at Martin.

"No, I get it, man . . ." the cop said skeptically.

"Actually, I noticed that the gentleman did have a wallet with him," Snow White confirmed. "He put a bill into our piggy bank over there."

The officer looked at Martin with a still-doubtful expression, but he pulled out a notebook and pen. "Please give me your name, then."

"Martin Gänsewein."

The cop's head jerked up. "Gänsewein? The coroner who got stabbed?"

Martin turned bright red but nodded.

"And what, pray tell, are you doing at a homeless shelter?" Martin shrugged.

"Aren't you a friend of Gregor Kreidler's?"

Martin hesitated and then nodded.

"I think it'd be better if Detective Sergeant Kreidler takes your statement, then." The cop pulled out a phone and spoke into it briefly. "Wait here for him. I'll be taking off."

As for the Zombie, he was allowed to leave the shelter after the other officer took down his information, but he apparently agreed to report back for questioning under hypnosis sometime in the next few days.

Meanwhile, Martin helped Snow White fold the blankets and sweep, but the physical work was a serious strain on him. His hands were trembling when Gregor finally arrived.

"We'll get to you in a moment," Gregor said, his voice icy. Then he turned to Snow White and took her statement. No, she hadn't noticed anything unusual, but she slept in her convent cell and not at the shelter. (She actually called it a "cell"!) Yes, everything had been quite normal last night when she left the dormitory. Most of the men had been sleeping, and the door had been set to emergency release. What did that mean? There is this little lever on the lock that one pushes down from the inside; then the door can still be opened from the inside but is locked from the outside. If one raises the little lever, the door can be opened from both sides. She always looked closely to ensure that the lever was down so that no one could break into the shelter overnight. The Zombie obviously knew about the mechanism, otherwise he wouldn't have been able to come back inside after his excursion.

Gregor thanked her kindly and then turned to Martin. "Come with me."

He didn't wait for an answer, only turning and hurrying out of the convent. Martin slinked behind him with drooping shoulders. The gelato café was already open. Gregor sat down at a table on the patio, which was just being hit by the sun's first rays. Martin sat down opposite him.

"*Buongiorno,*" the waiter said, welcoming them. If he was surprised to see Martin yet again, he didn't show it.

"Two tall cappuccinos, extra hot, and four croissants," Gregor ordered.

Martin stared silently at the tabletop.

While we were waiting for the waiter to return, Marlene showed up.

"What have I been hearing in the convent?" she asked me, all excited. "One of the men may have seen the arsonist?"

I detailed all the less-than-relaxing events of the night for her. Marlene was all restless, as though we had already ID'd the perp and his arrest were imminent. I had to repeatedly stress that this, unfortunately, was not the case.

She came back down from her excitement only slowly. At least I didn't need to worry about her blood pressure or heart. Whether a ghost can explode with excitement, I don't know, but I consider it unlikely.

When the order finally made it to the table, Gregor took a sip of coffee, a bite of croissant, and then turned to Martin. "What on earth are you doing here?"

"Drinking coffee," Martin said, taking a big sip.

"Martin!"

Martin's defensiveness immediately collapsed. He was at the end. Not fully recovered yet, hardly slept all night, and frozen to the bone. He opted for the truth.

"The newspaper reported that they now suspect the nuns of having set fire to their own convent. I can't just sit by and watch them take the blame for it."

"Why not?" Gregor asked, annoyed. "What are the nuns to you?"

Martin didn't say anything.

"Martin, the case with the car smugglers two months ago nearly cost you your job and your life, and yet here you are again poking your nose into a case that does not concern you. This is a matter for the police and not for a forensic pathologist on sick leave. What is wrong with you?"

Since Martin's strength had reached its limit, his psychological compartmentalization wasn't working either, and I could read his thoughts as clearly as the balloons in an *Asterix* comic. How was he supposed to tell Gregor about what his motivations were when he couldn't mention me? To say nothing of Marlene? And what was with all of Gregor's lame-ass questioning when he knew perfectly well that Martin was communicating with a ghost but had categorically prohibited himself from making any mention of this ghost? What kind of answer did Gregor expect if he didn't want to hear the truth?

Martin didn't say anything.

Gregor sighed. "At least tell me what exactly happened last night."

Martin recounted every minute detail, but without mentioning me or Marlene, of course.

"And you think that this guy traipsing around the convent last night saw the arsonist?" At least now Gregor had adopted a professional, objective tone.

Martin shrugged but nodded with his head cocked pensively at the same time. A pitiful sight!

"And why didn't he report this before?"

"He doesn't know that he sleepwalks, and apparently no one else has noticed it so far either."

"Was he even there the night of the fire?"

Martin shrugged again.

"And can he even ID someone if he saw the person while sleepwalking?"

Now Martin was in his element. He straightened up and spoke in complete sentences and with confidence. "It may be that he will recall this under hypnosis, even if he swears with a clear head that he never sleepwalks and never saw anyone."

I could sense that Marlene was also impressed by Martin's transformation, now that he was back within his specialty, the field of medicine.

"All right," Gregor forced himself to say. "First things first. I'll go and find out whether the sleepwalker even spent that night at the convent."

Martin had to eat the last croissant while Gregor silently watched. Then Gregor drove Martin to the closest precinct so he could report his wallet stolen and then home.

Marlene started jetting toward the convent and invited me to join her. Because I was afraid she wanted to jump back into her endless prayer loop, as a precaution I asked: "What's up?"

"Mr. Baumeister, the contractor I mentioned, is coming to discuss the renovation. It's always very interesting. And entertaining. He's very charming." She literally chirped the last word.

A contractor who was lining old rocks back up at a convent? He was supposed to be charming? Well, I was game to see what was up with this dude. Martin was long home in bed and thus unavailable to me anyway.

We reached the convent gate at the same time as the contractor, who had parked his car on the cobblestones right in front of the steps up to the church. In a tow-away zone. Propped up under his windshield, however, was a permit exempting the driver of this panzer from that rule. The panzer was actually a ginormous Land Rover. With a bull bar. Black. Dusty. With sprays of dried mud up to the door handle. A car that apparently actually drove the kind of roads for which it had been built. I instantly liked the guy.

Until I met him. He looked like some English country squire. Horse breeder, maybe. Waxed jacket, corduroy trousers, boots made of thick leather. He smelled a bit like saddle oil and a little bit like men's soap. Several nuns were fluttering around him like electrified hens.

"That's the mother superior," Marlene explained, referring to a no-longer-very-perky but surprisingly tall nun with the shoulders of a wrestler and a cross hanging from her neck. She herself could easily have been taken for the contractor, with the country squire as her secretary. The habit muddied the impression somewhat, of course. "She's strict, but popular. And she manages the convent very prudently."

She had no comments on the other nuns, but I sensed she had greater fondness for some than others. Marlene seemed to particularly like one petite Szechwan sister with a delicate smile and deep laugh lines, who was standing back a bit. She looked about as sly as they come.

"Who's the, uh, Asian?" I asked, striving to find a politically correct term for the Mao frau.

"She's the mistress of novices," Marlene said, then added tersely: "Remember: the novitiate is off-limits to you."

I confirmed this, although I could imagine the young novices having a lot of fun with their *mistress*.

Meanwhile the contractor was flirting with the nuns, paying them compliments on their appearances, although the only thing to be seen under each of their hoods was a face from eyebrows to chin. He got them grinning with his little anecdotes, and then he inquired with sudden seriousness about the health of Sister Martha.

The smile on every face was suddenly extinguished.

The mother superior clapped her hands. "Back to work, women."

The nuns quickly said good-bye and scurried away in all directions.

"Unfortunately, Martha's condition remains critical," said the mother superior when she was finally alone with contractor. "The doctors are doing all they can, but we have no idea whether she will make it."

"I'm so sorry," the contractor said, shaken.

"He's got a soft spot for Martha," Marlene whispered to me. As if someone might have overheard us if she'd spoken louder. "Martha works in administration and together with the mother superior is responsible for the construction plans. She's very smart."

I tried to imagine the nuns standing under their full-body drapery in front of copiers and computers, but the image was pretty ridiculous, so I had to giggle. Marlene thought I was being silly. That made me giggle even more.

She tried to keep serious, but I felt her self-control giving way. Finally she giggled with me.

"Now what are *you* giggling for?" I asked.

"I don't know," she said and burst out laughing.

"Yes you do," I said. "Care to share?"

She tried to control herself but was no match for the fit of giggles. "We once had a sister whose habit got caught in the shredder," Marlene said before another attack of the giggles set in. "We had to call in a technician." She started snorting with laughter again. "But he couldn't come until the next day." Now there was no stopping her. If Marlene had still possessed a body, tears of laughter would be pouring down her face and she'd be doubled over in spasms from laughing so hard. "So she spent the night with the shredder in her bed."

"Weren't there any moral complications?" I asked.

Marlene roared even harder.

"Why didn't she take her habit off?"

"She wore one of the old-style habits; you used to have to wear an underskirt, a tunic, and a scapular. Her underskirt was fastened in back, the tunic had a button at the shoulder, and the scapular was pulled over her head. None of the openings lined up, and every layer was so horribly tangled in the machine there was no way for her to get out again. And she didn't want to cut anything off, under any circumstances."

"So what did the technician do?"

"Cut everything off, of course," she said, gasping for air. Without warning her hysterical silliness transitioned seamlessly into uncontrollable sobbing. I didn't know how to help her in the pain of her grief. I couldn't pat her on the shoulder or hand her a snot rag. Other ways of consoling her, like taking her in my arms or something, were out of the question anyway. That was girl stuff. A man doesn't pull a fat, medieval nun into a hug. Just doesn't happen. So I awkwardly waited for her to pull it together again. After a few minutes things got back to normal and we were following the conversation between the mother superior and the contractor again.

". . . it would make sense in any case to renovate the columns along the cloister after we finish the roof," Baumeister said.

The mother superior shook her head. "The columns are purely cosmetic, so they're less important to us," she said. "The only critical thing is to maintain structural soundness. It may be possible to reinforce the columns less expensively using concrete supports, correct?"

Baumeister stared at her, horrified, and opened his mouth to say something.

"But first," the mother superior continued without letting him get a word in, "we should talk about the plan for the roof one more time. Based on your blueprint, the dormers and turrets will all be conserved and restored exactly the way they once were. We can't afford that."

"But it's important to maintain the value of the property," Baumeister lectured. "Just like the columns. I've been in touch with the Office of Historic Preservation again."

The mother superior stopped him with a wave of her hand. "We've tried that before. The official there informed us that the convent no longer qualifies for historic preservation subsidies because of the changes made to it when it was repaired after the war."

Baumeister lifted his right hand and pompously wagged his index finger in front of the mother superior's nose. "Yes, but I've found two examples of convents being designated as historic sites despite similar changes, and those convents did subsequently receive public funding. But if you redo the roof now without the turrets and dormers, you will lose this chance forever."

The mother superior sighed. "All right then, fine. We'll put off making a decision on the roof and columns for another few days. But I would like to award the contract by mid-May. If you haven't made any further progress with the Office of Historic Preservation by then, then the simplified design will be executed."

Baumeister bowed slightly.

"You see?" Marlene said, now back in control of her voice. "The mother superior knows what she wants. She's fought her way through several tough debates with Baumeister already."

Actually, it seemed logical to me that the person paying for the work should determine what would be done. That did not appear to be the case in the construction industry. Anyways, it made no difference to me if the nuns redid their roof with or without dormers, turrets, or whatever other nonsense, so I stopped following the conversation. And no one can really say anything else about preserving historic sites now that they've started registering decommissioned coal mines along the Ruhr River and barf-ugly eyesores from the nineteen fifties.

Since a new prayer circus was getting underway for Marlene and her sisters, I switched gears and went to see what Martin was up to.

I found him hunkered down in his armchair, reading, obviously well rested. As I floated through his front hallway toward him, the ceiling light flickered. And a little light on top of a box next to his armchair started glowing red. Martin looked up.

"Hello, Pascha," he thought. "Well, is everything OK?"

He was acting so weirdly normal that I wondered what kind of scheme he was up to now. The mosquito toaster had disappeared, in any case. Instead I noticed a new mirror in the front hallway. A metal thingy that looked like a mirror, about fifty centimeters from the ceiling. Much too high for Martin. And it was all cloudy. And it had two cables coming out of it plugged into the outlet next to the living room door. Modern art? In the front hallway, up by the ceiling, and in an apartment whose walls were otherwise plastered with old city maps? I went up closer. The flicker in the ceiling light picked up, the light next to Martin's chair started glowing steadily, and an alarm started beeping. I pulled back from the mirror contraption, and the beeping stopped.

"What is this?" I asked, dismayed.

"A capacitive magnetic field sensor," Martin said.

The virtual gears of my virtual brain fell into turmoil.

"I'm guessing you didn't pay very close attention in physics in school, huh?" Martin said. I thought that sounded a teensy-weensy bit bitchy.

Physics? Of course I'd paid attention. But mostly just to the topics that somehow had to do with cars. Performance, speed, and power. Acceleration. Combustion engines. *Real* physics, you know. Magnetic field sensors, by contrast, sounded suspiciously like electric currents, resistance, potential . . . Stuff you can't see. For that I had tuned out.

Only nutcases were interested in that stuff. And now Martin had suddenly transformed into an electronics hobbyist. The mosquito zapper in the outlet had more amused than annoyed me, but now I was getting really worried. What if Martin found some kind of ghost repellent? Given his triumphal grin, in any case, I suspected the worst.

But his grin quickly went out the window when I tested the range of his weird-wired metal plate. I had to fly directly in front of it for Martin's little red light to turn on. So for fun I zoomed about fifty times from his apartment's front entry to the doorway into the living room and back—just above the floor. Nothing happened. No flickering, no flashing, no siren at all. Martin's grin vanished, and he picked his book back up and got engrossed in it again.

Birgit finally arrived. At least she would inject some life into this joint. Sometimes I wondered whether Martin survived the stabbing just so he could resume sitting around and quietly reading. Or pretend he was reading. Birgit by contrast was unambiguously alive.

"Hey, I did something quite exciting today," she said, greeting Martin. Her blue eyes were gleaming, and she was fidgeting excitedly from one foot onto the other.

"Oh," Martin said, slowly and suspiciously. "What then?"

To me it seemed like he'd had enough excitement for now. I was bound to ruin it for him again in not too long; after all, we were in the middle of a murder investigation. But right now it was Birgit's turn.

"I was sitting in the cafeteria with some of my colleagues from the loan department," she began, taking a pregnant pause.

Martin had as much a clue about banking as I did of Einstein's theory of relativity. But I presume he did grasp that whole relativity thing, which I have exactly zero clue about. What I'm trying to say is that Martin is pretty bright when it comes to theoretical sciences, but he is totally the wrong guy if what you want is a normal member of a civilized society. His banking transactions consist of regular withdrawals of smaller sums of cash from his checking account, which is replenished by regular direct deposits of his salary. Surplus funds go into savings and get logged in a passbook. Yes, a passbook. One of those thingies that people last century used to get as gifts for first communion or confirmation or to secure the family fortune on the occasion of Grandma's admission to the nursing home. Turns out Martin doesn't trust anything else. Well, fine. Lots of investors are probably wishing they had relied more on their savings passbooks instead of buying shares in debt-backed American securities, but Martin had never had anything other than a passbook savings account. He hasn't even tried one of those savings lottery programs German banks run to encourage people to save more.

So Martin was at a complete loss trying to imagine what Birgit was hinting at with the loan department at work. Consequently his expression looked more suspicious than interested.

"These colleagues manage the account of the Order of the Charitable Sisters of Saint Mary Magdalene."

"Ah-ha."

Martin was doing a passable impression of a cold, stiff lizard slowly warming up and starting to move.

"I alerted my colleagues to the suspicion that the newspaper raised about the nuns, you know, that the nuns set fire to their own convent because they were stuck in some sort of financial trouble and wanted to collect the insurance payout."

Martin nodded vigorously. He was now paying full attention and hanging on every word from Birgit's lips. Figuratively speaking, of course.

"One of my colleagues said that the convent was up to its neck in debt last year, and the bank's real estate division was tasked with finding a buyer for the property."

"For the whole convent?" Martin asked, puzzled.

Birgit laughed. "You'd be surprised if you knew how many churches are being sold these days."

"Even Cologne Cathedral?" I interjected. "Man, that would make a kickass club."

Martin deliberately ignored my point.

"A real estate agent contacted the bank last January to inquire about purchasing it on behalf of a client of his. The purchase contract was already at the lawyer's office ready to be signed when the convent received a bequest."

That was true; Marlene had told me about it. The Good Lord had hung one of his lambs out by its hind legs and transferred its money to the convent.

"For how much?" Now the scientist in Martin was shining through again. Data, facts, and figures—those were his thing.

"Two and a half million," Birgit said.

Martin gave a slight cough. This time it wasn't my fault, because I was speechless.

"That's a lot of money," Martin said.

"Yeah, I guess it is," Birgit replied.

Sure, the chick works in a bank with millions of euros flashing past her all day. But for a forensic pathologist, a dead car thief, or a couple of modest nuns, two and a half million was a pretty decent little sum of money.

"The order had debts, but they settled them quickly. However, the convent is apparently in a pretty deplorable state, structurally speaking, and it's in urgent need of repair," Birgit continued.

"So the order is rich now?" I asked.

Martin repeated the question.

Birgit shook her head. "Based on an appraisal in the loan file, the cost of renovating would be more than four million euros."

"Who did the appraisal?" I asked.

"A general contractor named Baumeister," Birgit said.

I was not surprised. It apparently works the same in construction as in automotive repair. See, in Germany nowadays the standardized repair estimates that dealers pull up on their computers apply only to compact and midsize production vehicles, since manufacturers force dealers to use a fixed schedule of replacement parts and hours of labor for a given repair. It doesn't matter if the shop takes more or less time to get it done: customers know every shop will charge the same price for the same repair. However, with *exclusive* vehicles and *special* models, there are no such rules. Any workshop that thinks it might land the gig will run up as high an estimate as possible. So I suspected that that was where Baumeister's not-inconsiderable sum of four million euros just to realign some convent stones came from.

"Where does the order intend to obtain the millions it needs?" Martin asked.

"That's the big news," Birgit said. "The contractor is donating one euro to the convent for each euro it pays him. So if he does a job that costs one thousand euros, he charges them only five hundred and donates the rest to the convent."

Shoot, so there goes my overestimate theory down the drain. Why would Baumeister set the value so high only to give up half the amount later on when he does the job? Or just for the hell of it? And then how did that work with the donations? In the last years of my earthly life I never had any above-board income, so I never filed any taxes or deducted any donations, but I knew charitable donations were totally popular with the moneybag set out there. They waste money to save some. Unreal, huh? Even Bill Gates squanders a few billion a year to buy granola bars for malnourished Africans. Presumably the American secretary of the treasury has to get shitfaced as a coping mechanism every time he reads about another billion-dollar Gates donation and calculates how many millions in taxes just slipped through his fingers.

Martin reflected, "If I understand correctly, the order had been bankrupt but then received a bequest upon someone's death. It has also been receiving considerable donations from the general contractor, so now it is financially secure again."

Birgit nodded.

Martin sighed with relief. "Then the detectives on the case will figure that out very quickly. That should remove any suspicion that the nuns set fire to their own convent."

I knew exactly where this was heading, and I did not agree at all. "Hey," I yelled. "You can't just wash your hands of responsibility now."

"The issue has been addressed," he shot back, softly.

"At least ask Birgit to get some information about Rolf von Berg," I pleaded.

"I don't have time to keep playing private eye anymore, anyway," Martin said aloud. "Tomorrow I'm going back to work."

SIX

Martin would not change his mind, so I made my way to the convent to find Marlene. I had to convey the bad news to her about her disloyal investigator, who was closing the case right in the middle of the investigation. Of course I looked first in the church, but—surprise!—she wasn't there. I finally found her in the annex, hovering over the chalk lines that marked the spot where they had found her body.

"Hey, Leni," I said. "What are you doing here?"

"Hello, Pascha. I'm trying to remember."

I was picking up waves of shame. So now she was feeling embarrassed that she couldn't contribute anything to the investigation, although she had been not only at the scene but also basically right in the middle of the event. First in her earthly existence and then as a free spirit who might have thought to look around the scene to see the person who had locked the doors and thus blocked her escape routes.

I had struggled with the same self-reproach at my death as well. Someone shoved me off that bridge, but I couldn't name that perp either. Even though you might think the first thing I'd have done once my spirit left my body would be to take a look around for my murderer. But I didn't.

"Don't blame yourself," I said. "In the beginning, right when you first give up the ghost," I began, pleased with my wording, and even Marlene showed a tinge of amusement, "the whole supernatural-being thing doesn't really click for a while."

She sent me waves of gratitude, and for the first time in a long time I felt good, because I had done something good and been thanked for it. A pretty awesome feeling. Seriously.

"You're all right," said Marlene, who was apparently picking up my feelings more clearly than I would have preferred.

"Yeah, yeah," I said, playing it down. Way embarrassing. Here I'd been working for years on my tough-guy image, and now this? I was going soft, like I said before. Hanging around these hallowed halls totally screwed a guy up. I definitely needed to distract myself, and so I took a quick look around the annex.

"Have the police actually removed the barrier around the crime scene?" I asked.

"Yes. But the work in the annex has been idled until everything with the insurance is resolved and they decide whether to reroof the annex or tear it down," Marlene said.

Uh-huh.

"The rest of the work is proceeding. The drainage around the foundations . . ."

I supposed the list of other work would be great to know if you were interested in the restoration of medieval convents. But I was not. I was interested in arson and murder.

"So are any of the cops still on scene interviewing your sisters?" I said, cutting her off. "Are any government officials actually stopping in on-site to make sure everything is in order?"

Marlene sighed. "I think the police have turned to other priorities."

Ooh, very bad, I thought, which Marlene picked up on immediately.

"How so?"

I told her about our private eye throwing in the towel.

Marlene sighed again. "I think I'll say a few rosaries and pray that the case is solved quickly."

"Don't get angry with me, but I think instead we should try our luck again with your Sister Martha. If she saw anyone, we've got to find that out. You can always pray later."

Marlene agreed. We zoomed over to the hospital, snuck into the ICU carefully, and took up position in front of the window looking into Martha's room.

"Let me go by myself first," I whispered to Marlene.

I could feel that that was going to be hard for her, but she agreed. After all, I did have more experience.

Very cautiously and keeping an eye on the monitors over the hospital bed, I approached the mummy.

"Martha?" I thought very carefully.

No reaction.

"Martha, your Sister Marlene is also here. Right in front of the windowpane there. You might be able to sense her."

No reaction.

"So, Martha, we urgently need your help. Marlene died in the fire, you may know that already. And specifically because the arsonist locked the doors so Marlene couldn't get back out. We think you shook on the door and couldn't open it."

No reaction, not even the hint of assent.

"We're also thinking you may have seen the arsonist, because he had to be in the vicinity when you tried to save Marlene."

No reaction.

I felt Marlene come into the room. Her boundless compassion and sadness about her sister's situation suffused the stuffy room. The peaks and valleys on one of the monitors began to flutter.

"Careful," I whispered at her.

"Oh, my dear, sweet Martha, we're worried that the arsonist will strike again, but the police aren't making any headway with their investigation. If you know anything . . ."

"But I don't know anything," Martha answered pleasantly.

At that moment all of the alarms on the equipment went off, the displays flickered, and the cycles of peaks and valleys on various instruments started ebbing and showing flat lines. The prolonged beeps started testing our nerves.

"Oh no," Marlene whispered. "Martha, what's wrong?"

"Don't worry," Martha replied, sounding totally relaxed, utterly serene and calm. "I'm on my way into the light."

Marlene's waves were shimmering like the air in the pit lane at a Formula One race.

"Hey, Sister, not so fast," I interjected. "We'd still like to get a couple of answers to our questions."

"I ran to the door," Martha said, "and I almost had my hand on the handle when out of the corner of my eye I noticed someone was there."

"A nun?" Marlene asked, alarmed.

"I'm not sure. I screamed, 'Fire! Quick! Call 112!'"

"And then?" I asked.

"Something hit me on the back of my head."

Marlene and I were speechless.

"You got hit? What with? How?" I asked this because I know from Martin that forensic pathologists always like to know the presumed sequence of events to compare that with their findings at the autopsy.

"I don't know what with. But it was hard."

Marlene couldn't decide whether to rage in disgust or wail in compassion. She chose tears of rage. Figuratively, you know.

"And then the door exploded."

Nurses and doctors rushed into the room, all of them yelling chaotically. One picked holes in Martha's dressings and stuck electrodes onto the largely burned tissue underneath. The sight was grisly.

"Clear!" someone yelled.

The mummy's body jerked.

"Martha!" Marlene called in a clearly hysterical tone.

"I love you, Marlene. But I have to go now."

"Where?" Marlene cried. Panic waves radiated out from her.

"Into the light," said Martha. Then she was gone.

We stayed there for a little while as the doctors' and nurses' efforts to save Martha continued. Marlene was still hoping that Martha would come back, and I didn't want to rob her of this hope, even though I knew better. Once ghosts were gone, they never came back.

Eventually Marlene accepted it too.

"I'm going to say a few prayers for Martha in the convent church," she mumbled. Visibly shaken and sad, Marlene slinked away.

I, by contrast, spent the evening and half the night at the movies with that silicone babe who keeps adopting children from the third world. But I don't really care about that aspect of her as long as she shoots hot movies with tons of action and some sex now and again. I saw the eight thirty and eleven o'clock shows. They don't have a late-night showing, unfortunately. But that's no problem. There are plenty of people who conk out in the front of the TV, which then blares on through the night without anyone watching. If you find a TV with a good channel on, you can spend a whole night relaxing that way. It's almost as entertaining as the emergency room, although there isn't much going on in the ER during the week. Anyway, I needed all the distractions to keep myself from asking the same question again and again: why did most souls find their way to another world right away, but not Marlene or me? Were we stupid? Or indispensable? I tried to short-circuit my brain with action flicks to keep from mulling over that question.

On Thursday morning Martin entered the Institute for Forensic Medicine around nine o'clock. He usually starts work no later than eight, but today his doctor had wanted to see him one more time. No one could make sense of Martin's excessive zeal. Not the doctor, not Birgit, and not me. The only one who really seemed pleased that he was starting work again was Katrin.

WELCOME BACK! it said at Martin's workstation. The letters had been printed out in bright colors in one of those joke fonts that come on the computer, laid out across his desk. The office was empty, but no sooner had Martin set down his lunch box and apple on his desk and hung his jacket neatly on its hanger (the only one!) in the closet, all of his colleagues gathered around, led by Katrin.

"Martin, at last," she said. And hugged him.

I wanted to insinuate myself into Martin's thoughts so I could feel Katrin's cheek on Martin's cheek and feel her arms around Martin's chest and her awesome, full, tight knockers against his ribs, but Martin's sentiments totally turned me off. Technically his thoughts were correct, but without the appropriate dose of testosterone they were dead-boring. He felt pressure points on his cheek, shoulder blades, and ribs, otherwise nothing else. And I knew that Martin was capable of performing sexual acts. That is, to a certain point. That one time he got distracted and unfortunately couldn't . . . No matter: I was sure he would have made the most of what is expected of a man in a situation like that. With Birgit.

Now, in most of the men I know, the testosteronitos get all excited even with hot chicks they're not dating, and Katrin is clearly the hottest of chicks. Martin by contrast seemed immune to all feminine charms, apart from Birgit's. A scientist through and through.

The other colleagues gave Martin pats on the shoulder or shook his hand, and someone held out a nicely wrapped gift to him. Martin opened it. A city map. Surprise! Still, an unusual specimen showing the city of Cologne—or at least, that was what the title said at the top. I wouldn't have recognized it. The map had tons of unfilled gaps in the middle of the cityscape I knew, and those gaps had large areas colored green. The neighborhoods I used to haunt during my lifetime were labeled as a national forest. It must have been quite a while since this map was up to date. Martin thanked his colleagues enthusiastically, and his colleagues were pleased, asking if he was sure he was really feeling well enough to return to work. I was sure they meant that in a not-purely-physical sense. His behavior in the last few days before the stabbing had been really bizarre. For which I was not entirely blameless.

Martin was pleased with the lively welcome, but soon it got to be too much for him. He exhaled in relief when his colleagues took their leave, put his desk and computer back into use, and got to work. The institute's temporary offices still weren't quite ready yet, but in a few weeks the asbestos-removal project was going to start here and the offices would move off-site. Only the cold room with the morgue drawers and the autopsy room would remain in this building. The stiffs would have it all to themselves. Most of them didn't care, of course; they required no further attention.

I paid my pals in the morgue drawers a visit. Here in repose was the usual mix of suicides, murders, car accidents, household accidents, and autoerotic accidents. Which doesn't have anything to do with the eroticism of autos, as I had initially thought. Rather, they are people who have to pull a plastic bag over their head or tighten a cord around their neck to get off. Things like that go wrong sometimes. Pretty embarrassing if they find you like that. Bag over your head and hand on your pecker. I tried to catch a sign of other spiritual souls, but there wasn't anything. Only dead bodies.

Two pallbearers entered the cold room with a box. They were met by an institute employee with a clipboard in hand who checked some data and then pulled out one of the drawers. The pallbearers set down their box on a table, moved the lid aside, and lifted out the newcomer.

Martha!

Of course. Obviously she'd have to end up here, because her death was from unnatural causes as the result of an arson. I hadn't thought about that last night at all.

It was time for me to head back to Martin. With any luck, he could take on Martha's autopsy. After all, I had specially interrogated Martha to serve Martin up an important clue. The forensic pathologist of my choice was unfortunately not at his workstation. I zoomed through the offices and break rooms and found him in with the boss.

". . . sure that you've recovered completely, Dr. Gänsewein?"

"Martha's here," I exclaimed.

Martin's mouth, which he had already opened for the purpose of answering, stayed stuck open for a moment. "Uh, yes, of course," he then squeezed out. However, the boss had noticed his hesitation, as we both could easily discern from the worried wrinkles on his forehead.

"We should probably take it a bit easy on you to start with."

"No!" I screamed. "You've got to do Martha's autopsy. Marlene and I talked to her last night."

"Talked? How?" he asked back in thought. "Were you able to communicate with her?"

"Yes, but only after she was dead."

Martin turned visibly pale. "Is her ghost now also . . ."

"Are you not well?" the boss asked.

"Yes, uh, of course," Martin replied. "I'm fine."

"At the moment she died, her soul briefly buzzed by Marlene and me, and then she disappeared."

I could see Martin's tension recede. And if I could see it, the boss could too.

"Dr. Gänsewein . . ."

"I would like to take on the postmortem examination of the nun who died in the fire," Martin quickly said.

"But her body is already gone," the boss replied, surprised.

We thought for a moment about what he meant, and then Martin understood: "No, no, not the one who died in the fire."

The boss raised his eyebrows.

"The sister with the critical burns over most of her body," Martin added.

"But Dr. Gänsewein!" the boss interrupted. "We're all still hoping that she recovers!"

"No," Martin said. "I . . ."

"You do not share in this hope?" The boss's expression was clearly horrified.

"Unfortunately, it's too late," Martin stammered, his whole head bright red.

"Has she died?" the boss asked.

Martin nodded.

The boss frowned. "I haven't heard anything about this. I wasn't notified."

"She died last night," Martin mumbled.

"How did you come by this information, Dr. Gänsewein?"

"Um . . ."

"Radio!" I screamed.

"Radio," Martin said. "Yes, from the radio."

"And why are you so interested in this autopsy?"

Little drops of sweat started forming along Martin's brow. "Because I, uh, because I haven't autopsied a fire victim for a long time. I would like to keep in practice."

The boss agreed, reluctantly. "You know Dr. Zange; she will assist you."

I zoomed off to get Marlene, and I found her in the convent church, of course, presumably saying her two-thousandth Hail Mary of the day, and it was only with difficulty that I was able to pry her away from the holy hollow and her prayers for Martha's soul. Of course, I was of the opinion that Martha's soul required no further advocacy, having already taken the direct route to heaven. But I guess it takes time for nuns to shed their habits. So to speak.

Marlene and I made it back just in time for the start of the autopsy.

Martin was standing in his green scrubs at one of the three stainless steel tables in the slaughterhouse, as I call the autopsy room for obvious reasons. Tile on the floor, walls, and ceiling with drains for blood and other bodily fluids, shelving for delicate instruments and electric bone saws alike, and scales to determine the precise weight of each individual organ.

"Sorry, I had to talk to the boss for a moment," said the person who came rushing in, hardly recognizable under the green full-body condom plus face mask. But from the bust and voice I immediately recognized her anyway: Katrin, a.k.a. Dr. Zange. What a pleasant surprise, for once.

"No problem," Martin said warmly. It seemed like he was almost looking forward to the autopsy. "Shall we get started?"

"By all means." Katrin took the clipboard and read off the identification data. Then she turned on the Dictaphone. "Autopsy of a female body for the Cologne District

Attorney's Office. Identified as Astrid Kammschneider, age: thirty-seven, height . . ."

"Astrid Kammschneider?" I asked Marlene. "I thought her name was Martha."

"Martha is her religious name," Marlene said.

"And your . . ." I began, but she interrupted me.

"My name is Marlene." She made it abundantly clear that that was the end of that topic.

Martin began the autopsy as always by removing clothing, or in this case by unwinding the bandages. What was revealed underneath was, let's just say, *unpleasant*. Marlene was hit hard by the sight. She began to weep. Great! Crying is like puking. A lot of people turn green riding the bus, but they all manage to keep it down—until the first one revisits breakfast. Then everybody starts blowing chunks. I made my best effort to console Marlene without starting to bawl myself.

"Leni, there's no reason to cry. Where Martha is now, she doesn't need skin, eyelashes, or eyeballs anymore."

That made her cry more, not less.

"If just this first glimpse is too much for you, then maybe you'd better spare yourself the rest of the autopsy."

By this point she was sobbing like a howling hurricane.

"You could also just wait outside. Say, did you actually ever see the morgue drawer you were in? It's Number Five, right next to my old drawer. Maybe that'll take your mind off things."

She'd gone category 5. I didn't know what else to do now.

"Pascha, what's going on?" Martin asked.

Oh, right, he was probably picking up my utterances but not Marlene's. I explained the situation to him.

"Just tell me what you need me to know," Martin thought, "and then take Marlene to a friendlier place."

Yeah, right, you'd just love to get rid of us. "Martha told us that she took a strong blow to the back of her head from the arsonist right before the door exploded."

Martin, who had just finished the external examination, froze for a second. "A blow to the back of the head?"

"Yes."

"Before the explosion?"

"Yes."

"OK, I'll watch out for that."

Meanwhile, Marlene was calming down a bit. It seemed nuns were much like little kids and regular chicks. They stop wailing as soon as they realize it's not getting them any more attention.

"Is there a body-discovery report?" I asked.

"Of course not," Martin said. "She wasn't dead when they found her."

Crap. I was trying to show off a bit to Marlene with the expertise I'd now acquired in forensic medicine, but it totally backfired. Obviously the police do investigations and write reports like that only at actual crime scenes. But when the fire department and an ambulance get called out to a fire with casualties, they all scramble around thinking they're cool blowing a massive jet of water through a big hose over the whole area and hurling the victims into the closest ambulance. At that point no one is thinking about an incident report to document the discovery of a dead body. They have time for that only if they're not burning their asses off at the scene and the victim is no longer in any particular rush.

As Katrin and Martin found their forensic rhythm, she dictated everything that Martin said and did, and Martin completed his part of the work routinely, neatly, and precisely . . . until he got to the back of Martha's head.

"The skull presents multiple fractures." He listed off several technical medical terms. "The type of fractures largely matches the police report detailing the events at the scene. However, it cannot be excluded that the victim sustained one or more fractures prior to the explosion."

Katrin switched the Dictaphone off and stared at Martin over her mask. "What are you doing?"

Martin attempted an innocent expression, which always makes him look like a schoolkid who's just been caught peeing into the coffee machine in the teachers' lounge.

"It cannot be excluded," he repeated.

"But nothing suggests that either, right?"

"But nothing suggests the contrary, right?"

"The police report from the night of the fire says that the woman was flung back by the shock wave from the explosion and that the back of her head impacted the stone wall that separates the convent hill from the square below," Katrin countered. "Then the woman received emergency medical care on scene followed by intensive care at the hospital. All the wounds were cleaned. She spent days lying in the hospital wrapped in ointment gauze. There isn't anything left that might suggest one over the other as the cause of the injury."

"Exactly," Martin said. He sounded defiant.

"Not 'exactly,'" Katrin replied. "There is no evidence that she sustained trauma to the head prior to the explosion; in this respect, it is inappropriate to single out this possibility explicitly."

"If my report avoids addressing the possible manner in which this injury was sustained, then anyone who reads the report will interpret this injury to clearly support the sequence of events currently assumed at the scene of the arson." Martin took off his mask and looked at Katrin.

"So what?" Katrin asked.

"What if that sequence of events was not at all how it happened?" Martin asked.

Now Katrin took her mask off too, walked around the body on the table, and stood right in front of Martin. "Did the nun regain consciousness before she died?"

Martin shook his head.

"Then how would someone know what happened the night of the fire?"

The two stared at each other in silence.

"Man, Katrin," Martin said at last. "You know . . ."

"No," Katrin said. "No, I do not know."

I felt Martin beginning to panic.

"*But*," Katrin said knowingly, laying a hand on his arm, "I suppose it's fine for you to mention *all* of the possibilities in the report. If you think it's important . . ."

Martin felt a surge of gratitude and relief.

You may recall that with Katrin, Martin had the same problem he did with Gregor. Katrin knew about me, as did Gregor. There were thus three people who knew about my presence, but two refused to acknowledge it openly, so sometimes it was like the third had cooties.

"OK," Martin said coolly. "Can we continue, then?"

The rest of the autopsy didn't yield any further findings relevant to the case, only a few things that had nothing to do with her death. Martha's left cheekbone had previously been broken in several places and healed badly; she was missing a few teeth that had been replaced with a bridge; and there were more nails and screws hidden in her arms and wrists than in the toolbox of the average do-it-your-selfer. Oh, yeah, and there were also a couple of badly knit broken ribs too. Martin didn't comment on the type of injuries; he mentioned only that they were several years old.

"Car accident?" I asked, again trying to show how much I'd already learned. Rib fractures from hitting the lower half of the steering wheel, the broken wrist from holding the steering wheel, and the fractures on the left half of the face from hitting the A-pillar. Classic patterns in cars without airbags.

"No," Martin replied, surprisingly. And surprisingly monosyllabically.

"Then what?"

He didn't say anything. And made an effort not to think anything.

"Man, Martin, I'm just trying to learn something. So out with it. Did she get stuck under a steamroller?"

He still refused to think anything.

"Marlene, do you know where these older injuries came from?" I asked.

"Hail Mary, full of grace . . ."

That was the last straw. One of her sisters from the order was lying filleted into thin strips on the stainless steel table, and here was Marlene starting to pray again.

"What is wrong with the two of you?" I asked, irritated.

"Even the dead have a right to dignity and the right to keep their personal information private," Martin lectured.

I could certainly fathom why he didn't clue in all the friends and family of an autoerotic accident victim about the state of arousal that the dude had passed away in, but what harm could there be in telling me how Martha's old injuries had come about? It would've only been for teaching purposes. But no, instead Martin and Marlene agreed, although they couldn't coordinate with each other directly. Great. Now if the only two souls I can communicate with could both team up against me, my somewhat unilateral social life was going to be taking another nosedive. Such developments need to be nipped in the bud.

I swore revenge.

And I got my chance right after the autopsy. Martin took Katrin's voice recorder, attached it to his computer, and ran the recorded autopsy notes through his speech recognition software. He corrected a few transcription errors of the sort that crop up occasionally. Then he put on his cordless headset and filled out all the different forms that are part of an autopsy report.

The cover sheet asks for the victim's name, his or her personal information, and information about who requested the report and the scope of the examinations performed. Martin dictated, "Astrid Kammschneider, religious sister, member of the Charitable Sisters of Saint Mary Magdalene, religious name Martha." He said her dates of birth and death, last known address, and ID number. "Examination requested by: Cologne District Attorney's Office."

The scope of the investigation performed was checked off using a preprinted list. Autopsy of body, check.

Toxicological examination, no check. Genetic analysis, no check. "Other examinations," Martin dictated: "None."

"Ah, Dr. Gänsewein," the boss called out through the office. "How did the autopsy go? I hope your feet aren't too sore from standing so long over the autopsy table."

Martin's eyes left the screen, and he confirmed for the boss that everything had gone OK, he was feeling fit, and there weren't any problems. The boss walked around the desk and looked at the screen.

"Oh," he said with an expression that apparently couldn't decide between amusement and horror. "I think a small typo made it through there."

The line in question read "Chewable Sisters" instead of "Charitable Sisters of Saint Mary Magdalene," and the examination had been requested by the "Cologne District A-go-go's Office," and the ID number read "abc123."

"What's the big idea?" Martin hissed at me.

"Where did Martha get those old injuries from?" I hissed back.

Martin typed quickly on the keyboard, correcting "Chewable" to "Charitable."

I changed it back again.

"What the . . ." the boss said. "What's going on with your computer?"

Martin tore the headset off his head and switched it off. "Sometimes this headset gets some weird interference, and then the software doesn't work properly," he stammered while making the corrections on the keyboard.

"The injuries," I reminded him.

"Battery," Martin mumbled.

"What did you say?" the boss asked.

"Uh, battery. A friend mentioned that the little lithium batteries in these cordless headsets can cause problems when they get close to empty, so I should check on that."

"Oh, I see," said the boss. The look he gave Martin was thoughtful. Or worried. Or both. "Try to not overdo it right out of the gate. Ramp up to your previous workload slowly." He laid his hand on Martin's shoulder. "It's not a sign of weakness if you take it easy for a bit. Rather, it's a sign of good sense."

Martin nodded.

"And give me the report when you've finished it."

Martin nodded again.

"Why are you doing this to me?" he asked me in his thoughts as soon as the boss had left the office. OK, it wasn't a question, it was an accusation. Followed by, "Why can't you just leave me in peace?"

A rhetorical question, in all likelihood, because Martin knew the answer every bit as well as I did.

SEVEN

I left the Institute for Forensic Medicine after Martin had so
rudely dumped me, and I zoomed back over to Mariental.
Of course some devotion or other was yet again going on
in the convent church, and the whole prayer posse was bab-
bling and reciting canticles to God the Father, his son, and
the latter's mother. Talk about a blended family, just like the
hundreds of thousands there are nowadays. Nobody ever
heard anything else about Joseph, did they? Poor guy. At
least in all the prayers I'd heard in the last few days he never
got mentioned. Instead there are all sorts of saints who are
constantly having to intercede and pray for us. Nobody was
praying for me. Not that I was sure praying for me would be
a productive use of their time anyway.

Hey, God, some angel would say. *Now they're praying for
Pascha.*

Pascha? Who's he?

Um, I think he's the one who stole cars.

At this point I wasn't sure how it would continue. Was
the Good Lord a real man who'd say something like, *You
know, I could go for a Porsche with deep-dish wheels too, one that
would hug the road nicely, what with driving over all these clouds
up here.* Or would he respond, *A car thief? Let him grease bicycle
chains in hell!*

"He would forgive you if you repented," Marlene said,
suddenly right next to me.

Oh my God, she scared the bejeezus out of me.

"But you don't regret the things you've done, right?"

Caught! But I do know that theft is against the law.

"And against the Seventh Commandment," Marlene added.

Well, that too, but what do I care? The rides I stole were insured up to the roof rails. So basically no harm was done.

"Well, now you listen to me—" Marlene started, indignantly.

"No, no," I interrupted her. "Really. Our economy functions much better with car theft."

If only she'd had eyes, they would be staring at me blankly, all bugged out like the headlights on a 2CV.

"Pay attention: A man buys a car. He insures it in case it's stolen. If the car is not stolen, its contribution to gross domestic product stops right there."

Marlene nodded, although somewhat reluctantly.

"Now instead, let's say the car gets stolen. The insurance company has to process the claim, and for that they need personnel, whose salaries and health insurance and retirement contributions they pay. The man gets the money from the insurance company, which is paid through a bank with a staff, whose salaries and health insurance and retirement contributions they pay. The man buys a new car. That creates jobs for some gearheads somewhere. The stolen car stays in traffic somewhere in the world and needs replacement parts, which again creates jobs. That's what they call a 'circular economy.'"

Marlene gave a subtle cough. "Actually, I wanted to talk to you about something else."

You cannot have a rational conversation with chicks who are also nuns. About cars. Or sex.

"Tonight there's going to be a preelection rally for Germania Ahead."

I vaguely remembered having heard that name once before.

"That's the right-wing populist party that's running for city council, and they've been polling as much as ten percent—which would make them the third-largest bloc on the city council."

Yowza! Marlene was totally clued in on events outside her convent? I was pretty surprised.

"And can you guess who this campaign event is being hosted by?"

I hate guessing games. She didn't push it.

"By the Allotment Garden Club."

"Oh-ho," I replied, now very interested. "Are they joining forces out of common interest?"

"It very much looks that way," said Marlene. She sighed. "Even though my sisters are still in extreme shock from the fire and two deaths, they are slowly getting back to business as usual. They are still in danger, right?"

I nodded.

"So we should definitely stick with the case."

I nodded again. "And Martin has to attend that rally tonight."

"But he doesn't want anything further to do with any of that," Marlene said. "Right?"

"Don't worry. I'll find a way to talk him into it."

We agreed to meet at twenty past seven at the Allotment Garden Club in the middle of the garden area, and then I zoomed off to Martin.

On the way through Martin's front hallway I caused the light to flicker again, and one look at the wall showed me why. Instead of that weird metal mirror thingy at ceiling height, now Martin had screwed pieces of sheet metal about a meter wide onto the walls on either side, from floor to ceiling. When I flew through this "gate," the lights flickered. What did he call this contraption again?

"Capacitive magnetic field sensor," Martin yelled to me from the living room.

Well, thank you very much.

He was sitting in his chair with a hat on like my pig-tailed cousin used to wear when she was about five years old. Color: hot pink. Material: probably angora. Style: with ear flaps. And a little tie under the chin.

After a moment of flabbergastment I shrieked with laughter.

"Just wait," thought Martin. Then he took a plastic bag, pulled it over his hand, and rubbed it like a madman all over the hat. The fur took on static charge so that every bit of fuzz was standing on end.

"Well, ow t d ou nk?" thought Martin.

At first I didn't say anything at all because I was still doubled over laughing. But eventually I calmed down enough to respond to this strange creature from Planet Pink. "Well now, if you just screen the front part of your skull with a photonic shield as well, then your plan might succeed," I suggested. Incidentally, I had to explain to my editor what a photonic shield is. She'd never seen *Star Trek* . . .

Martin shrugged. "You'll stop laughing soon enough."

At that moment I couldn't really imagine that happening, but since I'd come all this way to convince Martin to attend the rally of "Germanists" among the garden gnomes, I finally managed to hold back.

"Marlene is asking if you'd be willing to visit a campaign event being held tonight by that right-wing rabble group that's making a stink about the convent," I began.

"No, I have a date with Birgit."

"You can bring her along."

"No."

"Martin, please! The nuns are still in danger, but the police are sitting on their asses not doing anything anymore. You can't let the nuns down now too."

"Yes, I can," said Martin, but I could feel that he was not comfortable saying that. He is a do-gooder after all; there's no doubt about that. A do-gooder who's clearly a little off his rocker, yes, but a do-gooder all the same.

Birgit's arrival interrupted our friendly banter.

"Are you cold?" she asked wide-eyed, staring at his hat.

Martin tore it from his head. "Uh, no, well, I'm just doing some physics experiments."

"Uh-huh." Birgit's gaze moved from the metal plates in the hallway over Martin's hat to the stack of physics and electronics books lying next his armchair.

"I'll explain it another time," Martin muttered.

"All right," she said, seeming slightly unsettled. "And have you given some thought to what you'd like to do tonight?"

"Now's your chance!" I yelled at Martin.

"Well, there is a campaign event tonight for Germania Ahead," Martin said, hesitantly.

"What, you want to go to *that*?" Birgit asked, horrified.

Martin nodded unhappily.

"Well, now, that's not something I'd have thought you'd be interested in."

"Tell her why," I prompted Martin.

"Germania Ahead's party platform actually opposes the homeless shelter at the convent too, just like the allotment gardeners."

"Oh!" Birgit said, relieved. "So you haven't completely given up on the investigation."

Martin nodded. He looked just as unhappy now as before.

"I think that's great. It would be terrible if the arsonist were to strike again. Then we'd be kicking ourselves for not having done anything."

Martin shook his head. "Well, really it is a police matter. The detectives on a case are not at all pleased when private individuals interfere in an investigation."

Birgit shrugged. "If there are any detectives at the event tonight, then we can make ourselves scarce."

"Bravo!" I cried. That chick not only looked hot, but under all that angel hair she also had some serious wattage in her high-beams. And she's practical. And she's built.

"PASCHA!" Martin barked.

"Why do you look so angry?" Birgit said, insecure.

"Uh, what? Me, angry?" Martin stammered. "No, no, it's nothing. It's just because I've got those rabble-rousing brownshirts on my mind. They've got my blood boiling already."

Martin and Birgit wanted to grab a bite to eat before heading to the rally. I followed them to Veggie Paradise, but did not join them. Instead I waited across from the french fry street vendor's stand until they'd both satiated their hunger with steamed lawn clippings, and then I accompanied them to the Allotment Garden Club in Mariental. I don't assume the worst of anyone, at least not very often, but I wanted to be sure that the two of them actually did make it to where I wanted them. And they did.

The registered nonprofit "Magdalene Convent Allotment Garden Club Foundation" was laid out like the cloister inside the convent. The outer hedge that went all the way around the clubhouse garden in the middle was actually made up of two parallel hedges spaced three meters apart. They were pruned so that they met high in the center, forming a tunnel. The inner of the two hedges had regularly spaced gaps in it that opened into the middle. It was supposed to mimic the cloister, Marlene explained upon arrival. I couldn't make out anything in the darkness other than a dreadful amount of green, but I got what she was trying to tell me: these garden gnomes *liked* the convent. At least, they had liked it in 1952 when they set up the allotment gardens and piggy-backed onto the convent in name and planting plan.

"They still bring us fresh flowers every week for the church," Marlene explained to me.

"Do they have a key for this purpose?" I asked.

"No idea."

I rolled my eyes. More and more, the convent struck me as a regular coop of birdbrains.

"That's not true," Marlene retorted. "Each of us sisters is responsible for something different, and within her own area each sister knows everything there is to know. Sister Hildegard is responsible for the church decorations; she will know whether the allotment gardeners put the flowers only in the church itself or whether they have a key to the sacristy."

"We should definitely pin that down," I made clear. "After all, the bell's rope was cut, and the wood was soaked with the oil for the sanctuary lamp. So anyone who has a key to the sacristy could have stolen the oil and cut the rope."

I could sense that Marlene didn't think the allotment gardeners were capable of setting the fire, but clearly she had a totally warped view of people. Although I didn't want get into that now.

Even if the allotment gardeners still harbored love for the convent or a church decorated with flowers, that great love did not by any means extend to the bums. The signs the club had put up everywhere spoke for themselves: NO SOLICITING, NO ACCESS TO NONMEMBERS, NO CAMPING, NO ALCOHOL IN GARDENS (ALCOHOL PERMITTED ONLY IN CLUBHOUSE). Now, surely no paying allotment garden club member would ever be hit with a fine for enjoying a frosty Kölsch while sitting in front of his garden plot's little summerhouse. But I had no doubt if a bum was downing a forty on one of the benches that he'd be ordered off the property lickety-split.

So we were dealing with a club of type-A uptight upper-middle-class assholes. The ideal hosts for a Germania Ahead campaign rally.

Martin and Birgit stayed in back, as much as they could. It wasn't working for Birgit. She had a problem—she looked like the winner of Hitler's Model of the Year. Blonde hair, blue eyes, athletic figure, good posture. In addition, she was the only woman there under fifty. And she arrived with a companion whose physical presence dissuaded no one from casting covetous glances at her.

134

Martin strained his neck and stood on his tiptoes, try-ing to subject every visitor at the rally to scrutiny. He was obviously looking for plainclothes, whose presence would give him the rest of the night off. Optimist. Of course the cops weren't here.

"Good evening," said the guy who stepped up to the microphone.

To his left stood living proof that the genetic cross of man and animal had been successfully achieved about twenty-five years ago. The result had escaped from the lab and was now standing wide-stanced and motionless beside the speaker. Unfortunately, the lab researcher at the time had apparently been able to find raw material only in his immediate personal environment and had hence gotten hold of some pretty low-grade genes. The human half may have come from the researcher's slightly mentally retarded brother, whereas the animal donor was clearly the family dog—a pug by the looks of things. Every roll of fat on the front of the neck, on the back of the neck, and over the ribs had withstood the interspecies leap, and the pushed-in snout betrayed his animalian origin. Pug-Man was squeezed into a tight black suit with an earpiece in his ear and hands folded in front of his crotch. The typical stance of a Secret Service agent standing next to the president of the United States, waiting for a terrorist so he could throw himself between the boss and the bullet.

Martin and Birgit had to stand along the back wall because the hall was already packed when they came in. At least a hundred fifty authentic adherents of Germania Ahead were there—each recognizable by their armbands with the party's logo, which featured the German eagle and a laurel wreath. Another thirty or so figures were squeezed tightly together in one corner, probably the allotment gardeners. I saw two or three ladies and gentlemen from the neighborhood association, but there was no sign of Susanne Gröbendahl or Rolf von Berg. This scene was probably beneath them. Or else they had walked into the allotment garden area but turned off toward a dark corner and were now fooling around behind some bush.

"Do you recognize anyone?" I asked Marlene.

"Just a few of the neighbors, who I know only by sight." She pointed to the heads that I'd already recognized too.

"What about the guy at the mic?" I asked.

"No, I've never seen him."

"I am pleased to see so many people turn out tonight who are not indifferent to the destiny of our homeland," the Germanist said, beginning his leisurely address.

Applause.

"I am pleased to see that there are people who want to make right those things that have gone wrong in recent years."

Applause.

"It is time for us to again remember that we are Germans and we live in Germany—our policy should not be set in Brussels!"

Applause. Now from the allotment gardeners too.

The speaker took his time. He calmly took a sip from the glass of water sitting in front of him on the lectern. He gave a totally relaxed impression. And he didn't at all look the way I'd always imagined wing nuts, with boots and bald heads and everything. This guy here was also wearing a suit, just like his bodyguard, although his fit well. Dark-blue suit, light-blue shirt, open collar. He didn't look half bad. And in fact, each female allotment gardener seemed to have totally forgotten her lawfully wedded *Rosenkavalier* standing in cords and plaid shirt next to her; instead, with faces alight, all the women were hanging on each word emanating from the lips of this gasbag.

Martin and Birgit looked embarrassed, standing in the back holding hands.

"This financial crisis has its origins in America. The European Union wants to ban German cars because they are too good, too fast, and too safe. The Indians are snagging all our jobs, and the Chinese are buying up the whole world's supply of coal and steel."

Applause.

"With so-called farm subsidies, we have been financing every farmer between Gdańsk and Moscow."

Applause.

"German money is financing roads from Riga to Belgrade—but are German companies ever awarded the contracts to build these roads?"

"No!" someone shouted from the audience.

The gasbag didn't flinch at all.

"They cannot. Calls for bids on these projects are being made throughout Europe. But because German companies are already financing this insanity with their tax money, they can't offer the penny prices that the Latvians, Bulgarians, and Czechs do. They are not only *not* getting the job," artificial pause, "but with their tax money they are also actually paying the Czech entrepreneur who *is* allowed to perform the job."

Applause.

"Is that true?" I asked Martin.

"Yes and no," replied my otherwise oh-so-precise scientist.

"Good to know," I replied sarcastically, but Martin wasn't at all annoyed. He was much too fascinated by what was transpiring in this hall. How calm the speaker was, how well educated, how he avoided words that had to do with racism or violence or Teutomania.

I was starting to wonder if this speech was going to turn into a lecture on European Union subsidy policy, but apparently the speaker had already moved on.

"And how do things look here?" the speaker asked quietly. He didn't shout the whole time; now he was almost whispering. "Could it be that things are better here?"

It seemed like the audience members were all holding their breath just to avoid attracting attention by disrupting the ensuing silence. The gasbag was drawing out the artificial pauses after his rhetorical questions so long that I half-expected the nearest potbellied garden gnome to keel over out of his chair due to lack of oxygen—but no one was actually passing out, so the pauses must not have been *that* long.

"A skilled German worker with two children has less money to spend than does an equivalent family of Kurdish immigrants, none of whom is working and all of whom are receiving their second year of German unemployment benefits. And they are not able to work specifically because they cannot speak German."

No one was shouting agreement into the hall anymore, but a lot of heads were nodding.

"For heaven's sake," said Marlene. "Those people were driven out of their homes specifically because the government was banning their language and culture."

"And now they're planting bombs," I replied.

"Individuals are," Marlene replied sharply. "There are murderers among ethnic Germans as well, but most Germans are upstanding citizens. So too with Kurds."

There she went again, laying on her usual love-your-neighbor charity drivel. If it were up to Marlene and her charitable sisters, we'd presumably invite the whole world in and let them sponge off us.

"Yes," Marlene responded, simply.

Oh, please.

"Retirees who have slaved for forty years and paid into social security the whole time hardly receive enough money to live on. But teenagers who graduate high school unable to read and write, people who prefer 'hanging out' to working, immigrants who haven't paid one cent into social security, and any random EU citizen who decides to take up residence in the welfare paradise known as Germany: these people are all receiving the money that you earned with all your work and retirement contributions."

Now the allotment gardeners were all applauding, without exception.

"What an asshole," Birgit whispered into Martin's ear.

"How so?" I asked. "What he's saying is true, isn't it?"

"No," Martin said. "It's not as simple as that."

"If you pay money in and another gets it out, that seems pretty simple to me. Simply shitty, actually," I explained.

"And to which of those groups did you belong?" Martin asked.

"None of them," I said. "They don't have a professional association or a retirement plan for car thieves."

The speaker resumed his speech. "We donate school-books to children in Africa, but in this country our schools are dilapidated. We provide reconstruction aid after earth-quakes in Pakistan and Afghanistan, and the inhabitants of these countries thank us with terrorism and bombs. We send rice to North Korea while that country builds its nuclear bombs against the West."

Applause.

"The rice is for the people," Marlene argued. "Those in power make bombs while the people starve. Are we just sup-posed to stand by and watch them die?"

"German soldiers defend the Hindu Kush—and what for, actually? German interests? Or is it sooner for American interests? British? Perhaps even Indian interests? Or what interest do you have in the Hindu Kush? Or you? And you?"

The individual audience members that the speaker addressed and pointed at stopped breathing and froze; one shook his head, unsettled. Then the tension erupted into applause.

I was slowly getting bored with the sermon. While on several points I thought the guy wasn't really that far off the mark—even though Martin and Marlene reprimanded me immediately for thinking such things—he was beginning to ramble on in generalizations, as all politicians do. I used to think politics was interesting, but only when I understood what was in it for me. For the life of me, I couldn't see what the Hindu Kush had to do with Marlene's sisters. So if this event here wasn't going to turn up any new information for our case, I thought I'd head right over to the movies, because today was Thursday, and Thursday's the day when they start showing the new releases. There were a few action flicks I didn't want to miss.

I was just transmitting to Martin that I'd see him later when the speaker suddenly transitioned to close combat.

"In our immediate neighborhood we can observe similar trends," he said very quietly. "The streets have as many holes as the government's budgets do. School buildings are falling apart; there is no money for educational materials, let alone a hot meal for all schoolchildren. By contrast, food handouts to the unemployed and homeless are practically growing on trees. The coddling pedagogy used in our schools encourages teenage offenders to commit violent acts, and foreign criminals are happy that they are living better in German prisons than they do in the hut villages of their homelands."

Applause.

Martin and Marlene were on maximum alert. Even Birgit, who I unfortunately wasn't getting any thought signals from, looked like she wanted to throw something at the guy.

"It has become the hallmark of German politics and our society that for those who do nothing, everything is done, and for those who do everything, nothing is done."

Pff, that convoluted wording was probably a challenge for some of these garden gnomes to follow since some of them had already started on their second liter of Kölsch, but the thunderous applause showed that the majority had gotten at least a basic understanding of the message.

Martin and Birgit refused to applaud, and Marlene kept shouting, "Stop, stop"—but obviously I was the only one getting reception.

"We must again start showing both respect and consideration to those who are making a contribution. And cure of their parasitism those who intend to live at the expense of honest and upstanding citizens. Alcoholism is not an excuse. Foreign origin is not an excuse. Laziness is not an excuse."

Applause.

Each of the people who were clapping their hands so enthusiastically here were undoubtedly sponging off the government themselves. Tax evasion, child allowance fraud, skimming off the balance on Grandma's savings account so the social security office doesn't seize her money to refinance the nursing home. Playing hooky from work. Just normal things that any middle-class asshole does. I used to too. However, I never denied I was a criminal. I just never got caught.

But if people like this gasbag were to hold power, it wouldn't take long for at least half of the people attending this rally to land in the can for offenses exactly like those. The other half would know someone inside the government shielding them in some way or other.

Then the speaker suddenly took on a worried expression. "We live in a country of Christian traditions."

At the demagogue's sudden reference to Jesus Christ, Marlene exploded in incandescent outrage.

I was curious to see what was coming next.

"The Sermon on the Mount is a central tenet of our faith and of our tradition. As we read in the Gospel of Saint Luke, chapter six, verses thirty-five and thirty-six, Jesus tells his disciples: 'But love ye your enemies: do good, and lend, hoping for nothing thereby: and your reward shall be great, and you shall be the sons of the Highest; for he is kind to the unthankful, and to the evil. Be ye therefore merciful, as your Father also is merciful.'"

The audience hung on his every word as though Jesus himself were standing before them. Marlene recited the words with him. By heart. But you would expect that of a nun.

"Even two thousand years ago there were parasites who believed they could enjoy a comfortable life at the expense of society without personal responsibility and without personal labors, and they also interpreted Jesus's words in the way most convenient to them. And it is to them that Saint Paul addresses his second letter to the Thessalonians in chapter three, verses ten and twelve: 'For also when we were with you, this we declared to you: that, if any man will not work, neither let him eat. Now we charge them that are such, and beseech them by the Lord Jesus Christ, that, working with silence, they would eat their own bread.'"

The audience awoke from their surprised religious stupor and started clapping, stomping their feet, and yelling, "Yeah! That's right!"

Marlene shrieked as though someone were ripping all her fingernails and toenails out at the same time.

"We ought to remind ourselves that we can be the masters of our own country. We need only the desire. Thank you very much."

Apparently no one had reckoned with such a quick end to the speech because there was a scary moment of silence before applause thundered through the hall, shaking the plastic flowers in the plastic vases on the red-and-white checked plastic tablecloths.

Martin and Birgit quickly exited the place in silence, still holding hands.

"Hey," I yelled at Martin, "the event isn't over yet. Go back and ask him what he intends to do about shelters for bums."

"My goodness, that guy really scares me," Birgit whispered.

"Yes," Martin agreed. "With his suit and elevated language he's made himself socially acceptable to a lot of people."

"But do you think he's the arsonist?" Birgit asked.

"He himself, probably not," Martin said. "But his followers are entirely capable of something like that." He was picturing the pug-man playing bodyguard.

"We shouldn't write off Rolf von Berg yet either," I reminded him. "Did you ask Birgit to get that info on him? And maybe she could find something out about the speaker while she's at it too."

He wasn't responding to me.

Birgit laid her hand on his arm. "Come on, let's go get a drink somewhere and think about other things."

"No! Back into the hall!" I shouted. "The evening's not over yet!"

"If you say so," Martin mumbled.

I don't know exactly who he was talking to, but since he spoke his assent out loud, Birgit thought he was talking to her and pulled him with her, bundling him off into the passenger seat of her convertible, and they zipped off. I couldn't take more celery/rhubarb virgin daiquiris at Veggie Paradise or ginger/cinnamon/lemon balm infusions at some esoteric tearoom. Plus, I didn't consider our research into the right-wing political scene complete just yet, so I went back in and hovered beside Marlene under the ceiling light of what had since become a very stuffy event room full of human-sized garden gnomes.

"Did I miss anything?"

"It's unbelievable," Marlene whispered. "All this frustration and hatred for human beings who are really struggling."

"Did I miss anything?" I asked her again.

"And to top it off, justifying his tirades of hatred with passages from the Bible . . ."

"Marlene!"

"Hail Mary, full of grace . . ."

Not this again! For fu—

I managed to pull it together and left Marlene by herself for a while, trying to get the big picture of the throng below us.

It took a while for me to get the gasbag back in view again. He was chatting with a guy who I'd seen somewhere else before. Oh yeah, at the neighborhood association meeting.

". . . a tragedy right here in our beautiful neighborhood."

The gasbag nodded.

"However, we've already taken a few steps to put an end to these shenanigans."

"Ah-ha" and a raised eyebrow were the speaker's only responses.

The neighbor raised his chin. "Because you are quite right. One simply cannot abide everything. We have invested our sweat and hard-earned money into the redevelopment of this neighborhood, and now property values are going down the tubes because vagrants are continually hanging around our square."

"Mmm."

"And if the nuns cannot be gently convinced that this kind of charity is not desired here, then other ways will simply have to be found to close the shelter."

Just spill it, I thought, irritated. *Just admit you set the fire and took out Martha, and then I can go to the movies, finally.*

The busybody took a deep breath, presumably to at last describe his heroic act in every detail when the sound of breaking glass came from outside. The attendees froze for a moment, and then they rushed outside and ran down the main path to the rear exit from the allotment garden area. From there the convent was only a stone's throw away— and in the truest sense of expression, because several window panes on the long side of the building facing us were broken. I tried to remember what rooms lay behind these windows, but Marlene, who suddenly appeared next to me, spared me the trouble.

"The novitiate," she whispered.

Lights were turning on, women in baggy T-shirts and unkempt hair peering out through their windows toward us. One of them yelled something out the window that sounded like, "Fuck off, you assholes," but that couldn't be right, could it? Surely I'd heard wrong. In any case, that's the only comment I heard because all of the lights went out simultaneously, as though on command. Or as though someone had cut the power to the whole wing of the building. But that couldn't be right either, could it? I was pretty sure that in this whole henhouse of nuns there wasn't one with the common sense to cut the lights to protect the clearly recognizable women standing in their well-lit windows. No, considerations like that would be more typical of those of us who come from a criminal milieu. At any rate, the windows were dark again, and no further window panes were getting broken, so the allotment gardeners quickly returned to the glasses of beer they had left behind in their clubhouse.

The police must have been called because they showed up quickly in two patrol cars and tried to interview as many witnesses as possible. The first two officers to arrive on scene stood akimbo and tried to usher all the people in the vicinity back into the meeting hall where they wanted to take down their personal information. Most of the people stumbled back toward the hall in the dim light, left exact change next to the half-full glasses, and hightailed it out of there. Others, unfamiliar with the area, ran right into the arms of the second team of cops, who were waiting at the main entrance to the garden area, and others vanished down the dark paths and through little side gates into the night. The ones who got caught all recited the same story: No, they hadn't noticed anything unusual. No, they didn't know anyone who had anything against the convent. Yes, this had been a perfectly harmless city council campaign event. Yes, they attended every campaign event for all the parties running. Purely out of civic interest. Basically they wanted to know what kind of people the candidates were, they all said.

Marlene had immediately returned to the convent to find out what was going on and what the nuns were saying about it. My company was not desired because her sisters were all in their nightclothes or bathrobes in the refectory. That was bullshit, of course, because if I wanted I could watch the nuns in their beds, in the shower, getting dressed, or taking a dump. *If I wanted to.* Though I must confess that I can imagine much sexier stimuli.

Plus, someone had to keep an eye on the police work, so I stayed with the garden gnomes. But the cops were not exactly putting their shoulders to the wheel. In the end, they simply wrote up a vandalism report for broken windows that the nuns could use to submit to their insurance company. And that was that.

Before long Marlene whooshed back over and told me that the nuns hadn't seen or heard anything. Just the shards of window glass plinking down, which had woken them up. Then she whooshed away again.

As for me, I stole a glance at a passerby's wristwatch. Perfect! It wasn't yet quite eleven o'clock. I could still make the late movie. A decent action flick was exactly the right medicine now to take my mind off things.

EIGHT

I spent the night first at the movies and later in front of the boob tube in an apartment where this single guy indulges in awesome pay-per-view titles but always sacks out on the couch around eleven thirty. I discovered him a couple of weeks ago by accident, and I didn't have anything else planned tonight, so I went over to his place to watch TV. From my position in front of the premium-television programming, I could also see through the window that there had been a multiple-car pileup in the fog out on the A1. So I gadded around over there a while, watching the scene, but no one died. That would have been too convenient. Most often, people quietly peter out alone in their apartments, and then their souls zoom away, so I never get a chance to chat them up. That's what keeps drawing me back to accidents and disasters of all kinds. I'd actually encountered a few souls this way, but not once had anyone spoken to me. They always zoomed single-mindedly past me, seemingly unaware of my presence.

I arrived at Martin's apartment shortly before the punctual ringing of his alarm, zoomed through the apartment's front door, and felt a very unpleasant tingling in the front hallway. The metal plates in the hallway were plugged into the outlet and had several hundred volts surging through them. I was pissed off. Martin was really trying every means conceivable to banish me from his life. However, he had not thought all this through to its logical conclusion. Although I was still kind of stuck in my former earthly habits, such as coming into his apartment through the front door, it's not like I *had* to come in that way. I could just as well walk or fly in, or however you want to describe it, through windows, walls, roofs, and even people, and I decided to immediately start coming through his living room window, thus rendering his groovy Ghostbuster gate pointless.

I was going to whisper that in his ear right now, even before the soft beeping of his alarm started. I zoomed into the bedroom—but immediately recoiled. Martin was not alone. Birgit was lying beside him. Her blonde hair covered her face, and a single hair was blowing up and down to the rhythm of her breathing. Apart from the natural hair on her head and body, she was naked.

I couldn't believe it.

The two of them had screwed.

In secret!

"Did you screw her?" I asked Martin, ignoring our usual morning greeting ritual.

He grumbled vaguely.

"DID YOU TWO HAVE SEX?"

"Shut up," mumbled Martin.

"Did you say something?" Birgit asked.

"Good morning." He beamed at her, she beamed at him—Martin's beaming made perfect sense to me.

"How was it?" I asked.

"You'd better pull something on," Martin said.

"What for?" Birgit mumbled, stretching cozily.

"Because we've got a peeping Tom in the bedroom who lacks even a flicker of decency," he thought toxically in my direction.

"So you don't catch a cold." He tossed her his fleecy pajamas with blue-and-white horizontal stripes.

"I'm going to take a shower, and then I'll be getting dressed anyway," Birgit said.

"Awesome!" I thought, looking forward to a steamy shower orgy with sexy Birgit.

"Uh, no," Martin called. "The shower's broken."

"Broken?" Birgit asked.

"Broken?" I asked. "It was working fine yesterday."

"Yes, that is, the shower works, but there's a leak in the drainpipe somewhere. Whenever I take a shower, my downstairs neighbor gets stains on his ceiling," Martin stammered.

"Liar," I yelled.

"Oh, you poor guy," Birgit said. "Something needs to be done about that."

"Yes, the super is taking care of it today."

"Great," I said. "Things will be back to normal again tomorrow. Invite Birgit over again."

"OK, I'll take a shower at home then," Birgit said.

She walked, naked as she was, into the bathroom.

"You stay here," Martin scolded me.

"That would be pretty stupid," I replied, following Birgit as soon as I heard the toilet flush.

She took a quick sponge bath, combed her hair, plucked the hairs out of the comb, and then made faces into the mirror. Then she snuck back into the bedroom and jumped onto Martin's bed.

"Don't you go back into your burrow, you little ground-hog," she yelled. "Go make me some coffee."

Martin tried for a few minutes to fend off her advances, but then finally managed to push her to the side and wrap her up in his duvet before getting up to make coffee. He measured the water, measured the beans, ground them in the hand mill, filled the espresso machine, and set it on the burner, all with this totally ridiculous grin on his face.

"So, how was it?" I asked him, man to man.

"Shut up," Martin thought.

"I'm going to be here next time," I promised him.

"We'll see," he said, but I followed his thoughts to the stack of physics books next to his reading chair. I was starting to get worried. What if he actually found a way to cut me out of his life? Or maybe even disintegrate me? Was that possible?

My dark thoughts were interrupted by Birgit, who strode into the kitchen. Dressed. Unfortunately.

"With to-o-ons of sugar," she said. "What should we do tonight? It's Friday. Let's celebrate this weekend somehow. It's the first weekend you've had free in weeks." She stepped behind Martin and hugged and kissed him. On the ear.

Martin turned around, giggling. "I don't know. A movie, perhaps?"

"Great," Birgit said. I felt like today she would think anything would be a great idea—even if Martin proposed collecting garbage in the Rhine Park or sorting and labeling histological organ preparations. "Something fun, OK? Maybe something romantic. But definitely no horror movies, no vampires, no action movies, and nothing heavy."

Martin nodded happily. OK, so I wouldn't be joining them.

"What's in store for you today at work?" Birgit asked.

"Marlene's funeral," I answered before Martin could inhale. He turned pale.

"What's wrong?" Birgit asked, worried. "Are you OK?"

"Yes, uh, no, there's nothing wrong," Martin mumbled. And to me he thought: "I see no reason to attend that."

"Of course you have to go," I replied. "Marlene and Martha were murdered. The perp always goes to the funeral. So we should too."

"You can fly over and keep an eye on everyone," he thought.

"Of course. Except I can't ask anyone anything."

He sighed. "When, where?"

I gave him the information he needed, and he disclosed to Birgit that he wanted to attend Marlene's funeral.

"Oh. I'd love to join you, but I can't get away from the bank today. But you'll tell me everything tonight, right?"

Martin promised. He prepared himself a tea—loose-leaf, with a dishwasher-safe infuser, preheated cup, triple-brewed. The two turtledoves were now sitting harmoniously with irritating cockeyed smiles on their faces, sipping tea and coffee and eating sugar-free muesli soaking in fresh, organic whole milk out of little bowls. Was this love? Well, it certainly looked different from *my* usual after-sex break-fast—a cigarette and a beer, hoping that the chick would shut up. So, you know, Martin was just a total wuss.

Before the funeral, Martin had a long morning of forensic medicine ahead of him at the lab. He greeted his colleagues as he walked down the corridor toward his office, smiling at the usual jokes about his dictation fixation.

He arrived to find Katrin waiting for him at his desk. She was asking if she could run some information by him about the strange injuries of a resident of a nursing home—Martin was known for his recollection of the details of thousands of autopsies, and he was faster than any database when it came to recognizing parallels to past cases—when the boss burst in.

"Dr. Gänsewein, what were you thinking? Oh, Dr. Zange—I'm glad I caught both of you together."

Martin and Katrin looked at each other nervously.

"What's the matter?" Martin asked.

"It's regarding your autopsy report on the fire victim from the convent."

While Martin had been talking with Katrin he switched his microphone to sleep mode so that the program didn't keep transcribing everything he was saying. I woke the microphone up with a friendly command.

"Is something wrong with it?" Martin asked. The sentence appeared on his screen.

"What motivated your analysis of the head trauma as the possible result of willful assault?" the boss asked.

Divine inspiration, I wrote.

Katrin noticed the activity on the screen out of the corner of her eye, looked more closely, and then turned pale.

"I added it as a possibility because that possibility exists," Martin muttered.

Bullshit, I wrote. *It's because Martha told us.*

Martin frantically pressed various keys on his keyboard trying to sever the wireless connection from the mic to the computer, but in his nervousness he kept hitting the wrong ones.

Hello, Katrin, I wrote.

"Stop that," said Katrin. But she wasn't talking to me; she was talking to Martin. The anxiety had turned his cheeks blotchy and the tip of his nose white, and he took his hands off the keyboard immediately.

"But the wording in your report characterizes this finding as though you were certain that the trauma was sustained from assault. You don't have any evidence of this even though you mention it specifically."

Exactly, I wrote.

"Exactly," Martin read out loud.

"I beg your pardon?" the boss asked in disbelief.

Katrin stood pale and trembling next to Martin, unable to turn her eyes from his screen.

"What's wrong with you, Dr. Zange?" the boss asked with a worried expression.

Tell him you're pregnant, I suggested via the screen.

Katrin put her hand over her mouth as if suddenly nauseated and ran out of Martin's office.

"Is she pregnant?" the boss asked, bewildered. "I had no idea that Dr. Zange was even in a steady relationship."

As a medical doctor, this man should actually know that pregnancy is an issue between sperm and egg—it doesn't have any sociological relationship as its prerequisite. I mean, even a quickie on the hood of a car is enough to create life, right?

Drops of sweat appeared on Martin's forehead, and his hands were trembling on the desk next to the keyboard.

"Dr. Gänsewein, you're not looking well. I would like to ask you to set up an appointment with a psychologist. Even before the, uh, incident, you were already very tense, and then this terrible injury and weeks spent hovering between life and death"—Martin grew a bit paler—"and now jumping right back into a full load at work . . . I think you may have overextended yourself. Psychologically. And physically. Please take the rest of the day off. Get some psychological help. And bring me a note from your psychologist saying you really did get some help."

Martin's shoulders drooped; he nodded. Then he turned his computer off, put his apple for his midmorning snack back into his bag, and left his office.

The door to the break room was open. Katrin was leaning on the dishwasher, and Gregor was standing in front of her. They were whispering secretly to each other, but the way they were acting and the expressions on their faces were serious. Gregor was the one who noticed Martin slinking past them.

"Martin, hi. How are you doing?"

"Hi, Gregor. What are you doing here?"

"I was actually just stopping by to pick up the report about that brawl from Monday night."

And that's when Katrin took the opportunity to leap into Gregor's arms, I suspected.

"Is there any news about the convent fire?" Martin asked.

"Not that I know of," Gregor replied with a suspicious look. Katrin jabbed him in the side.

"I'm going over to Sister Marlene's funeral right now," Martin said. "Are you attending as well?"

Gregor shook his head. "You know, the notion that perpetrators always come to the funeral is something that uninspired crime writers invented."

Martin nodded. "Or bored ghosts," he thought.

"Thanks a lot," I replied.

"Do you want to go out and grab a beer later?" Gregor asked.

"Sure."

Martin raised his hand to weakly wave good-bye and started walking again. I stayed with Katrin and Gregor.

"I feel so sorry for him," Katrin said. "He's at the end."

"I feel sorry for him too, but we can't help him," Gregor said.

"The guy talked to me," Katrin said.

"Talked?"

"With Martin's speech recognition software. You remember."

Gregor nodded.

"The boss has got to—"

"No," Gregor urgently whispered. "Then he'll think you're completely loopy too. You have to understand. Detectives and forensic pathologists are not allowed to talk to ghosts. Period."

Katrin nodded unhappily. "But Martin . . ."

"He'll make it through," Gregor said. It sounded harsh, but there was a certain compassion unmistakable in his tone. "It's not like there's anything we can do to help him anyway."

Katrin took a deep breath and tried to smile. "OK, you're right." A single tear escaped the corner of her eye.

Gregor carefully wiped the tear away with this thumb and took Katrin into his arms. She didn't resist. "All we can do is try to keep him from doing anything majorly stupid.

We cannot let him land in as dangerous a situation as the last time, when he almost died."

Katrin nodded and cuddled a bit closer to Gregor. He noticed and was happy to let it happen, reciprocating the pressure. "You pay attention to him here at the institute, and I'll try to keep an eye on him outside."

I waited for another few minutes, but since they weren't saying anything else about me and, despite the body check, there was no prospect of any hot hay-rolling, I left the break room and looked for Martin. I couldn't find him. He wasn't at home or at Veggie Paradise, or at any of his favorite organic grocery stores. I didn't give too much thought to it because he'd promised to come to Marlene's funeral, and I'd probably catch up with him there.

The convent's chapel was filled with five times the normal quantity of flowers and candles, and up in front between the sanctuary and the first pews there was a casket.

"Looks nice, what they're doing for you here," I said when Marlene came.

"It's the season," she replied. "There are a lot of beautiful flowers in the spring. People who die in the winter have the church decorated with a lot of pine boughs and things like that."

I thought for a moment Marlene was suddenly channeling the spirit of some dead hippie when she started singing a verse from "Seasons in the Sun," a tune from a thousand years ago when women still had hair on their legs and sat on the grass in tiered boho skirts with a guitar on their knee, singing of love and peace. At least it was something other than this interminable "Hail Mary, full of grace" shtick. Marlene actually had a really nice voice. I wasn't clear on whether she was singing for me or herself, but I didn't care. It was just beautiful, hanging out with her here in the empty church and listening to her. I was so moved that I almost started to tear up. So embarrassing! As a ghost you lose any sort of hard shell you may have had; all that's left is your soft core. Good thing my old buddies couldn't see me like this.

Meanwhile, a few people started arriving and taking seats in the fourth and fifth rows of pews. Susanne Gröbendahl was there, looking good in a black dress with matching hat. More neighbors, some totally in black and lots—especially the men—in a mixture of dark blue and black. The allotment gardeners all arrived together, even the guy who'd been showing off to the gasbag and who I still had not deleted from the list of arson suspects.

Last to slip in were Martin and the contractor, Mr. Baumeister.

Next the nuns moved into the church, entering in total silence through a door in the chancel. There were considerably more than fifteen of them; I bet it was at least twice that. All their heads were bowed, their hands clasped in front of them with the sleeves of their habits pulled together so that neither faces nor hands could be seen. They moved past the altar and walked down the three steps into the nave. Some of them raised their heads almost imperceptibly, but after a quick whisper they bowed their heads again. The nuns took their seats in the first three rows. When they were all sitting, the organ began to play and a priest appeared from the sacristy. Following him in long shirts were two acolytes. One of the reasons I've probably never been able to take Catholics seriously is because they run their so-called dignitaries out onto stage in long skirts with negligées on top. How are you supposed to respect men who are dressed that way?

It turned out that this ceremony was actually a mass. Not a funeral service, not the Liturgy of the Word, no: a whole, interminable Catholic mass. Marlene prayed along with every prayer, she sang along with every song, mumbled every amen, chimed in with every *Kýrie* and *eléison* in exactly the right spots, as well as the responses to other phrases said by the dude up front in the skirt. Most of the nuns of course did exactly the same, but quite a few of the sisters joined in the singing and praying only sporadically. They seemed a little confused at times, many of them even hesitant about when to stand or kneel.

I asked Marlene what was up with that, but I didn't get any answer at all, at first. She was pretending to be lost in her devotion, but I sensed that was not the case. So I asked again.

"Those are the novices," she whispered at me.

I'd have expected more of a clue about the rituals even from women who were relative newbies. After all, no chick goes into a convent without already having occasionally been to church, right?

"Wow—so they must be *very* new, huh?"

"Exactly. Now please don't interrupt my prayers anymore."

Once the guy who was literally tied to his mama's apron strings up there trotted out the story about water transforming into wine, I floated over the chalice and determined much to my unsurprise that it was wine in there the whole time. What a scam. I was sure Marlene knew that. And yet she still believed this stuff.

I could not quite figure out the extent to which she believed the drivel about death, resurrection, and life. Of course the priest spoke of the eternal life that Marlene was now enjoying at Jesus's side. If he only knew that she was actually floating right in front of his cassock, he'd probably choke on the body of Christ in terror.

The ersatz saint proceeded to ramble on about Marlene, a member of the Order of the Charitable Sisters of Saint Mary Magdalene, the sinner who had found Jesus and walked with him as his disciple.

"Sinner?" I asked, puzzled. "Disciple? I thought the Twelve Apostles were a boy band."

"Wrong," Marlene said. "His circle of disciples included more than twelve men, and there were a number of women who saw to his subsistence. Luke chapter eight, verse three."

"Those chicks who did the cooking? That doesn't count."

"When Jesus died on the cross, the men fled, but Mary Magdalene stayed with him. Matthew chapter twenty-seven, verses fifty-five and fifty-six."

"She just didn't know where else to go."

"And in chapter twenty, verses fifteen through twenty, John says that Mary Magdalene was the first to see Jesus on Easter morning after his resurrection."

"He probably came to her first because he was hungry," I said.

"Sister Marlene made it her life's work to help women in need," the priest intoned.

"Women?" I asked.

Marlene remained stubbornly silent.

"She did good in so many places, showing affection to many people and making God's love felt. She alleviated despair through the love of Christ that she brought to this world."

I thought the wording there was pretty vague, but maybe the guy in front didn't really know what role Leni had actually played in the convent either. She was pretty reticent when it came to that.

"That's completely irrelevant," Marlene whispered at me. "Everyone serves in the place the Lord puts us."

Well, the Lord has a sense of humor, then, because he had put me in a place to redistribute horsepower. So I guess you could say the recipients of these blessed cars could look at them as gifts from heaven.

"Perhaps you simply haven't recognized your true place yet," Marlene said. "Or perhaps this is your place, right here. Your life may have just been the prelude."

Now she was just being mean, and I didn't get why. What had I ever done to her? Maybe she was offended because I didn't take any pleasure in all of this pseudointellectual holy talk, plus Marlene and I both knew firsthand that eternal life with God wasn't exactly all that people on earth claimed it would be. But I couldn't help that. Besides, I wasn't the one who got her into this state. Women make no sense.

After just about an hour we had finally gotten the ceremonial kerfuffle behind us, and the funeral procession began. The nuns exited first, of course, followed by the rest of the attendees, their hands and faces still hidden under their habits.

The convent grounds included a cemetery that was still in use today. It wasn't big, but for a convent that used to have seventy nuns it was big enough. Now that fewer nuns were living here, fewer were dying here as well, and of the ones who died here a lot of them were interred elsewhere with their families, so there was still plenty of space. Especially since the graves were small and modest. They lay along the side of the convent farthest from the allotment gardens.

A small pit had been dug up. Marlene's casket was now positioned over it. The dude in the skirt stepped forward again, offered some more sanctimonious babble, and then the casket was finally lowered in. The nuns, who formed an impenetrable wall of black dresses and cowls, sang a weird-sounding hymn in trembling voices. Then they bowed and exited to the left. All together. Almost in lockstep, apart from a few stumblers—the novices again.

"Are your funerals always so—dry?"

"The earthly body is being buried, nothing more," Marlene said. "Tonight there will be another small memorial service. Not open to the public."

"A rip-roaring wake with tons of booze and chow?" I asked. "And music and whatnot?"

"No. A reading of the Bible and a conversation where everyone says what she misses about me and what she wishes for me."

Well, presumably a rip-roaring party by cloistral standards, I suppose. I can totally picture it. But before I could bury my thoughts in the topic, Marlene sent me an unambiguous rebuke and dispatched me to Martin.

"Well, what did you think?" I asked him.

"Stupid question," he snarled. "Now the sisters are all gone. So what's left for me to do here?"

"Just talk to people. For example, you could talk to the convent's neighbors or to the allotment gardeners. How should I know?"

Martin dutifully turned around, took a step to the side, and stumbled over a headstone that looked like it had been there for a few centuries at least. Baumeister caught Martin before he fell into Marlene's grave.

"Thank you," Martin wheezed as he pulled himself together and was able to stand on his own two feet again. "You're Mr. Baumeister, right?"

Baumeister was clearly flattered. "Have I already had the pleasure?" he asked as he shook Martin's hand.

"No. I wanted to tell you how great I think it is, what you've been doing for the convent," Martin said. "Nowadays you don't see that kind of generosity very often."

"Thank you, that's very kind, Mr. . . ."

"Gänsewein, Dr. Gänsewein."

Baumeister had the good manners not to bat an eye at Martin's silly surname. "Yes, I love medieval architecture. Not just architecture one might encounter in the area, of course, but especially architecture that is still being used as originally intended."

"Although it is certainly difficult for the order to maintain a complex like this," said Martin.

Baumeister made a troubled face. "Very difficult. Fortunately, the order does have financial means. But that of course isn't the only problem." Now his mien turned downright gloomy. "Poor Sister Marlene died in a fire that was deliberately set. And to tell you the truth, I'm a little worried the sisters here might be in danger."

"Ask him if knows more about where the danger comes from," I yelled.

Martin waved me off internally. He was already on it. He cautiously pressed Baumeister on the topic.

"I've heard rumors that there was some kind of attack last night when Germania Ahead was holding a campaign event with the allotment gardeners," Baumeister whispered with a sidelong glance at the garden gnomes. "Naturally, I don't wish to impute bad intentions to anyone. But I find the scapegoating of the weakest in our society to be very unsettling."

"Mr. Baumeister," a shrill voice rang out right next to Martin's ear, making him wince. "I was hoping to run into you here because I simply must compliment you."

Martin was pushed aside by a gelatinous steamboat of a woman in a black pants suit, black hat, and comfort slippers, which with their low heels were apparently supposed to give the appearance of elegant shoes.

"Who is that?" Martin asked me mentally.

"Neighborhood association." I'd noticed her that night at Susanne Gröbendahl's house, not because of her speaking skills but her cocktail-snack gluttony. I mean, at least thirty of those swollen pretzel sticks had disappeared between her puffed-up lips alone.

"Oh, a compliment?" Baumeister turned to the lady, visibly flattered.

"I was just in Belgium. In Deigné. You already know exactly what I'm about to say, right? I'm sure you've heard it a hundred times already."

She winked at Baumeister, who towered over her by at least a head, in a way she probably intended as sexy. Or coquettish, in the event that that's what it's called in circles like this. It might have been too, if her double chin didn't wobble with every blink, as though neurons connected the rolls of fat around her neck directly to her eyelids.

"The Hôtel du Cloître is pure poetry. A fairy tale. Heaven on earth."

Baumeister strained a bit to smile. "Yes, thank you. That's very nice of you to say."

"No, really. You've achieved a miracle with it. *Sssuperbe.*"

In her Gallic hypersibilance, she sprayed saliva onto Baumeister's shirt.

"I'm pleased you liked it." His eyes went over her shoulder toward Susanne Gröbendahl, who was approaching, chin held high.

"Ms. Gröbendahl, good day," Baumeister said, greeting her courteously.

Geez, everybody really knew everybody around here.

"Hello, Mr. Baumeister. Say, didn't we have an agreement about the times of day the heavy trucks could not be driving through our quiet streets here?" Her voice was as sharp as her nose, which was jutting out below her little hat.

"Of course, Ms. Gröbendahl, of course. I've already been told that the building material supplier wasn't complying with the agreement, and I notified him in writing that I won't tolerate this behavior. If it happens again, I will order the material from someone else."

I couldn't have heard that right. This conversation was going quite differently from all of the other conversations of its kind that I was familiar with. In my world, if a jackhammer starts pounding at seven in the morning, you throw open the window and bellow, "Turn off your fucking dildo or else I'm going to jam it so far up your backside it'll never see the sun again!" The guy at the hammer would give me the finger, and that'd be it. But here somehow the script was going unexpectedly wrong. Whether it was due to Marlene's open grave or to Mr. Baumeister's especially Christian attitude remained unclear to me.

"Then I should hope that something like that will not happen again. We're having enough trouble with all of this," Ms. Gröbendahl said, then turned, tottering off on her high heels.

"Don't take her too seriously," the fat groupie whispered to Baumeister. "She just had breast implants put in, and then the affair with the plastic surgeon started, and now she's having marital problems. That kind of stuff will make a woman ornery."

What the . . . ? Rolf von Berg was Susi Sweetie's tit-smith? First he consulted on the shape and size of the silicone upholstery, and then he ordered up a round of sex to get in some experimental boob-groping under realistic conditions? Huh. Was that creepy or cool?

While I was still contemplating the merits of natural nipples versus firmness factor in knockers, the mother superior chose this moment to rescue Baumeister from the conversation, pulling him away from the flabby wobblemonster and asking him to come inside the convent to talk. He sighed visibly.

All this drama was getting too lame for me. People don't lie anywhere else as much as they do before an open grave, so I wasn't sure anymore if this event was going to be helpful for our purposes. Plus Marlene was missing again. Why was I the only one actually taking this thing seriously and driving the investigation? Martin was proceeding only under sustained pressure and even then reluctantly. Marlene, who ought to have had the greatest interest in solving the murders, was constantly busy with other things or nowhere to be found. Like right now. Sighing, I made my way into the church. That was the only place she could be. Of course I was right.

Marlene was hovering in front of the big crucifix hanging over the altar, speaking with her beloved Jesus. But it was nothing like the conversation I expected to hear.

". . . just me? Obviously I don't want to complain, but—oh, damn it. Of course I want to complain."

Her voice had lost its patient quality and sounded unambiguously bitchy.

"I've devoted more than half my life to people who live in filth. People who largely have only themselves to blame for it. I've consoled them, helped them, defended them against hostility from society, and shown them your love. Doesn't that mean anything? Haven't I earned some reward for this? Or," she laughed cheerlessly and whined, "is this perhaps my reward? To share all eternity with an uneducated idiot, an incorrigible, sexist jerk?"

My jaw hung open in surprise. Well, figuratively, you know.

"I've always had faith in you, even in my darkest hours. I've had faith that you are our hope. That you are the light waiting for us at the end of time. But now?"

Marlene zoomed a bit closer to the crucifix and raged in a swirling electron storm.

"There's nothing *there*. Nothing. You're not there. You don't exist. And there's no heaven *or* hell—oh, wrong. Hell exists. Hell is this existence between life and death with a lowlife like Pascha at my side."

Well, my decision was obvious: she knew what she could do with her off-limits rule. Obviously now I *was* going to take a look around in the novitiate, yes I was. That was the very first thing I was going to do after Marlene finished her hateful tirade. You couldn't possibly expect a brainless lowlife like me to comply with the orders of a nun who was out of her mind. I didn't owe this self-righteous hypocrite another ounce of loyalty anymore anyway. I had stuck to our bargain because I had believed in the connection between us. In a kind of friendship because we were sharing the same fate. I had always been too honest with her and had volunteered to help her. But this was the end of that.

Marlene's anger evaporated so suddenly that I hardly noticed the reversal of mood. But when I heard her heartbreaking sobs, I knew it didn't sound like anger, but despair. I could have comforted her, but I wouldn't dream of it now. Me, the lowlife, the sexist jerk, the uneducated idiot. It was time for her to finally get that all of that sanctimonious drivel is just the opiate of the masses. Ha, even I was educated enough to know that quote. From Gandhi.

My mood was at absolute zero when I reached the patched-up windows behind the scaffolding. I spared myself the trip through the convent because I didn't want to run into any bitter old nuns. The younger girls might not be as jaded yet. I jetted directly into one of the bedrooms and thought I'd been blown off course. A young woman was lying stretched out on the narrow bed. She was wearing tiger-pattern pants with a red-silk corsage and black-lace blouse. Her feet were bobbing up and down to the beat of the music that a white iPod was blasting through the mini headphones into her ears. And when I say blasting, I mean blasting. The sound waves almost blew me back out the window.

This chick was anything but a nun, that was clear to me at first glance.

I jetted next door. Miniskirt instead of tiger pants, skin-tight gold lamé shirt, a bit more melody and fewer beats in her ears, but the same caliber as the peahen next door. The next few rooms were empty, but I found the other girls in a lounge where they were sitting together painting their toenails and braiding each other's long hair. Fourteen women lounging around bored in the nun bunker on cots under Jesus on the cross and looking like sin itself. Had I not known I was inside the convent in Mariental, I'd have thought I'd landed in a whorehouse during the midmorning break.

Then it struck me: Maybe I had. Who was it that told me the convent's sudden windfall had been a bequest? Maybe the nunnery was offering love for sale, the way the Vatican used to OK the pill? Awesome idea. Something new for once. I'd actually seen pretty much everything already. And now a nun whorehouse? Aw yeah! It would explain why Marlene was keeping the novitiate so secret.

But then I thought for a second how the whole thing was supposed to work, and my enthusiasm disappeared. I was sure that the johns weren't coming into the convent, because the whole time I'd been there I had not yet seen any man enter or leave. Apart from Baumeister, but there was no way he was keeping fourteen fillies in racing shape all on his own. So were they more like call girls, perhaps? If so, their conspicuous clothing would be an impediment, wouldn't it? And if a nun were constantly visiting one of your neighbors in your building, you'd ask about it at some point, right? That's what I'm saying.

So something else had to be going on. I did a second flyover and took a closer look. Six of the girls had facial lacerations that were poorly concealed with makeup, or black and blue areas on their arms. One had an arm in a cast. In one room there were two sitting side by side, one crying.

"But I had to tell her everything was fine," she sobbed.

"I know, I know," the other softly said, "but it was risky all the same. If he finds out where you are . . ."

"My mom won't tell anyone where I am."

The doubtful look on the face of the other chick clearly revealed what she thought about that statement.

So that was it. If the girls were being kept here as the cardinal's harem I couldn't have been more surprised. And maybe that's what they were too. No, joking aside, although the chicks were professionals—but on a sort of vacation. The nuns were apparently hiding abused hookers who had escaped their pimps. A kind of pound for prostitutes. Hence the hints from the dude in the dress that Marlene had helped women in need.

Another memory flashed in my mind: the other night I *had* actually heard one of these women yelling, "Fuck off, you assholes." Hopefully no one else had picked up on those words.

I made a beeline back to Marlene in the church. Sure, I was actually still pissed and had just sworn to never say another word to her again, but knowing that the nuns were hiding escaped sex slaves made it clear to me how deep the shit was that these penguins were in. Pimps do not think it's funny when people steal their little fillies. For one thing, then they're not earning money anymore. And for another, they lose face—and that's just as bad. Any pimp whose girls can just jump ship without showing up two days later as a corpse on a local news flash then loses his most important argument when it comes to maintaining trust-based cooperation from the other girls: their fear of ending up the same way. A women's asylum is thus the mortal enemy of a pimp. So an arson with only two fatalities actually made for a pretty restrained warning—and one that I didn't think Marlene's sisters had understood, otherwise they'd have evacuated the women long ago.

I absolutely had to talk with Marlene, but I couldn't find her in the church. Or in the convent. I looked at her gravesite, in the Institute for Forensic Medicine where Sister Martha was still lying around in Morgue Drawer Five, and in the hospital chapel—but I couldn't find her anywhere. This was unsettling. Maybe the Good Lord had sent her directly to hell after her outburst of rage? I had wished that, after all. I hoped I hadn't put a stupid idea into his head.

Regardless of Marlene's disappearance, there remained the problem of these women who were stretched out on their narrow cots in the convent worrying about their future job prospects, given their training to date, and holding off on the obvious choice, at least for the moment.

Given this new information, we'd clearly been looking in the wrong direction. So I raced straight to Martin's apartment to tell him we needed to think up a new strategy, lickety-split.

NINE

I found Martin at home with cardboard boxes of every imaginable size cluttering his living room. Some were already unpacked, and he was excitedly fiddling with another. Once again I'd forgotten to avoid the front hallway, so I set the light flickering again.

"Hello," Martin thought. "Perfect timing."

To me that sounded like a threat, so out of caution I kept my distance from him and all the equipment he was arranging on a tray and wiring together. The only thing I could recognize was a digital camera at the end of the tray. Another thing looked like a double-glazed pane of window glass sitting in a bowl of water.

"Martin, we've been thinking about this case all wrong the whole time. The convent is a whore asylum."

He said, "Oh, I see," but I got the impression he was not listening that closely.

"Martin, there are fourteen chicks hanging out in the so-called novitiate; they're so hot that the wooden crosses hanging over their beds are already half-charred."

Now he stopped tinkering with batteries and user instructions and looked up in the direction he thought I was. "And what, if you don't mind my asking, are they doing there?"

I sighed and projected into his mind a short film in which an abusive pimp, a crying hooker, and a do-gooder order of nuns played the leading roles. He was dismayed. And: he immediately thought one step further. After all, he is a doctor of forensic medicine. People who are good at that job are able to reconstruct what happened to a victim by diagnosing the injuries.

Martin thought back to Martha's autopsy and the evidence of old injuries. His thoughts painted a grisly picture. A fist hits Martha's cheekbone and knocks her teeth out. As she raises her arms to protect her head, the bones shatter like glass under the impact. She falls, and as she lies on the floor, a few kicks to her ribs finish the job.

"Martha too?" I asked.

Martin nodded. "I suspect so. The nature of her injuries in any case is indicative of an extremely brutal batterer. It wasn't a fight between equals; it's the work of a professional."

"But Martha was really a nun, right?"

Martin nodded. He had dealt with all the paperwork for the autopsy himself, and, precise as he usually is, he had absorbed every detail into his legendary memory. "Yes, she's used her religious name for a few years now already. She likely found she took pleasure in convent life. It was presumably a good alternative to the life she led before."

Boy, today was really the day for big surprises. A convent turns out to be a hooker bunker, a hooker renounces the world and becomes a nun. I wasn't sure I could take any more surprises today, which is why the sight of all Martin's boxes made me queasy. But if we revised our investigative strategy, he wouldn't have any time for his physics foofaraw anyway.

"We're going to have to plant a spy in the convent," I told Martin.

In response to his raised eyebrows, I told him about the chick who'd apparently blabbed to her mother about where she was staying.

"So what?" Martin asked.

Sometimes when cause and effect are not as directly related as decapitation and onset of death, Martin can be really slow on the uptake.

"We need to know *when* she clued her mom in on where she's been staying. Plus we need to know who her pimp is. And then we need to find out whether the mom may have passed this on to some nice man who stopped by to express concern regarding the current whereabouts of her daughter."

Martin thought.

"OK, we'll pass a tip on to the police and they'll find everything out."

For cripes' sake, he still hadn't fully gotten that these weren't medical students but hookers. At least half of which were presumably not born in Germany, did not have valid residence permits, and for that reason alone could not talk to the police. Or wouldn't want to.

"Yes, but . . ." Martin said.

I made it short. "Birgit."

"No way."

"She's our only chance."

"No."

"Martin, she's smart, she doesn't look like a police officer, she'll find out the names of the mom and the pimp in, like, no time, and the police will take care of the rest."

"But . . ."

Ah-ha, the resolute *no* vanishes so quickly.

"Tomorrow morning, Saturday, in broad daylight, she goes to the gate, says she's a persecuted hooker, bunks in, and she's out again before lunch. She doesn't need to spend the night there. It's totally safe. But without this information we'll just be running in circles, and the cops are never going to clue in on what's been going on under their noses in the convent."

The doorbell rang.

Martin opened the door.

When Birgit came through the front hallway, the light flickered briefly. The thought flashed through Martin's brain that he should lower the sensitivity on his capacitive magnetic field sensor. Birgit noticed the flicker, blinked in irritation, but didn't ask Martin about it, instead excitedly announcing: "Rolf von Berg is as good as broke." She let that sink in, her eyes twinkling. "He's a plastic surgeon and had to pay damages after a malpractice lawsuit."

"Surely he was insured for that," Martin said.

"Gross negligence is not covered by malpractice insurance," Birgit replied. "And a blood alcohol level of one point two while performing a surgical procedure is the very definition of gross negligence."

Martin winced. At one point two, Martin wouldn't have been able to stand anymore, let alone wield a scalpel.

"He owns the building he lives in. So now he wants to sell the other lofts as condos so he's liquid again."

"That shouldn't be that hard," Martin theorized, but Birgit shook her head.

"The building has pros and cons. On the positive side, the building is located in that quiet, upscale residential area, and the building is in great condition because it's just been remodeled down to the studs. But on the negative side are its proximity to the homeless shelter, the excessive snootiness of the neighborhood, and the fact that the lofts are not move-in-ready yet."

Martin, who muddled along in his one-bedroom rental apartment, nodded slowly.

"Either way," Birgit said, "he can't finish the renovations because he doesn't have the money. The only screw he can turn is the homeless shelter."

During her torrent of words Birgit hung her jacket up in the front hallway wardrobe and then walked out into the living room.

"So what's going on in here?" she asked. "Are you leading a Young Scientists team this year?"

Martin was embarrassed, standing amid all his books and the boxes filling his living room.

She stood in front of the tray and looked at the experimental setup with an interested smile. "What is all this?"

"Ask her if she'll go into the convent as a spy," I intervened.

"I will, I will . . ." he thought.

"No, right now," I insisted. "There are quite a few things we have to discuss so she'll act correctly and not scare the hookers. If they don't trust her, they won't tell her a thing. So go on, ask her."

Martin stood next to Birgit and carefully put his arm around her shoulders.

"Birgit, I got some news today from the convent that casts our investigation in a wholly new light."

How poetic.

"What's that?"

He gave her a summary of the latest information, but he exclusively used politically correct terms such as *prostitute* and *pimp*. We were just going to have to banish all those words from her vocabulary in a few moments, so why use them now?

"How do you know all of this?" she asked.

He told her about Martha's old injuries and that he had suspected it at the autopsy.

"But that was only a suspicion."

I always say, Birgit may be blonde, but she's pretty frigging smart. And she had all kinds of follow-up questions. Which can of course be useful when sounding out hookers, for instance. It's just that this typically womanish way of asking endless questions was pissing me off at the moment. Martin, in any case, was able only to stammer strange things out.

"Have you told Gregor?" Birgit asked.

Martin explained to her why that wouldn't work.

"But what are you going to do next if you can't tell anyone?"

Martin eyed her coyly.

Her eyes turned rounder, bluer, bigger. "Me?"

Martin wanted to deny everything, he wanted to cancel everything, I could clearly read it in his thoughts, but Birgit's eyes started shining. "Yes, of course I'll help you. What do I do?"

With a sigh, he explained our idea to her.

We did our planning for about two hours, during which time I made an effort to convey the necessary vocabulary to the two lovebirds. Martin could hardly let the words pass his lips, and Birgit wondered how Martin knew all the jargon that was an everyday part of a hooker's language. But at last I thought I'd gotten the two of them on the right track.

"And now I want to know what all this crazy equipment is you've got lying around here," Birgit demanded.

My God, this woman had stamina; it was just incredible. Normal girls can't concentrate on an important topic for even three minutes, and then their thoughts wander back to money, shoes, or tit enlargement, but Birgit was displaying no signs of fatigue. So now there was going to be a little physics lesson. I was hoping that the two of them would turn to biology as quickly as possible. Particularly the birds and the bees.

"The equipment on the tray is an experimental setup to do some Kirlian photography," said Martin. He blathered some garbage about objects that have an aura that you can make visible through long-term exposure. Then he explained the rest of the equipment using key words that meant nothing to me or, apparently, to Birgit.

Now Birgit's concentration waned a bit, and her eyes wandered to the stack of books next to Martin's armchair.

Discovering the Supernatural. Experiments with Paranormal Phenomena. Electronic Surveillance and Security Technology. Cellular Communications, Electrosmog, and Microwaves. Electromagnetic Radiation and Shielding. Parasciences. Measuring Mystical Phenomena—and Making Them Visible.

Birgit's expression grew more and more pensive, and then even troubled. "Martin, what is this all about?"

Martin sat on the couch with his shoulders drooping, looking at her helplessly.

"A few days before your, uh, accident you were acting so strangely too. So oppressed. Hounded. And you still seem a bit that way even now."

Martin's gaze moved down to his genuine-wool slippers.

"Did you have a near-death experience?" Birgit asked.

Martin laughed bitterly in his thoughts. I had no idea what was so funny. He had been only near death, after all. I had taken a significant step further.

"You can tell me anything," she said. "I won't laugh."

Martin nodded hesitantly.

"Did you leave your body?"

He nodded again.

"And did you see the tunnel of light?"

Martin shook his head. He hadn't had the time to see a tunnel before I started screaming at his fledgling soul to slip back into its body and keep living. A pretty big shock for him, I suppose.

"What did you see, then?" Birgit asked. She sat down right next to Martin and held his hand. Sweet as sugar.

"Do you know what a medium is?" Martin quietly asked.

Birgit turned pale. "You mean people who can communicate with the dead?" Her voice was shaking.

Martin nodded.

"And you can do that too?"

Martin rocked his head side to side. "It's more like there are certain spirits who can communicate with me."

Birgit swallowed. She had apparently been ready for bad news—but not this bad.

"What are you waiting for?" I asked. "Tell her about our bromance!"

"What spirits?" Birgit asked.

"Well, for example, there is the spirit of that car thief who was pushed off the bridge."

"When was that?" Birgit whispered.

"Right after you and I got to know each other. During his autopsy he explained to me that he was pushed and didn't fall, as we thought at the time."

Birgit was now white as the wall. "You mean, while you . . . And he, uh, spoke to you?"

Martin nodded.

Birgit put her hand over her mouth. I was worried she was about to puke on Martin's experiment. She swallowed a couple of times and took a deep breath.

"Are there others?"

"Sister Marlene."

Birgit gasped.

"She herself doesn't . . . or always . . . more like . . ."

Alas, the moment Martin leaves his academic field, his eloquence completely bails on him. We're going to have to work on that.

"And so now you're trying to do some physics experiments to prove that these spirits are really there and that you're not crazy."

Martin nodded.

Birgit looked like she'd just seen a ghost herself. It's presumably pretty creepy when the most precise, most analytical, most natural-sciencey guy you know suddenly starts rambling on about ghosts busting his balls. And about wanting to take pictures of them too.

"How is that supposed to work?" Birgit asked.

She was actually addressing the question by applying the scientific method. Incredible what this woman has both in her sweater and in her braincase.

"OK, for example, the setup here on the tray is for what they call 'Kirlian photography,'" said Martin feebly.

"Normally this technique is used to make the auras of inanimate objects visible, but it may also be possible to use it to display an electromagnetic anomaly."

"An electromagnetic anomaly?" Birgit repeated, confused. She could juggle numbers and currencies and even stock market crap in her head no problem, but when it came to physics she was about as clueless as me. God, I love her.

"Between this glass and the film there is an electrolytic . . . Oh, it doesn't matter. Anyway, the theory is that a soul or spirit consists of electromagnetic waves that can be made visible using this experimental technique."

Birgit didn't look convinced, but did seem to be fiercely determined. "So what do you have to do for this?"

"You place this setup in an absolutely dark room, set the camera for a long exposure time, and then wait and see what happens."

"But what if during the exposure time the spirit doesn't . . ."

Even though Birgit was totally with it, she still had no clue what was actually going on here. Martin had rambled on only generally about occasionally hearing voices from the Beyond. What she didn't know was that I'd been hanging around constantly, chattering his ears off and becoming his best friend, in a way. His constant companion, in any case.

"And she won't find out about that either," Martin mentally roared at me.

Whoa—now what was his problem? It'd be nice if Birgit knew that she could talk to me anytime . . .

"You stay away from her!" Martin ordered in his thoughts. What he did not say but what was writ clearly in his brain was his worry that Birgit would no longer feel relaxed in his presence if she knew that there was always someone around she couldn't hear or see.

"But what are you telling her all this metaphysical stuff for, then?" I asked.

"Because I can't stand everyone thinking I'm totally cuckoo," he said, both riled up and exasperated. "Katrin and Gregor refuse to let on what they know, my boss is sending me to the psychologist because he thinks I'm completely bananas, and I continually have to lie to Birgit whenever I have to explain where I know this or that from."

He was close to tears.

"So you want to tell her that you occasionally get helpful hints from the Beyond but not that this is a two-man frat house here?" I asked.

At the expression "frat house" he had to bite his lips to keep from moaning out loud.

I was disappointed. He was denying me as a person and friend, content merely to use me for the information that I was kind enough to keep feeding him. It's not like I could fill Birgit in on everything myself, so I was left with two options: sulk and steer clear of Martin's gizmo or suck it up and press my nose onto the pane of glass in his rig so Martin could prove to Birgit his apartment was haunted.

Birgit was now standing closer to the setup, carefully studying the device. Fortunately she wasn't picking up on Martin's mental state and our fight. Martin took a couple of deep breaths and had more or less regained his composure when Birgit turned back toward him.

"When do you want to do the experiment?" she asked. "Is there a certain time . . . ?"

I guessed her concern about time came from reading *The Little Ghost* when she was a kid, with all the "witching hour" stuff. Ridiculous!

"We can try it now," Martin said loudly for my benefit. And in his thoughts he added: "If ever in this life you were to do me a favor, please let it be now."

For that stupid comment alone I should have made a beeline out of there and left Martin by himself with his stupid experiment. As though I'd never done him a favor!

He didn't wait for a response, instead carrying the tray with the setup into the bathroom. The bathroom?

"The experiment has to be done in total darkness," he explained with a deadpan expression.

Martin and Birgit placed the setup on top of the toilet seat, walked out of the bathroom, and closed the door.

"Now," Martin said in thoughts to me.

I aimed for the keyhole and whooshed through. Though I wasn't sure I wanted to do him this favor, I was actually kind of curious. I moved very carefully, and after a few seconds I could even dimly make out the outlines of the equipment. Right, a tiny bit of light was making it into the bathroom through the keyhole. I flew right in front of the glass, paused a moment, and then went even closer. The moment I touched the glass I got zapped.

"What the fuck," I cursed. That was really unpleasant. All my electrons were whirled up, kind of like the time I accidentally whooshed through a wall into a microwave that was in use. I put myself back together, as it were, and zoomed back into the living room.

"What the fuck is that all about?" I roared at Martin. "Did you want to disintegrate me?"

Martin droned something about needing directly applied voltage to make the electromagnetic impulse visible, blah blah blah.

"Well I've had it up to here with that," I said, envisioning a "here" to have had it up to.

Martin made such a soft sigh Birgit couldn't have heard it and then dismantled the rig in the bathroom to retrieve the picture.

"Let's see," said Birgit, who was bouncing around him excitedly as he removed the wires and carefully slid the pane of glass out of its holder.

She pressed the little buttons on the camera and then suddenly fell into a kind of shocked stupor.

"That's insane," she whispered.

Martin's head whipped around. "What?"

Birgit held the display on the camera out in front of his nose without saying a word. Martin took the camera out of her hand, flipped open his laptop, plugged some cables in, and opened the photo on the big screen.

Just about centered in front of a black background there was an eddy of red and yellow dots. Like an alien galaxy observed from far, far away.

Crazy.

That was me!

We were all speechless.

OK, I admit I was pretty shocked at first, but this galactic whirl was way cooler than my old passport photo. Even if it didn't look all that . . . human. I swallowed. I could finally be seen again, after months of incorporeal invisibility, but I looked like some graffiti from a spray can. The finality of my separation from my body hit me like a hammer, worse than at my funeral. I looked for Martin's thoughts but found him focused entirely on Birgit.

She reached for Martin's hand, and then she turned around and hugged him. Really tightly.

"You are a very special guy," she said quietly. "I like that about you."

Martin almost wept with happiness.

Not me. Not with happiness, I mean. But I pulled myself together and left Martin to his delirium of joy.

I'd have preferred some honest, hot sex over this gushy melodrama, but my wishes didn't count for anything around here. The ghost had done his duty; the ghost was now permitted to zoom off. I left the cloyingly sweet lovefest and took in a couple of action flicks at the movies.

TEN

Late Saturday morning, Birgit rang at the convent gate. She was carrying a fairly big shoulder bag with her cell phone, some cash, and a few clothes in it, as well as emergency hygienic supplies, to bolster the credibility of her story of escape. She looked terrible. First, she had borrowed a totally slutty outfit from a friend of hers who had worn it in the mid-nineties to a Carnival party for work and had kept it for sentimental reasons, although it had long since stopped fitting her. It consisted of skintight pink jeans with giant holes in the knees and a glittery pink top and a little black faux-leather jacket. Second, she had shoveled on the makeup and then sliced three onions to generate the tears needed to mess up the makeup, making her look like a melted Neapolitan ice cream cake—three days after the power had gone out in the freezer.

After endless discussions Birgit and I had successfully convinced Martin that it'd be best if he stayed home. If Martin were hanging out around the convent, it would only have drawn attention. Or so we thought . . . quite incorrectly, as it turned out. In fact, Martin later surmised that his presence might have spared Birgit the subsequent drama, but of course that's bullshit. Anyway, according to our plan, then, Martin was just supposed to wait by the phone for Birgit's call. The second there was any cause for concern, but no later than when she finished her job, she would call him right away. What Martin knew but Birgit didn't, of course, was that I'd be with her the whole time.

When Birgit arrived at the square in front of the convent, she stopped, stunned. The whole square, including the patio of the gelato café, was packed with people. Parked in front of the convent's wall was a gigantic semi with the logo for West German Broadcasting on its side. The long side of the trailer facing the square was open, and the cargo area was set up as a stage with several people seated on it. Some chick with a microphone and notes in her hand was playing the moderator, talking with the others on stage and occasionally fielding comments from people in the audience.

One of the women sitting on stage was Susanne Gröbendahl, from the neighborhood association. Over her head hung a banner announcing the topic of the program: UPSCALE ADDRESS FOR HOMELESS SHELTER?

Out in the audience, Birgit paused and took in the scene. She was standing in the lee of this super-tall guy with long hair, a long beard, and a dingy, police-green parka who had sunk his hands deep into the pockets of his baggy jeans. He was somehow exerting a calming influence over the sea of thrashing people, and I got the impression Birgit was hiding behind him. Then I realized he was probably doing surveillance for the German domestic intelligence agency, which conveniently happens to be here in Cologne. Domestic intelligence was not a part of Birgit's mission, however, but I promised Martin I'd stick with her and be on my guard, and so that's what I did.

"Obviously we should take care of these people, but not necessarily in a nice, middle-class residential neighborhood," someone on stage was telling the audience.

"But by all accounts," said the moderator, "as recently as five years ago, this was not a nice, middle-class residential area."

Ms. Gröbendahl literally stole the second, unused microphone and put it to her mouth. "But back when we were interested in buying our house, the city made very clear to us that it was going to focus on improving the surroundings. To date this has not happened."

"Mr. Berger," the moderator said to a man in an ill-fitting suit sitting on stage, "you're here representing city hall. How do you respond to this accusation?" She shoved her own microphone so forcefully into the guy's squinched-up face that he had to lean way back. Recovering, he grabbed the mic out of her hand.

"We have implemented traffic-calming measures to quiet down the area. We have planted trees to line the streets, giving this area the traditional character of a country village. We have taken out the regular streetlights and replaced them with antique-style lanterns instead. In addition, the city just updated the local playground and installed new equipment."

"That is all well and good," Gröbendahl said, "but—"

The guy in the suit would not be interrupted. "The neighborhood association's request that the city revoke the permit for a homeless shelter that has been in place for several decades was made only recently. Thus far, the city council has not made any commitment to comply—and frankly, it does not see any urgent need to do so."

The moderator took back her jabberstick and turned away. "Let's go to another question from the audience."

A short, fat woman in the crowd spoke into a microphone on the end of a five-meter-long boom that an assistant had shoved into her face.

"Why aren't the nuns up on stage too, so they can take
part in this discussion?"

"We did ask the order to take part in our discussion, but
unfortunately they did not send a representative," the moderator explained. "We received a statement from the order,
however, which I would like to read now."

She fished through her bag until she found a crinkled
piece of paper, unfolded it, and read: "The patron saint of
our order is Mary Magdalene. It is written that she was a
sinner who repented and followed our Lord, Jesus Christ,
and that she did this with unwavering loyalty and admi-
rable courage. Mary Magdalene did not flee after Jesus
was arrested, as his disciples did. Joined by two other
women, she remained with Jesus through his crucifixion
and death. The Gospel of Saint Matthew recounts this in
chapter sixteen, verse seven. Since the founding of our
order seven hundred years ago, we the Charitable Sisters
of Saint Mary Magdalene see ourselves as successors to
Mary Magdalene's legacy. We are an order of women who
are repentant sinners working courageously for the outcast. Although the lot of the outcast has improved over the
past seven centuries, we do not believe this improvement
has been enough. Even today in an era of relatively great
prosperity, there are poor and weak people who for widely
divergent reasons are not recognized as full members of
society. Standing at their side is our sacred duty, which
we take on with joy. We serve God by serving humankind,
especially those who are in need of our help. For, 'as long

as you did it to one of these my least brethren, you did it to me.' Thus saith the Lord God."

There was a moment of devout silence in the square before Susanne Gröbendahl spoke up. "That's very lovely. But why here, specifically?"

An animated murmur bubbled up from the audience. Birgit winced at the comment, shook her head, and left the square, squeezing sideways through the audience up the stone stairs leading to the convent. As she rang the bell at the convent gate, I kept close to her.

The nun on gate duty today welcomed Birgit warmly, her sharp eye immediately recognizing the kind of woman who stood in front of her. She pulled Birgit in through the door, carefully scanned the area outside, and then locked the gate twice from inside.

"What we can do for you?" the nun asked.

"I don't know where to go," Birgit stammered. "I need a place to hide, and I heard that you might be able to help me."

"From whom do you need to hide?" the nun asked.

"My boyfriend," Birgit whimpered. "Well, I mean, I thought he was my boyfriend. But actually . . ."

"Come with me."

The nun put her arm over Birgit's shoulders and led her into the novitiate. There the good sister of Szechwan came out, dismissed the other nun, and took over Birgit's care. Ah-ha, I realized: so this was Marlene's favorite sister—her successor.

"I'm Sister Johanna. I take care of the women who seek refuge with us. Is that what has brought you to us?"

Birgit nodded.

"I'll show you to a room where you can settle in. If you'd like to be alone, you can stay in your room, but if you'd like some company you can come out into the lounge. There'll always be someone there."

Sister Johanna pointed to the door to the lounge and then brought Birgit to a convent cell. "I have to leave in a few minutes and will be gone for a little while, but this afternoon I will be all yours—if you want to talk or have questions or just need someone to hold your hand. OK?"

Birgit nodded.

Sister Johanna turned around and hurried back down the long corridor. I wanted to follow Birgit to her room when a wave of indignation and outrage practically drowned me. Marlene.

"What is the meaning of this?" she yelled.

"Marlene, where have you been all this time? I thought you had to be stewing in hell by now after the obscenities you were hurling at sweet little Jesus."

My objection was apparently not well received.

"I ask again: what is the meaning of this?"

I tried to update her on the whole business as gently as possible, but she had flipped her lid so bad she couldn't process anything. "Against my express wishes you have broken into the novitiate? And you've dragged your coroner's girlfriend in here now as well? And she is lying to poor Johanna and all the other women because she wants to find out something that is none of the business of anyone outside these walls!"

"That's exactly the problem," I shot back. "News of your little asylum here already *has* leaked out. One of the women here blabbed to her mother where she is. Now you're all in danger. Birgit wants to find out when the girl passed on this information and how. And who the girl's pimp is, so we can put a tail on him in case he figures out where his hoo—um, his, uh, coworker is hiding."

Marlene was so upset that she wasn't open to any argument. She had turned into a raging storm of white-hot clouds of anger swirling around me, insulting me and accusing me of not being able to stick to the actual case.

Meanwhile, Birgit had put down her bag and started looking around the little room. There wasn't much to discover, of course. A narrow bed with a nightstand with—surprise!—a Bible in the drawer. A table, a chair, a narrow wardrobe, and the ubiquitous Jesus suspended on his cross with hanging head, spreading gloom. Some wise guy had stuck a green branch behind the cross. If it was meant as a friendly, spring-themed design element, it missed the mark by galactic proportions. The leaves were dry and dusty and looked at least as dead as the guy on the cross.

I couldn't read Birgit's thoughts, but her face spoke clearly enough. She left her bag on her bed and went out to the lounge. The other women greeted her warmly, introduced themselves, and asked Birgit her name and a whole slew of other questions, but Birgit was silent, tears in her eyes and lips pinched together. No one took it personally. Probably all women were bumming when they arrived here.

"Do you want some tea?" asked their spokeswoman, Danni, if I'm not mistaken. She was tall, skin and bones, with long brown hair; if she packed another twenty kilos on her frame she might even have been pretty. Right now she looked like the demonstration skeleton in biology class that someone had stapled some duds onto.

Birgit nodded.

"Do you have family here in town?"

Birgit shook her head.

"Do you have somewhere else you can go?"

Birgit nodded. "But . . ." she whispered, perhaps because she felt embarrassed she was lying to the girls, "but I don't trust myself to head there by myself. And no one can pick me up, because I can't tell anyone where I am."

Awkward silence unrolled through the room.

At that moment Marlene showed back up. "I want her to leave the convent immediately."

"Then tell her," I snarled, irritated that Marlene was making it hard to hear what the women below were saying.

"I can't establish contact with her, as you well know," Marlene said in a huff.

"Well I can't either," I replied with equal venom.

The conversation in the lounge was heading in the right direction; the girls were bitching at each other because one of them had blabbed to someone on the outside about where they were hiding. Danni wasn't the tattletale; it was the diminutive one I'd eavesdropped on during my inquiry, but I couldn't hear over Marlene's shouting what accusations they were hurling at each other.

At that moment the door flew open. Two huge guys in black leather jackets stormed into the room, followed by four more, and each grabbed two girls and pulled them down onto the floor by their hair or arm, or whatever else they got hold of. The other girls were already being dragged from their rooms and hauled toward the stairs. Some of the hookers screamed to high heaven, but not for long. Standing in the hallway was a guy sticking duct tape over shrieking mouth after shrieking mouth. Even over the mouths of those who had kept quiet out of terror. A second guy cable-tied the girls' hands behind their backs. Once the last shriek-leak had been duct-taped, the ensuing silence was downright eerie.

Only Marlene was screaming, as loudly as she could, but all she was doing was driving me—and only me—crazy. I circled wildly over the events, trying to keep my eye on things. What kind of operation was this? I had to make sure I stayed with Birgit, who, eyes bugged out and hands bound, was reeling around behind the guy whose left hand was clawing into her long hair.

The whole thing had taken hardly thirty seconds and incredibly had gone off without a single hitch. The guys had entered through the gate the construction supplies were delivered through, secured only with a ridiculous Easy Pickin' brand padlock. The kidnappers had pulled a metallic-black Mercedes-Benz cargo Sprinter up right in front of the gate; with military precision, they opened the van's rear doors and shoved the girls inside. None had had time to grab their cell phones, not even Birgit, because hers was in her bag on the narrow bed in her new room.

A few nuns appeared in the yard, apparently having heard the screams, but it was too late. The van with the girls and the two SUVs with the kidnappers were roaring down the rear access drive past the allotment gardens, long gone before the good mother superior could even dial 112.

Marlene finally stopped shrieking and fell silent. Acoustically this was actually quite pleasant but extremely ill-suited to the immediate need for action.

"Marlene, stay with the girls and stay in contact with me as long as you can," I yelled at her.

Marlene was still hanging around distraught and discombobulated in the yard where the van had been.

"Leni: lights, camera, *action!* Stay with your lambs. And stay high over the van so I can find you again."

She pulled herself together some, repeated "my lambs" as though hypnotized, and zoomed off. I did too, but in the opposite direction. I had to get to Martin and give him the information and the license plate on the van so that he could fill the cops in. I flew as fast as I could.

Martin was hunkered down, cross-legged on his bed, which was completely enveloped under a giant mosquito net. There were four hooks attached to the ceiling that the very dense metal-mesh fabric was hanging from like a box-shaped tent. There was a zipper on one side, and it was shut. Under the bed he'd put a pad on the floor that was attached to the netting with zippers. What kind of trip was this guy on now?

Martin was holding his cell phone in his left hand and staring excitedly at the display. I yelled to him, but he didn't seem able to hear me. No problem, I'd just move slightly closer and pester him from closer up to his wrapper. I zoomed right up to the dense mesh netting and tried to whoosh through—but bounced off.

Shit! What was up with that?

I flew up super close to the netting and could see that the display said NO RECEPTION. Furthermore, Martin seemed to be very happy about that.

"Martin!" I screamed. No reaction.

"MARTIN!" Nothing.

I zoomed into the front hallway and zinged back and forth between the capacitive thingamajigger plates, but nothing happened. Apparently they were turned off while Martin was playing with his latest shielding technology.

I tried again, but for the life of me I couldn't get through to Martin. I inspected the packaging for the mosquito net beside the bed and read "Anti-Electrosmog Netting—Sleep Safe and Sound." *No frigging way.* So the electrosmog hysteria had actually resulted in the development of viable screening. I was really happy for all the hypochondriacs, Luddites, and smoke-signal fetishists out there who I really didn't blame for using such netting. But Martin had chosen the absolutely worst possible time for his exorcism. I was going to have to come up with something else.

I left Martin and raced back toward Mariental, sending out signals in all directions to reestablish contact with Marlene. Finally I got a response.

"Where are you?" I asked.

She passed on her current position in pursuit, properly including the name of the street as though she were driving along with her finger on a map of the city.

How terrific that I knew where the van was now too. So now there were two of us in the know. A spiritualized nun and a dead car thief whose sole human contact sat shrouded in electrosmog shielding. We couldn't help the girls by ourselves. I had to find a way to pass on our astutely obtained but thus far useless knowledge to someone who could. Chop-chop. If only the bad guys could run smack into a couple of cops. Did I just say that? Never in my life had I felt such a perverse desire.

I reached the convent at the same time as the two-man flashing-blue-light crew and listened in on the nuns' statements.

Yes, a kidnapping.

Getaway vehicle? They thought it might have been a passenger car.

Getaway direction? No idea.

Fabulous.

I flew slightly higher to contact Marlene when some nasty radiation tickled me. Radio waves.

That was it! The WGB truck was still parked in front of the convent in the square. On its roof stood a fat antenna, whose transmission signal I had just flown into. It felt like the purest form of electrosmog horror: cordless mics and microwave relays to some base station, distributing the signal throughout the country. But it could also make for the purest form of riding the waves.

It was worth a try, especially since I had no other idea for communicating quickly with the world of the living. So I steeled myself and flew into the microwave beam coming off the roof antenna. Instantly I was literally being scrambled like eggs and having trouble keeping my thoughts together.

What was I trying to do, again?

"Attention," I thought with the full intensity I could scrape together inside this whirlwave.

The normal programming being broadcast through the WGB truck's speakers continued unaffected. I tried again.

"Attention, attention. This is an important announcement for the police."

No go.

Meanwhile, I was starting to feel like I was in a hurricane. Pretty much tattered, splattered, and scattered. It seemed like my signal couldn't make it through the turbulence fanning out from the giant tube. *Damn it.*

Breathless, as it were, I left the beam of radiation and immediately felt worlds better. But only until it became clear to me that, although my unwanted blow-dry hairstyle could be tamed back down again, the girls were still in the hands of their kidnappers. I climbed higher and had Marlene update me on the current position of the van. Then I dove like a pterodactyl toward its prey back down to the broadcast truck. I had to try again in a different place.

The moderator was once again reading from her note cards. I perched on the antenna stub to her cordless mic and sounded my "Attention, attention!" cry one more time.

My words echoed out over the square. My voice! I hadn't heard it for months, and suddenly here it was, sounding out of all of the loudspeakers. A little tinny, but still unmistakably me. So with the right tools, I *could* still speak, even without vocal cords. Awesome! The mic matron was just as amazed as I was. After a moment of shock she turned to her sound engineer at the mixing desk and gave her the internationally understood gesture for "What gives, you idiot?" The engineer stared at her console then back to the moderator and shrugged.

I had to make use of this moment of confusion before it occurred to someone to cut the juice to the mic. I cleared the frog from my throat and quickly started gibbering again.

"Attention, this is an important announcement for the police officers who . . ."

Shit, now what should I say? If I tell the whole wide world here that a couple of hookers had been kidnapped from the convent, then within five minutes every pimp would know about the shelter, and the convent would be burned to the ground for protecting the women.

"This is an announcement for the police officers who are investigating the incident at the Mariental convent."

A commotion spread through the square. "Incident? Here? Huh? What kind of an incident? Did you notice anything?" people murmured back and forth, craning their necks, but only the convent's spires were visible behind the broadcast truck.

The moderator held her mic way out in front of her as though it might bite her nose if she held it too close to her face. The engineer slid the controls up and down and then gave a sign to cut the mic.

No! That couldn't be allowed under any circumstances.

"Keep the mic on!" I roared. "This is for a police investigation."

The radio ladies looked at each other, startled. Then a smile slowly crept onto the face of the moderator. Finally she'd realized that this unexpected incident was not even remotely likely to hurt her ratings. The mic stayed on.

I whooshed onto the roof of the truck to see what the cops were now up to. At that moment, the convent gate flung open and the two cops stepped out in front of the door. One holding a vintage 1970 portable radio to his ear he must have borrowed from the nuns to listen to the live broadcast from outside. They had radios at a convent? Surely only to listen to Vatican Radio. But it meant that my contribution was audible not only here on the square, but it was also being broadcast live. The whole country could hear me. OK, not the whole country, just the people who were tuned in to this particular publicly funded station, where the moderators speak German in complete sentences and administer musical interludes of ear-mollifying intellectual jazz in homeopathic doses. One thing was certain: the kidnappers would not be among the listeners.

"Set the microphone onto the roof of the tractor," I told the moderator.

For a moment she stared stupidly, but then she handed the mic to the beanpole from city administration and asked him to carry out the command. He climbed off the stage, opened the passenger-side door to the tractor, set one foot inside the cab, and then pulled himself as high as he could and did what I had asked, acting as though the mic were a bomb that might go off at any moment. Now I had an unencumbered view of the events at the convent while I spoke. The cops were still standing around in front of the convent's entry with the antique mini hi-fi to their ears.

"The, uh, the stolen property . . . was loaded into a metallic-black Mercedes-Benz cargo Sprinter. By the way it tore out of here, it was the 3.0-liter V6 common-rail direct injection turbo diesel, with an added tuning box."

The cops in front of the convent gate stared at each other, and the one pointed his index finger at his temple and started spinning it in a circle. *Not good. Not good at all.* If they tuned out now, the girls were lost. I had to pull myself together.

"The van's license plate number is a Cologne registration, K . . ." I slowly said the number and repeated it, because the law enforcement officials had to get out a pen and paper first. Then I climbed higher and picked up Marlene's excited data stream.

"Hey, Pascha, they've switched drivers in the van. Now they've got two young guys sitting in the driver's cab. The old driver disappeared on foot. I'm staying with the women. I've lost the original driver."

Good girl. We had to focus on the girls; that was absolutely our top priority. "Where are you?" I asked.

She passed on her current position.

The cops in front of the convent seemed to be arguing with each other, and the one was circling his finger at his temple again while the other was gesticulating wildly as they argued at each other. The gesticulator made a dismissive hand movement, stormed off to the squad car, picked up his radio, and yakked excitedly into it. But if you were to think I could now simply give up my radio career and start jabbering directly into the police radio, then you would be sadly underestimating the secret-mongering that typifies law enforcement in this country. Police radio is encrypted; I couldn't get into it. I had tried that weeks and weeks ago, of course. Too bad.

So the cop kept yakking, wagging his free hand around, listening, yakking some more, shrugging, and getting more and more excited. I had a bad feeling about this. This might all be for nothing.

"Notify Detective Sergeant Gregor Kreidler. Birgit is in that van."

The cop on the radio stopped short mid-sentence and mid-gesture, then apparently repeated my request. Good pig.

I climbed higher, but Marlene had since gotten too far away for us to communicate directly. So I whooshed off in the direction her last report had come from. I had been practicing supersonic flight, actually, so I caught up with her in three seconds. She was hovering over the quick-moving hooker truck, praying. Very helpful. Instead of waiting for the intervention of heavenly hosts, I whooshed quickly back to the radio and passed on the van's current position and direction, and then I jetted back to the abducted girls. The whole time I was thinking of a way to slow the kidnappers down a little more, since they weren't going to just keep riding the roads forever. As soon as these psychopaths reached their hideout, the rescue mission would become a whole lot harder.

Like all modern cars, a Mercedes Sprinter is a high-tech ride, the only remnant of its purely mechanical origin being the windshield wipers. Everything else is controlled electronically. I had to find a way in. Of course I needed a wireless transmission to patch into an electronic circuit, so I couldn't just shut off the ignition. Too bad. But somewhere there had to be some kind of wireless radio connection in a ride like this. Like with the power locks, which you can also control with the press of a button on the smart key. For testing purposes I fired a pulse into the locking system, and, as a matter of fact, all the door locks engaged with the familiar *ca-chik* sound. The front-seat passenger stared at the door lock knob next to his elbow, then back at the driver, whose hands had been firmly on the steering wheel the whole time. He took a breath as though he were about to say something, and then froze when the knob popped back up again. *Ca-chik.* The stupid look on his face was priceless. But there had to be a way to top it.

These rides also have preset seat adjustments for each smart key. So if multiple drivers use the same vehicle, each of them doesn't have to manually readjust the seat and mirror to the right position; that would be far too retro. Instead, each driver uses a separate key, and the onboard electronics detect the key and then signal the little electric motors to adjust the seats and mirrors to the positions saved for that key. Now, I didn't know how many keys there were with what codings, and I didn't know the actual codings either, but a stab in the dark couldn't hurt. So I gathered all my energy and connected with the sensor for the remote smart key control. Immediately the driver's seat dropped down and slowly slid backward. The driver was having trouble keeping his feet to the gas pedal. This was hilarious!

"Hey, what's going on?" the passenger asked.

"Shit, man, I got no idea," the driver stammered, keeping one hand on the wheel while he used the other to frantically search for the switch low on the left side of the driver's seat to slide his seat forward again. He was seriously weaving in his lane.

Maybe I was getting a little carried away. I didn't want the idiot to get into an accident. So I switched on the seat heater instead. It was turning out to be a fairly hot day today too, so his nuts would be roasting in no time.

"There's a fucking ghost in the machine!" the driver roared. "Shit, man! I've never seen anything like this before."

His forehead now glistened like his greasy hair, and sweat spots were starting to spread out through his shirt. He opened the window.

"Fortunately, it's not much farther to the warehouse," he mumbled, wiping the sweat out of his eyes.

Shit! Where were the police?

I jetted back to the convent. The two uniforms were now standing on the stage of the broadcast truck, asking the moderator stupid questions that she obviously couldn't answer. The engineer had also left her mixing desk and was making defensive gestures.

"Damn it, where are the cops?" I roared into the mic.

A collective wince passed through the figures on the truck and among the audience.

"The van isn't far from its destination now. If those bastards dig themselves in there, it'll be a bloodbath."

The cop who had just called in reinforcements fumbled with the second microphone, switched it on with the moderator chick's help, and spoke slowly and clearly: "They're en route; only seconds away."

"Set that mic back down!" I snapped at him through the same mic. "Or are you trying to make sure the gangsters find out live what direction the cops will be coming from?"

He set the mic back down as though it had horrifically burned his fingers. But he did leave it on, so now I had two mics to work with. One was down on the stage, and the other was up on the roof of the truck for a better view.

"Is Gregor with them?" I asked.

He just nodded.

"Good."

I jetted back to the van, caught up with the praying Marlene, who was lagging a bit, maybe because she didn't have that much practice in high-speed flight yet, and then I spun around slowly. From all four sides, squad cars were approaching the intersection where the kidnappers' truck was currently positioned on its approach to an industrial

park that was home to several shipping companies. One of
these big warehouses was likely their hideout. We had to stop
them before they reached the warehouse. Unfortunately,
the traffic light where the kidnappers were stopped had just
turned green. The van pulled forward, its blinker on. The
next driveway was only twenty meters ahead of them when
the first squad car tore around the corner.

The passenger-seat kidnapper saw it. "Floor it! It's the
cops!"

The driver stomped on the gas, and the van shot forward. I had to do something.

There was only one way: the electronic engine immobi-
lizer. Certain manufacturers, whose names do not matter,
used to have a giant problem with their engine immobilizers
going off erroneously and surprisingly often, even though
the right driver put the right key into the ignition. But if
the battery in the smart key wore out, then the key and the
engine immobilization system couldn't communicate with
each other anymore, and then the engine wouldn't start
again. It had happened to me personally more than once.
Just the kind of problem with brand-new technology that
insurance companies love, but these problems had been
mostly fixed now.

Even so, blocking communication between the key and
the antitheft system was the only way I could think of to stop
the car. No idea if would work. No idea if I could survive
it, because there was a ton of power flowing right where I
needed to create my interference. It wasn't a question of a
simple A-to-B interface; I needed to get into the heart of all
the onboard electronics. No matter. With the battle cry "For
Birgit!" I bolted into the ignition.

All around me there was hissing, crackling, and flashing—and then everything went quiet. It felt a little like that
time I'd ended up in a drumstick-shaped radar antenna at
the airport. That is to say, *awful*. Like I'd been napping with
two fingers stuck into an outlet and then simultaneously
pissed onto an exposed wire when I woke up. I felt woozy.
Everything going on around me looked totally warped. Like
I was underwater without goggles with that funny burbling
in my ears.

The squad cars raced up and surrounded the van, which
had come to a stop right in the middle of the road. Several
cops ripped open the doors, dragged the driver and passenger out of their seats, forced them onto their knees, and
handcuffed them before the guys could say, "I'm not saying anything without my attorney." More cops had ripped
open the rear doors and were helping the girls out of the
truck. They looked to be in pretty sad shape. Some were
probably seriously carsick—no wonder when you're getting
all sloshed around lying in the payload space of a van with
your hands tied behind your back racing through half the
city. The duct tape had come off of some of their mouths
because they'd puked all over themselves and the others.
Makeup smeared, lipstick smudged up over the edges of the
tape, noses running. But they were all alive.

Gregor leaped out of one of the squad cars and scrambled through the rear doors.

"Birgit!" he called in panic.

Birgit turned toward the sound and threw herself in his
arms, bursting into tears. With the tape over her lips and
snot bubbling from her nose, she was at risk of suffocating.
Gregor pulled off the tape, cut through the cable ties with

a pocketknife, handed her a tissue, and patted her blonde hair, in which the remnants of one of her fellow abductees' breakfast had almost dried.

Touching.

———•———

Martin turned pale as a corpse when Gregor showed up at his apartment with a calmed-down Birgit and a slightly sugarcoated version of the day's events (though a version that did make mention of the mysterious voice that had alerted the cops).

Although a few reporters had been startled by the radio show and had shown up at the scene of the rescue shortly after the cops, they all agreed to keep the hooker shelter a secret. The news coverage had instead focused on the interesting question of what mysterious guy had hacked into the live broadcast and given directions to the cops. West German Broadcasting kept replaying snippets of what I had said and asking their listeners for help in identifying the hero.

Gregor and Martin stared into each other's eyes at the mention of this strange manifestation, and then they both quickly looked away again. Birgit wasn't saying much at all; she was just holding Martin's hand, and then she hugged Gregor good-bye, full of gratitude, for a solid minute. Maybe two. I wished I was him. Even with the dried barf in her hair. Then she disappeared into the bathroom while Martin made a calming tea. Only then did she find her words again.

"That voice on the radio . . ."

Martin's thoughts went to DEFCON 2.

"Gregor says the voice asked for him by name. And that it mentioned me."

Martin's thoughts started doing loop-the-loops as he thought back through the day, realizing what had happened and when. And how he'd shut me out just when Birgit and I needed him most.

"Tell her about me," I ordered him. "Just come clean once and for all, and then you won't need to hem and haw all the time anymore."

Martin resisted with all his power. He only mumbled, "That is strange."

"It's mysterious," Birgit said.

"Yes," Martin said. "Mysterious."

"I wonder if it was a, uh, supernatural apparition like the voices you sometimes hear?"

Martin was clearly at his limit. He didn't dare answer for fear he would just spill his guts about everything. So he kept his trap shut and shrugged. Chicken shit.

"Let's wait and see what turns up from WGB's investigation," Martin said. "Most importantly of course is that this someone, whoever it was, passed on the right clue to the police."

"That someone was ME!" I roared, but there was no point. Martin was not going to tell Birgit about me.

Disappointed and pissed off, I left his apartment. Even if the living weren't prepared to pay the necessary tribute to me, maybe I could at least make up with Marlene.

ELEVEN

Marlene was in the convent church, praying. Properly this time, the way she should be. Without blasphemous comments. Although, this time she was praying to the Virgin Mary. I doubt she could have held her tongue so nicely if she were praying to a man.

"Hello, Marlene," I said carefully when she was finally done.

"I'm sorry for yelling at you that way," she said.

I felt a flood of relief. Now that we'd made up, sort of, I had a question for her. "Where were you yesterday after the funeral? I was looking for you everywhere."

"In Cologne Cathedral, downtown."

My amazement was apparently clear even without words.

"I had actually never been inside it, although I've wanted to for years."

"You've been living in Cologne as a Catholic nun for thirty years, and you were never in the cathedral?" I asked.

"Correct. But now I've seen it. Even better than if I had been able to see it when I was alive. Thank you, by the way, for saving the women."

"No problem," I replied casually; if I'd had to really say it out loud, I probably couldn't have got it out past the lump in my throat. Marlene's praise went down like a cold beer after a greasy burger.

She could sense this. "You're not at all as bad as you pretend," she said.

Careful . . . Now she was talking crap, that much was clear. I needed to change the topic.

"How long have you been running this emergency shelter for the women?" I asked.

"For thirty years," she said proudly. "I started it."

"You did?"

"I was seventeen when I ran away from home." She was almost whispering, so I had to make an effort to understand her. "I'd met a man. A very good-looking man. Older than I was. He used to pay me compliments. He made me feel grown up. Important. Something my parents couldn't do for me. He'd take me out, give me presents. When I showed up at his place one day with a big gym bag, he was really delighted. Today I know why."

I could not imagine Marlene as a young girl or as a little sweetie-pie in love, but I could sense that she was telling the truth.

"The realization that I'd fallen into the clutches of a pimp was a real blow to me. It took me almost a year to work up the courage to escape. The Lord led me here."

"How were you able to keep the shelter secret for thirty years?" I asked.

"The women who come to us know that secrecy is vital for them," Marlene said. "It used to be much easier, of course, back in the day. The area in the convent where the women are housed doesn't have a telephone. For decades they had to ask the mother superior to use the office phone, and then they were allowed to speak only under supervision. But nowadays each girl brings her own cell phone and develops withdrawal symptoms if she has to live for three days without sending a text message."

That was true, and not only for hookers.

"And how did the women used to find out that you existed, with all the secrecy?"

"The Holy Ghost."

I groaned softly.

Marlene giggled. "No, of course not. The Holy Ghost can't worry about these details. We get the information out in a very targeted way, just like other women's shelters. Social workers, youth outreach workers, women working for the health department or city administration: they all know about us and tell women that they can get help here, free of red tape."

I was impressed. For thirty years these ho-hum Catholic penguins had been hiding runaway hookers inside their holy walls, but neither the public nor the pimps knew a thing about it.

"Whenever we had to take the women to a government agency or a doctor, or on occasion to the police, they would wear a habit as a disguise. Then we could take the bus or the subway without anyone bothering us at all. No one pays attention to two penguins waddling down the street with their eyes down and hands folded."

"You said penguins," I noted.

"But it's all over now," Marlene said, close to tears. "The kidnappers found out where we are, and they'll sell this information to their colleagues at a high price."

I had no answer for what she'd said—it was true.

Marlene told me that she planned to spend the rest of the day with her protégées, who, after the shock of the kidnapping and rescue, had faced the next shock of their day when the cops tried to haul them all to the precinct to take down their personal information and question them. Fortunately, the mother superior and Sister Szechwan had showed up in time to collect their girls and bring them back to the convent. I had no idea how they managed to get them all released from government custody, even the ones who didn't have residence permits, but Marlene waved her hand dismissively.

"We've had years and years of practice at that," she said nonchalantly.

———•———

While Marlene watched over her girls, I paid a visit to Gregor. The questioning of the driver they had in custody was dragging on.

"Who gave you the job to take over control of the van and drive it to the specified address?"

"Geez, I dunno, man. It was anonymous."

"How did you get the job?"

"The guy who runs the bar I hang out at handed me an envelope with the money. There was a slip of paper in it."

"Why were there two of you?"

"If you're not sure what's waiting for you, it's better to have backup."

"How do you think your customer knew about you?"

Now the greasy bastard grinned smugly. "Geez, man, I'm the Transporter. People just know that."

A greater blasphemy I had not heard in a long time. Ugh. At this spot my editor wrote a huge question mark in the margin, so now I have to explain: I love the *Transporter* movies. The real Transporter is a god. The coolest dude you can imagine. A man who has only one condition: "I drive my own car," which he says before every job. And here was this junkie comparing his anonymous van-driving job to the *real* Transporter? Well, you could plainly see where his conceit had gotten him.

Gregor's colleague was having even less success with the passenger. Frustrated, they compared their results and had decided to call it a day when the captain interrupted their intimate tête-à-tête at the coffee machine.

"Whose voice *was* that on the radio, Detective Kreidler?"

Gregor's partner slinked out inconspicuously.

"No idea, Captain."

"Why did this voice use your name?"

"No idea."

"Who is Birgit?"

I had expected him to lob another "no idea," but this time he told the truth.

"What was she doing at an emergency shelter for runaway hookers?"

"I think she was looking for a friend of hers."

For a cop, Gregor wasn't that creative a liar. But he was confident. No blinking, no sweating, no stuttering. Masterful, actually.

Presumably due to the advanced hour on a Saturday, the captain articulated his displeasure by means of sullen grumbling and left police headquarters. Gregor hurried to grab his jacket and did the same.

Katrin was waiting for him in front of the building.

"What are you doing here?" Gregor asked.

That question was on the tip my tongue too. Had I missed something in the break room? Weren't these two already hooking up? Apparently no, not actually, because Gregor looked just as surprised as I did. Maybe also a bit suspicious—but not unfriendly.

"What's this whole story about?" Katrin asked.

I like women who get right to the point.

"How do you know about it?"

Katrin laughed out loud. "You're not serious, right? West German Broadcasting has been running tape of that voice on all its shows all day asking for tips about who the person is."

Now the two of them were standing close, facing each other, the air between them convecting in hot little eddies.

"I don't know the voice," Gregor said in a husky voice, something I'd never previously observed in a cop.

"But we have an idea whose it is," Katrin whispered into his ear.

He nodded.

She nodded.

Their heads were so close now, they were touching.

"Got anything planned for tonight?" Gregor murmured.

"If I were to say it in public, I'd be arrested for disorderly conduct," Katrin purred.

They smiled at each other.

Katrin took a step back and ran her fingers through Gregor's dark hair. "I'm hungry," she said in an almost-normal voice but with a still-volcanic glow in her eyes.

"Me too," Gregor said.

I did not get the impression they were speaking of comestibles. Nevertheless, they went out to eat. First. A solid foundation is never the wrong place to start. It took two and a half hours for them to finally get to the point.

Watching was far from exciting, despite what I used to think. Somehow it made me a little blue, so I didn't stick around to see Gregor and Katrin's crowning achievement. Instead I spent the night in the emergency room at the hospital. It's usually really worthwhile on Saturdays. During the time I needed to kill between the more interesting and promising emergency cases, I thought about what the next step in our case should be.

"We've got to find the pimp who had the girls abducted," I explained to Martin on Sunday morning when he woke up.

I'd been making myself comfortable for quite a while at the foot of his bed, watching Birgit. She was lying next to him, still asleep. This time she was wearing panties and a T-shirt. Pity.

"The fire in the annex and the hooker hijacking don't necessarily have anything to do with each other," I went on. "Maybe our neighborhood tit-smith set the fire to get rid of the bums. Or maybe it was the brownshirt in the black suit. But the kidnapper's more important right now in any case."

Martin reluctantly nodded. "Yes, but the police actually did arrest the driver of the van . . ."

I tried to be patient with Martin. He clearly hadn't yet reached the pinnacle of his usual mental capabilities.

"Forget the driver. Stones were being thrown into the windows of the convent last Thursday night when that hooker yelled, 'Fuck off, you assholes,' out the window, so anyone with more than fifteen grams of brains between his ears could have figured out where the girls were getting their shut-eye."

"Mmh."

"And due to the construction work the south gate to the yard is open and obstructed only with temporary fencing that any eight-year-old with a bobby pin could open."

The image of a barrette with daisies on it briefly passed through Martin's brain. He was wondering in all seriousness if someone could pick a lock with something like that. Martin is truly unfit for survival. That is an unfathomable but totally indisputable fact. So if it's survival of the fittest, I have to ask, why is he still alive and I'm not? The Good Lord has a sick sense of humor.

"So put something inconspicuous on, and let's get going."

"It's Sunday," he objected grumpily.

"That's what I'm saying. Everyone's got the whole day off. The hookers will be working at peak capacity, and you'll find a lot of people to interview for your research."

He looked at me blankly, so I explained my plan to him.

Once again Birgit was smiling over the breakfast Martin had made of fruit muesli, a coffee for Birgit, and an herbal tea for himself. The woman was a regular Sally Sunshine.

"I've got to head back over to the convent again to pick up my bag," she announced. "And then home to change. But after that we'll spend the day together, right?"

Martin repressed the image of him and Birgit holding hands in a summer meadow in bloom. "I'd really like to," he said. "But . . . I've got to make a few, uh, inquiries."

He awkwardly explained my idea to Birgit.

After a moment of shock, she was all on fire. "I can help you with that," she said.

Martin went pale. "I don't think it's a good idea to involve you again," he said. "I already feel responsible for putting you in such danger yesterday."

Birgit waved him off. "I'm definitely no heroine," she said. "But the women I got to know at the convent really need the help."

Martin nodded reluctantly. "But that's a job for the police. Or the nuns."

"Well, why are you butting your nose into police business, then?"

"I don't think the prostitutes are particularly eager to supply information to the police," Martin said.

"I doubt they'll be any more inclined to open up to you, since you're a man."

Right on, lady! Mind-blowingly brainy, that one. She'd managed to outwit Martin, an ace maneuver. He was still making a little fuss, but he abandoned his opposition as soon as he'd gotten that he was powerless against Birgit.

I accompanied Birgit to the convent, where she slid into the lounge where the remaining girls were hanging out and picked up her things. I looked for Marlene while I was there and found her in the mother superior's room, together with the contractor, Baumeister.

"Doesn't he have a house to go home to?" I asked her.

"He always comes to mass on Sundays, and after that he has coffee with the mother superior," Marlene explained. But she sounded troubled.

"What's wrong?" I asked.

"Listen for yourself," she whispered.

". . . terrible events as an opportunity to think about a mission for the convent," Mr. Baumeister was saying.

"What does one have to do with the other?" the mother superior asked.

"The existence of your shelter for girls who have, uh, strayed off the straight and narrow has leaked out now. If you won't be operating it anymore, you'll be needing a lot less space." Baumeister made a sweeping gesture. "Given the number of sisters in your order, minus the sanctuary, a quarter of the space would be enough for you."

The mother superior looked at Baumeister thoughtfully and nodded.

"And the neighborhood protests against the homeless are also getting stronger and stronger. I've heard the city administration wants to review the permit situation again."

The mother superior put her fingertips together and looked at her hands.

"At least thanks to the bequest you won't need to dissolve the convent. Actually, I might be able to help find a suitable building for you. There are several properties still within the city limits that would fit the bill. There are even churches for sale. An abandoned parish house with a church that is no longer being used would offer your convent a suitable new home. Then you wouldn't need to sink the entire bequest into renovating an admittedly beautiful but much too large building. Instead, you'll have more financial leeway for your charity work, which you can then conduct separately, outside the convent."

Overall that actually sounded pretty logical. "What would be so wrong with that?" I asked Marlene.

"We aren't some kind of social work service zooming around town in little sports cars offering house calls," Marlene said. "We are a religious order with a convent. The convent is a place of faith and love. A place to glorify God, here on earth where we live and where we offer sanctuary to people in need. A safe refuge. Where else are these people supposed to go? This cannot be made up for with money."

The mother superior waited for Baumeister to finish his comments, then said, "I value and appreciate your efforts, and I will think about what you say."

Baumeister nodded, smiling. "I'm certain we can find a beautiful new convent for you where you won't need to fear hostility from disgruntled neighbors. If nothing else, you should also think about your own delicate health."

"What does he mean by that?" I asked, surprised. For a woman her age, the mother superior looked not only amazingly healthy but above all surprisingly strong.

Marlene gave a sigh. "She has a congenital heart defect."

To cheer her up, I told Marlene that Martin and Birgit would be pursuing other leads in the case. Marlene insisted on accompanying us.

We met our turtledoves in Martin's apartment. They had taken a digital photo of Birgit. On the computer they then changed the color of her hair, pulled the corners of her mouth down, and put a distracting mole under her left eye. Then they printed out the picture to go with our cover story: The picture was of Birgit's "twin sister," who had fallen in with a bad crowd and had been missing for ten days. The sister had sent only one text message: IM SAFE. The plan was for Birgit to ask hookers around town about her sister and in this way find out what people on the street knew about the convent and hopefully also get the names of any pimps who had suddenly had a filly go missing recently.

Martin was going to masquerade as a reporter among the "gentlemen of the night," making inquiries about a widely rumored but off-grid women's shelter and offering considerable money for this information. We hoped that anyone who took the bait might also lead us directly to the kidnappers.

Birgit set out around four in the afternoon, a good time of day for the horizontal trade, and Marlene and I were fiercely determined not to let her out of our sight. As we followed her, we found the selection of prostitutes to be abundant, but the looks Birgit got from the streetwalkers were not exactly friendly. The women standing around here wanted to meet men willing to fork out half a C for a labor of love—*not* clueless, towheaded cherubs with hesitant steps and nervous smiles.

"Hello. I'm looking for my sister." Birgit showed the doctored photo.

"That's you, right?"

"My twin sister. Do you know her?"

The chick in the black fishnet stockings and yellow tube top held the picture up so close to her nose I thought she was going to snort it. "Uh-uh."

"She disappeared a few days ago," Birgit continued.

The yellow-bellied toad shrugged.

"But she sent a text message on her phone that she's safe."

"Then everything's good, right?"

"I need to find out where she is," Birgit said nicely but definitively. "Our mom isn't doing that well."

"I'm sorry, sweet pea, but I can't help you."

A car turned into the street and crawled closer. Birgit's unwilling interlocutor pushed her aside with a skillful, lightning-fast movement of her arm to present herself in her full yellow and black nastiness.

The car stopped.

"Hey, baby. I haven't seen you here before."

Marlene understood first and gasped. It took Birgit a moment to get that the guy was talking to her, and then she blushed to the roots of her hair.

"Oh, how sweet," the driver said. "I'm guessing you're still new?"

The yellow-bellied toad made a furious face but then quickly brightened.

"She's available only through me," she said. "How much are you offering?"

"She didn't just say that!" Marlene protested.

I had to chuckle; I couldn't help it. Mistaking beautiful blonde Birgit in her tasteful clothes with no makeup on, standing next to this sauced-up sore-throat-lozenge of a hooker, was so outlandish that I wondered whether the driver believed in angels.

"Can't you speak for yourself?" the guy asked.

Birgit pulled herself together again. She approached within arm's length of the car.

"Well, what's your name?" she purred.

"Jürgen."

"And are you married, Jürgen?"

"Unfortunately."

"Do you have children?"

Jürgen nodded.

"Is this your car?"

"Paid off. No lease."

"Then you be sure to head on home right now, Jürgen, because I've just memorized your license plate, and I'm going to pass it on to every uniform and plainclothes officer I work with, and if you ever show up here again or even just park a little crooked, then I'm going to ram so much trouble up your ass it'll make an incurable STD seem like a mild case of hay fever."

For a moment Jürgen stared at Birgit with his mouth agape (as did the yellow-bellied toad), and then he floored it.

The hooker burst out in laughter you could hear from four blocks away.

"Where could she be?" Birgit asked, returning to the original question as though nothing had happened. Man, this woman had a bite like an attack dog. Once she sunk her teeth into her prey, she never let go.

"There's no way you're with the cops," the hooker said once she'd recovered from her laughter.

Birgit shook her head, smiling.

"Who in the hell are you, then?"

"I'm looking for my sister," Birgit explained with a friendly smile.

"I wish I had a sister like you," the yellow-bellied toad said. For the first time her voice didn't sound dismissive.

"So what do you mean? Where could she be?" Birgit asked.

"At a women's shelter."

"I've got three telephone numbers from the police. But she's not at any of those places."

The yellow-bellied toad squinted at Birgit. "You know more than you're letting on."

"I've heard there's another one. A safe house where a woman can go when she has to disappear. Where even the police and Immigration have no access. But where is it?"

The woman bit her lower lip, then made sure no one was standing within listening distance and whispered, "The convent in Mariental."

"Do you think people on the street know about it?"

The look from the overly made-up eyes turned suspicious. "What does that have to do with your sister?"

"I'm just wondering if she might have known about it . . ."

"Any girl who's seriously thinking about getting out and asks around can find that out easy enough. Now get out of here, I've still got to earn some more today."

Birgit thanked her and said good-bye, and then she started walking up close to the buildings in search of a face that looked promising to her. She talked to a few women but was brushed off by most of them.

"Isn't it terrible how women have to offer themselves up this way," Marlene said while we trained our eyes on Birgit. I gave her the ghostly equivalent of a shrug.

"Ah, well," she said. "At least prostitution is legal in Germany now so it can be practiced out in the open."

I thought my ears were on the fritz.

"If we could manage to reduce hostile societal attitudes toward sex workers even more so they can publicly stand up for their interests just like the huge steelworkers' union, then we will have taken a giant step forward toward the safety and self-determination of women."

"Marlene," I yelled. "Get a grip! You're a nun!"

"So what?" she replied, unmoved. "Of course I don't personally think prostitution is good, per se. But the social exclusion it entails is much worse, especially for women. Prostitution is finally legal in Germany now, but the social ostracism remains. And that is the very definition of hypocrisy. How do prostitutes make their living? From their customers. If there were no customers, there would be no prostitution. There are estimates that up to twenty percent of the adult male population has made use of sexual services."

She paused briefly, perhaps to give me the opportunity to come up with a reply, but I made the greatest effort to conceal all memories in my eddy of electrons regarding my personal experience at a whorehouse. I wasn't sure if I'd succeeded.

"It's a service that, as a devout Christian, I disapprove of. If I believed that prostitution could be done away with, then I would fight for that. But that's completely impossible."

Well, on that point, at least, we were absolutely of one mind. As long as women withheld sex as an instrument of power, there would be hookers. And withholding sex was socially acceptable, and indeed even desirable, on the pretext of morality or religion or whatever other abstract reasons; as long as that was the case, prostitution could look forward to a rosy future. Even my editor appears to share this opinion, because she didn't delete this paragraph.

Marlene sighed. "I might have put it differently, but you're basically right. Prostitution is indispensible in a society like ours. Even useful, because it prevents sexual violence against women under certain circumstances. That's why it's one-sided and thus completely misguided to ostracize the women but not their customers. It is so hard to provide counseling, health care, and a stronger sense of self-determination to a woman in this trade because she isn't allowed to publicly admit what she does for a living. This is what causes most of the problems. As a society we are allowed to publicly discuss the working conditions of hospital nurses and demand improvements, but not those of prostitutes. There is no public oversight or social safety net, which encourages exploitation and abuse."

Had I not known it was Marlene talking to me, I'd have guessed she was one of those militant feminists who had long ago exchanged her orchid overalls for an ammunition vest and publicly demanded that doctors prescribe the welding-on of a chastity device for all males upon the onset of puberty, the removal of which would require the consent of his wife, her best friend, and his mother-in-law.

"If the situation of prostitutes is to improve, there must be something akin to union representation, registration of dangerous customers, and government benefits to compensate for the loss of income to the brothel operator when a woman is infected by a customer with a communicable disease."

Union representation. Cool. I could see the headline now: SERVICE WORKERS UNION CLAIMS DIRTY TRICKS IN BERLIN BACKROOMS. That could lead to some misunderstandings. And syphilis would be added to the list of officially recognized occupational diseases, like a flour-dust allergy and asbestos lung. And when a teacher asks her first-graders what their parents do for a living, one will say her daddy is a banking consultant, and another will say his mommy is a whore. And perhaps they might even know each other? I giggled like a schoolboy.

Marlene sighed. "Yes, it's hard to have a discussion about this, especially for us, since as religious sisters we obviously cannot publicly advocate these positions."

"Otherwise the pope would send a load of funeral pyre wood and a matchbook with the Vatican's coat of arms on it," I joked.

"Well, he would kick us out of the Church," Marlene said. "For a religious order, that's about the same thing."

We had not let Birgit out of our sight during our conversation. Now she had put away the picture of her sister, apparently changing tactics.

"Which pimp has recently had a girl go missing?" she was asking.

"Whatcha wanna know that for?"

"I'm looking for the guy who went on a rampage at a counseling center."

"You with the cops?"

"No, from the counseling center. I'm an intern. We don't have any money to fix the damage, the insurance won't pay because there was a broken window lock that let the guy get in easily, and so far the cops haven't been going out of their way to help us. But if we find the person responsible, we'll make him pay."

With this approach she learned three names and got lots of encouragement such as, "Hey, great that you're doing that," and similar praise. I had some reservations about how easy it was for Birgit to lie, but Marlene explained to me that her creative handling of the truth wasn't hurting anybody, apart from the guilty party, so it was OK. I was going to have to dramatically revise my worldview of the holy habit wearers. It was becoming clear to me that an association based on nothing more than faith can exist for two thousand years only if it holds onto a certain amount of pragmatism. Which I suppose shouldn't surprise me.

Birgit's undercover mission didn't even last a full hour, and then she rushed back to the agreed rendezvous point and reported to Martin. First and foremost, Martin was terribly relieved to see her again unharmed; he was also mighty proud of her.

He had her give him the three names and respective comments about character, assumed dangerousness, and whereabouts, then kissed her as though he were a condemned man on his way to the electric chair and snuck off.

"Martin is going to need our help," I warned Marlene.

"I know."

She was surprising me today about as often as a Hail Mary comes up on the rosary. In other words, pretty much nonstop.

Martin hauled off to the bar where Birgit's information indicated that he'd find one of the jockeys who was down a filly in his stable. This establishment was, according to Birgit's report, a mixture of bar and brothel. The bartender normally earned his money in the totally normal way, by short-pulling drafts, but the customers knew that the snack menu here extended well beyond beer nuts. At least one pimp was always present, hanging out on the outermost barstool, nursing the only full glass of beer the house ever served, and waiting for demand. His product line was waiting in a side street, where direct sales also took place. However, some customers preferred a man-to-man business conversation in a bar over haggling at the street bazaar.

Martin ordered a beer, compared the figure on the stool with the description that Birgit had given him, sipped his beer, and then sat down on the open stool next to the pimp. Sitting next to the two-meter man with shoulders like an ox yoke, our dear Martin looked positively cute. Marlene and I took up position directly behind Martin so we could lend him advice and support during his conversation.

"This beer isn't bad," Martin said toward ox, who was known by the name of Fatman. "But beer alone cannot make a man happy."

"Too poetic," Marlene said.

"Too poetic," I said.

"Too poetic, eh?" Martin echoed out loud.

The ox nodded.

"Occupational hazard," Martin said.

The ox shrugged. So far he hadn't acknowledged Martin with even a glance, instead training his squinty eyes on some undefined point in the upper third of the dusty wood paneling on the opposite wall. His beard hung down to his chest, his bald skull looked just as dusty as the rest of the bar, and there were rips with blood-red edges in the knees of his jeans. Birgit's informant had rated his dangerousness as "average." Whatever that meant.

"I'm a reporter, you see," Martin said.

"Not a poet?" the ox asked without moving more than his lower lip.

"Poems don't pay the bills," Martin said.

"And now you've got money?" the ox asked.

"Yes," Martin said. "And I want to give you some of it."

The ox turned his head and looked down at Martin. "I'll take it."

"I'll need a piece of information for it."

"Information is a bad word," Marlene interjected.

Before I could pass on this wisdom, the ox had already held up his palm. "I don't trade in information. I trade in experiences." He resumed his uninterrupted observation of the point on the opposite wall.

Martin helplessly and frantically pondered how to steer the conversation back in the right direction.

"Pimps usually say that that they can offer a man any experience he can imagine in his wildest dreams. That's the hook," said Marlene. She came up with a suggestion for how to put it, I interpreted, and, always the good boy, Martin dutifully recited: "This is an experience that even you cannot provide me."

It took a solid twenty-two seconds for the ox to look at Martin again. In silence.

"I want to write a story about a women's shelter," Martin said.

"They won't take you."

"Exactly."

Again, silence.

"And?" the ox asked.

"There are three official women's shelters in town," Martin said. "There have already been articles about all three of them. But I hear there's another one. Some big secret place. Five hundred euros for the address."

"Why do you think I would know it?" the ox asked.

"Careful!" Marlene yelled.

"Careful!" I yelled.

Martin snapped his mouth back shut.

"Don't say anything," Marlene warned. "You never, ever reveal your sources. The only character trait that matters in this industry is loyalty."

I passed on the info, and Martin squeezed his lips together. The ensuing silence lasted for a minute and a half. That can feel like a really, really long time. Especially if, like Martin, you hold your breath when things get all exciting. After thirty-seven seconds you could briefly hear a few frantic gasps, followed by more quiet.

At some point Martin couldn't take it anymore. He took a breath to say something. Marlene and I held our breaths.

"A reporter never reveals his sources," Martin said.

We relaxed again.

"Say," I asked Marlene. "Do the girls at your shelter ever talk about their pimps?"

"On occasion."

"Do you know anything about Fatman?"

She nodded.

"And?"

"Later. I don't want to influence your judgment. There!"

She pointed excitedly at Fatman, who slowly bent over toward Martin, draped a tree trunk of an arm around his shoulder, and pulled him in closer so that the only part of Martin still sticking to his stool was half his ass.

"Where I source my girls from, there are lots and lots more waiting to enter the Promised Land here. So if one takes off, I just get two new ones delivered. Why should I care where the girls run off to?"

"Well . . ." Martin began.

"Stop!" I shrieked. No reporter would be so naive as to assume that one of the hookers would run to the cops and file a report on Fatman, which is what Martin was going to say.

"Well, what?" Fatman asked Martin, whose face was still half-shoved into Fatman's beard.

"Well, then, I'll have to give my five hundred euros to someone else, I guess."

Fatman stood up without letting go of Martin, and then with his toilet lids of hands he grabbed the lapels on Martin's jacket, lifted him off his stool, held him up for a moment in front of his eyes, and then carefully set him back down. "Looks that way, poet."

Then with astounding dexterity he swung back onto his own barstool, inhaled the half liter of beer in his full glass, and resumed staring at the point on the opposite wall.

"What do your girls say about Fatman?" I asked Marlene as we watched Martin leaving the bar on shaky knees.

"He imports women through a human trafficking ring that can supply him ten new ones every week. He's never tried to retrieve a runaway. Although not many of his women take off because they have it comparatively good with him."

I passed on Marlene's information to Martin, who shook his head. "Then I could have spared myself that conversation, right?"

The second name on the list was Kuri. The best place to track him down was supposed to be a Middle Eastern bazaar that offered a Turkish bath, massage, and other services. The three of us entered the teahouse that served as the entrance gate and distribution center for the other blissful destinations. They really did serve tea there, incidentally, as well as everything else. But more of the "everything else" was being consumed.

In a Middle Eastern teahouse there is, of course, no bar, otherwise everyone would immediately know that the whole thing was just a front. So Martin took a seat at one of the small tables. Birgit's informant said that Kuri usually hung out in the leftmost of the three red velvet sofa areas and that customers would check in with him there. Otherwise, he was apparently a pretty average guy. Average mug—for a member of his cultural sphere, of course. That meant greasy black hair, black pencil moustache, Roman nose, gold jewelry. Also average height and average dangerousness. But shorter-than-average fuse and lower-than-average IQ. And probably castrated.

Not that you could tell by looking at him.

The one guy hanging out on the velvet sofa didn't match Kuri's description, in any case. This fellow was so fat you had to wonder how he even got inside. Maybe the real, average-heighted Kuri was buried underneath him. You might find his flattened shell if you lifted this blimp here off the seat with a crane. Years later.

"My goodness, Pascha," Marlene giggled. "You have a rather peculiar imagination."

"Medically that is plausible," Martin said after a moment's consideration. Then he reshaped his mouth into a slight grin.

I almost fell over backwards, mentally of course. Martin, my Martin, had made a joke. The first one since his resurrection from death. I just knew a proper murder investigation would be the best antidote for depression.

Martin smiled, a little embarrassed. "No," he parried. "This is the last case I'm going to get mixed up in. After this I'm definitely calling it quits."

I didn't contradict him, but I had my own thoughts on the matter.

Marlene had since started looking around a little and now called me out to a back room where three grease heads were having a gentlemen's discussion.

"Geez, I dunno, boss. It was just lying around here," said a guy in black jeans, a white T-shirt, and a black leather bomber jacket, whose shifty look, hectic gestures, and beads of sweat on his forehead were all a clear sign of stress.

"And you showed Kuri this letter?" asked the man who was sitting in a leather armchair behind a giant, old, overly ornately carved desk. On the desk was a single white sheet of paper.

"Yeah, sure. Kuri was pretty beat up about Leila going missing. I mean, yeah, he also knew he'd fucked things up. After all, he was responsible for them, but he was also sad."

The boss accepted this blathering explanation without visible emotion. Meanwhile, the third guy in the room stood silently by the wall like a cigar store Indian.

"And then Kuri picked up a few buddies and hit that convent."

Sweat was now running into the stressed-out guy's eyes, so he had to keep blinking. He nodded with his head hanging.

"And they used my cousin's car."

His head went lower and lower, and his nodding grew smaller and smaller.

"And it didn't occur to either of you to come to me with this letter so I could decide what to do?"

He shook his head. Two drops of sweat fell onto the tips of the guy's leather boots.

"Where is Kuri now?"

Shrug.

"Who are the two people sitting in the slammer?"

"Contract drivers. They don't know who their customer was."

"Who else was involved?"

The guy whispered seven names.

"Remember those names," I whispered to Marlene (although I could have yelled—it's not like anyone could hear us).

"Get the fuck out of my face," the boss said. "I do not want to see you again, hear about you again, or have to say your name again. You're lucky your mother is my cousin."

The guy slinked out of the room, the cigar store Indian continued to show no emotion, and the boss grabbed the letter and a lighter. Marlene and I quickly flew around the desk and took a look at it.

It was written by hand—in a most familiar script—and said: "LEILA HIDING IN MARIENTAL CONVENT." Below that was a hand-drawn map of the convent that pointed out the location of the novitiate and where one could drive through the south gate.

Marlene stared at the paper, seeing in its script exactly what I saw. "For heaven's sake . . . that can't possibly be true!"

Then the flames devoured the evidence.

Back in the teahouse, we saved Martin from his third Turkish tea with tons of sugar. He was already pretty twitchy from the strong brew. And he was pleased when we told him we'd made an important discovery—and more so when I shared with him my visual memory of the letter.

On the way to pick Birgit up, we filled Martin in on everything we'd heard in the back room. Then we all hurried back to Martin's apartment. During the entire trip, Martin remained fairly quiet. He was thinking—something he's good at. We had been looking totally in the wrong direction the whole time and were now hopefully and finally on the right track. Of course, we still didn't have a coherent image, more a puzzle with certain key pieces still missing. Fascinated, I followed his razor-sharp train of thought and witnessed an absolutely hair-raising picture slowly coming together in his head. We were damned close to the answer; now we just had to dig up a couple more pieces of evidence.

TWELVE

We assigned tasks by ability. Marlene was going to put together a list of all the events of the past twelve months that supported our theory. Of course she couldn't actually write anything down, we are ghost writers after all, but she promised to put some thought into it. To refresh her memory, she wanted to do her thinking work at the convent, so she said good-bye and was gone in a flash.

Martin and Birgit discussed individual issues that weren't clear yet, brainstormed about a motive, but couldn't get any closer to the answer. The next day at the bank Birgit would do some research—that's what banks pay credit reporting agencies and debt collectors for, after all. Martin really wanted to take a break and go back to work again, even though he hadn't seen the psychologist yet. But he had set up an appointment. Maybe that would satisfy the boss for now.

By eight o'clock that evening everything they needed to put some thought into and plan for had been covered.

"Do you know what, Pascha?" Martin asked with forced casualness. "Perhaps you should go monitor our suspect. That way he won't be able to get up to any mischief."

"You just want to get rid of me so you can hop into bed with Birgit," I answered lightning fast.

How fortunate Birgit was currently on the can; otherwise she'd definitely have asked why Martin, who was perched all comfy in his armchair, was suddenly blushing to the roots of his hair.

"But it's all right, man," I said magnanimously. "You do what you got to do."

I graciously left the apartment and got to work monitoring the suspect, whose address Martin had previously jotted down. Only three hours later I was tailing him inside the Turkish bath where Marlene and I had found the key piece of evidence that afternoon.

"What on earth is going on here now?" Birgit asked, surprised, when she showed up for her Monday break at the gelato café on the convent square.

Although the broadcast truck from Saturday wasn't there anymore, in its place was a temporary platform stage decorated in black, red, and gold. On stage workers were just finishing the last preparations, and a number of people had already shown up on the square to watch. Oh yeah. The city council election was coming up. While the right-wingers had held their event among the garden gnomes, the Christians apparently wanted to display an even closer closeness to the convent. You couldn't get any closer than this to the wall in front of the convent's hill, in any case. And it seemed like their tin-can phone to the sky did in fact have a good connection, because the air was warm and summery, the scent of spring blossoms wafted through the square, and the gelato café had opened its express window in hopes of doing some good business.

Martin and Birgit found seats on the patio and opted for the Lovers' Sundae, which was soon served with burning sparklers. Martin managed to burn himself on the stupid things, so Birgit was blowing vigorously on his hurt finger. I instantly tried to recall my slowly fading memory of high-functioning erectile tissue. Martin of course didn't notice anything and asked the waiter for a small glass of tap water with six ice cubes. With difficulty the waiter tore his eyes off the vision of Birgit's lips on Martin's finger and walked rather stiff-leggedly back inside to get the water. I think he and I could hit it off.

"What did you find out?" Martin asked.

"He's got his hands in all kinds of businesses," she continued. "You know about the hotel in Belgium already."

Martin nodded.

"He's done similar projects in the Saarland and Luxembourg. He buys the old ruins, renovates them, and leases them to hotel operators. Medieval properties are his specialty."

"And what else?" Martin asked.

"Currently he's got some kind of project in an early phase," Birgit said. "He's taken out a not-inconsiderable loan for it."

"So he has debts," I said excitedly. Martin passed that on.

"For private individuals one might speak of 'debts,' but loans are completely normal for businesspeople when financing projects. That doesn't necessarily raise a red flag for me in this case."

Martin nodded again.

Birgit shrugged. "I'm not sure what all this has to do with the case. We're probably on the wrong track after all. So that's why I also ran the name of the district party chair for Germania Ahead again. Ever since he was sued for libel, that man has been waist-deep in debt, but he pays the agreed installments every month."

"Being sued for libel doesn't sound bad," I said, but I was interrupted by the pealing of the church bells.

The midday prayer was over, so Marlene would be joining us. Meanwhile Birgit was diligently chowing down on gelato, whipped cream, brittle, chopped nuts, chocolate sauce, waffle cookies, and advocaat. Martin ordered the fruit plate, preferring healthier fare. Of course.

"Building on what we suspected yesterday, we still have no idea what kind of motive he may have had," I said when Marlene finally arrived.

"It's a mystery to me too," she confirmed. "Everything else adds up."

We compared the results from thinking up our lists, returning repeatedly to the issue of motivation, when suddenly an earsplitting screech shattered the quiet over the square. Two seconds later the technicians had fixed the feedback problem, and a local politician stepped to the front edge of the stage to speak.

"Welcome to one of the most beautiful squares in Cologne," said the guy in a suit, his tie loosened in a down-to-earth way. He went on and on for a while; we made a concerted effort not to listen as we kept trying to come up with a motive. Nevertheless, the balmy wind kept blowing snippets of the guy's glowing self-adulation into our ears.

". . . recently done a lot for our neighborhood . . . increased the quality of life . . . a couple of small businesses have also located here, such as the gelato café right over there . . . and now another piece of very good news . . . efforts have finally borne fruit . . . a large amount of money to the city's coffers by selling municipal green spaces . . . about the Heiligenbusch, as . . ."

Martin's long spoon smacked down into the melted mush in the bottom of the giant bowl.

"That's it!" he muttered.

Birgit stared at him. "What's wrong?"

Marlene apparently got it immediately. "Of course! We should have been able to come up with that ourselves."

I felt a sense of solidarity with Birgit, who also didn't get it at all and asked out loud, "Huh?"

Martin pulled the bowl under Birgit's spoon away from her and into the middle of the table, and then pointed seriously at it and said, "This is the Mariental convent."

A miniature palm tree in the form of a toothpick with glued-on plastic palm fronds marked the allotment garden area, and the two long spoons marked the streets that led through Mariental to the square in front of the convent.

"Here." With his fingers, Martin traced the shape implied by the two spoons and the edge of the round table, coming to a point at the convent. The shape was like a fat slice of pie that took up about a quarter of the total area of the table.

"The part of the table inside this triangle is the Mariental neighborhood, with the convent at the tip of the slice of pie."

Birgit nodded.

"What is the rest of the table then?" Martin asked.

Birgit shrugged. "Woods?"

Martin nodded. "It's what they used to call the Heiligenbusch."

Birgit eyed him. "How did you know that?"

Martin beamed. "My colleagues at work just gave me that old map of Cologne . . ."

I launched like a rocket and flew so high I had a good view over what Martin had roughly sketched out on the bistro table. Well, what do you know. The Mariental neighborhood was the only thing that jutted up into the woods, and the convent was pretty much right in the middle, with the allotment garden area flanking it to one side.

If our man had in fact bought these woods, then we knew his motive. When I got back to the table, Martin already had his buddy Detective Sergeant Gregor on his cell.

"Baumeister," Martin was just repeating. "Yes, exactly, the philanthropist. Come out here, and we'll explain everything to you."

Gregor arrived quickly, bringing Katrin with him, and ordered a large chocolate sundae for her and an espresso for himself. Then he whipped out his pig pad.

"In January," Martin began, "Baumeister made an offer for the convent, which was for sale at the time."

"Verified?" Gregor asked.

"No," Birgit answered for Martin. "The offer came through an attorney and a broker, but it will turn out to have originated from Baumeister." She sounded so convincing that Gregor only slightly raised one eyebrow and didn't argue.

Martin resumed. "At the same time he bought the entire wooded area surrounding the convent. Not verified."

Martin and Birgit grinned at each other, Katrin continued eating her sundae, and Gregor took notes.

"Then the convent got that bequest, and the sale fell through, and Baumeister was left holding his Heiligenbusch like an idiot."

Katrin's latest cellular toy rang, she slid a futuristic-looking earpiece into her ear, pressed a button on the device, and answered—quietly, so as not to disturb the detective work going on around her. I was picking up clear waves of radiation. Interesting.

"When the convent was looking for a general contractor to do the renovation work, the choice automatically landed on Baumeister because he's the renovation guru in this region with the most experience. He drew up a horrendously inflated estimate and pretended he would cover half the costs himself. As a donation. That way he could reliably shut out any competitors."

"Verified?" Gregor asked Martin.

Headshake.

Gregor sighed.

"He had to complete the renovation of the annex to the mother superior's specifications, but otherwise he was planning to do the renovation the way he would do it as the owner of the property. So he wanted to keep the turrets and dormers on the roof, restore the cloister around the inner courtyard, and so on."

"So . . ." Gregor prompted Martin.

"Baumeister set the fire in the annex to terrorize the nuns and force them out of the convent."

Martin's remarks were starting to bore me; after all, I'd figured most of this crap out myself. So I approached my beloved Katrin, because I always feel so nice in her company. I perched in my usual spot in the crook of her neck and purred my standard "Hello, Katrin" into her cleavage.

"What was that?" asked a woman's voice from Katrin's earpiece.

Katrin's head jerked up. The others hadn't noticed anything. I was stunned for a moment of course as well, but then it quickly clicked that her cordless earpiece didn't have as effective radiation shielding as the manufacturer would have liked its customers to believe. What worked with Martin's computer headset also worked here.

"I didn't hear anything," Katrin whispered while she fumbled the cell phone out of her pants pocket and held it to the other ear and pressed a button. The earpiece abruptly stopped radiating. Too bad.

"And he also hired the pimps?" Gregor asked, derisively.

"Yes," Marlene and I said in chorus, but this issue seemed to make Martin sweat.

"Baumeister is a regular at the Turkish baths. That's where he knew Leila from; he saw her at the convent and tipped off the supervisor at the baths."

"I'm guessing not verified?" Gregor asked.

Martin shook his head. Unfortunately, we weren't able to show Gregor the piece of paper with the sketch and the reference to the place Leila was hiding. And even if it had been available, Martin wouldn't have been able to explain how he knew that a dead nun had recognized Baumeister's characteristic handwriting.

"Why did he go to all this trouble?" Gregor asked.

"Baumeister closed on the purchase of the Heiligenbusch, paid in full, and now he's in debt up to his chin. The economy also just started tanking again, the mortgage crisis is scaring investors, and he doesn't have any new jobs coming in. If he doesn't get the convent, which will allow him to see his hotel project through, he'll be bankrupt with a whole bag of debts hanging around his neck."

Gregor studied his notes. "This isn't going to be easy to prove," he muttered. "Not one damned bit of it."

Marlene and I spent the rest of that Monday shadowing Baumeister, who spent the majority of his day in the convent and then drove home to his futuristic luxury pad, where he took a shower, changed his clothes, and then went out to dine at some temple of fancy food with the head of the Cologne Department of Planning and Development. No doubt Baumeister was already paving the way for his official building permit to convert the convent into a luxury hotel.

This, not surprisingly, had Marlene über-depressed. So once Baumeister finally hit the sack and started snoring off the wine he'd drunk with dinner, I prescribed an evening of amusements for Marlene. First a romantic comedy at the movies, then a stroll past the narrow medieval buildings and soaring cathedral downtown along the Rhine, and at two thirty, a visit to my favorite bakery.

Aurelio—yes, that's really his name—has a teensy bakery where he bakes the best ciabatta north of the Alps. Aurelio weighs about a hundred fifty kilos, has body hair absolutely everywhere, apart from one specific body part. You'll have to mull over which one yourself, because my editor deleted it. Anyway, Aurelio always wanted to be a professional singer, so when he starts work in the middle of the night, he switches on an old CD player and sings one opera after another along with Placido Domingo and other fat squallers. Depending on the drama of the aria, Aurelio kneads softly or roughly, rips the dough apart, or throws it against the wall, beats it or caresses it. The first loaf is always in the oven at five thirty, and a squad car always stops by at six to pick up a warm slice of paradise.

"Someone called again?" Aurelio asked this morning's pair of police officers.

They nodded. "Your neighbors simply have no culture."

Marlene wept with happiness as we took our leave of Aurelio. "It's so sad that I never got to know him while I was alive," she whispered.

As far as I was concerned the night was overly sweet and schmaltzy, and there hadn't been the least bit of action, but I reluctantly had to admit I'd enjoyed spending it with some company. *Gone soft*, I repeated to myself.

On Tuesday morning around seven thirty when we arrived back at Baumeister's spaceship of a house, Gregor was standing at the front door with a female colleague. Marlene and I cheered.

Baumeister invited the detectives inside, offered them espresso from his ultra-high-tech turbo coffee jet, and even served a couple of dry cookies on the saucers, sank down into the leather armchair opposite the detectives' couch, leaned back, and smiled warmly.

"What can I do for you?"

"We're investigating the Mariental convent arson, where two people were killed."

"Terrible, really terrible," Baumeister said, affecting a concerned face. "Have you had any leads, then?"

"Oh yes," Gregor said. "That's why we're here."

Baumeister flashed his smile again. But now it looked a bit more strained.

"Mr. Baumeister, a few months ago you purchased the entire wooded area surrounding the convent. May we ask what motivated you to make this purchase?"

Baumeister nodded slowly. "As you surely know, I am just crazy about the convent. My purchase is intended to conserve the entire area in its current state. It's dreadful to imagine what would happen if the neighborhood development plan were changed and the existing boundaries of Mariental were expanded. After all, this area here has recently become one of the most expensive in Cologne."

"That's a very selfless and not exactly inexpensive thing to do given that there is no evidence whatsoever of this kind of threat," Gregor's colleague said in a friendly way.

Baumeister gave the dark-haired, long-legged, full-bosomed, hot-blooded cookie a lecherous ogle before regaining control of his expression. "Now there you are mistaken," he said unctuously. "Efforts along those lines have in fact already been set in motion."

"By whom?" Gregor asked.

"I would prefer not to disclose the names of these construction companies to you. Our industry is small and dirty." Baumeister's smile now contained a dose of apology.

"Is it true that you had this real estate transaction done through a front company?"

"Exactly."

"And about one year ago it also tried to buy the entire convent on your behalf."

Baumeister's smile was getting noticeably smaller and more strained. "The front company, as you call it, is actually a respectable law firm. As discretion is often the deciding factor between success and failure, this kind of approach is standard procedure in our industry."

"Neither the Recorder's Office nor the Department of Planning and Development are aware of any parties interested in the woods parcel or the convent," Gregor's super-hot partner said.

"So you can see how important discretion is," retorted Baumeister with a smile that had again reached maximum width. "But please explain what these issues have to do with the fire. Do you think that a competitor set the fire?"

"No," Gregor replied. "Did you want to acquire the convent for sentimental reasons?"

Baumeister's smile died a little. "Listen, I don't know what all these questions have to do with the fire. But my strategic business planning is a very delicate matter. I am extremely averse to sharing the details with you here and now. I have to think of my business."

"Particularly since your business is not doing well at all," Gregor's partner said.

"That's not accurate." Baumeister's smile had disappeared.

"No?" Gregor asked.

"I am currently in a prefinancing phase. As soon as the project starts, the investor will have to settle previously incurred costs and cover the individual stages of construction."

"Which project does this pertain to?" Gregor asked.

"That's confidential." Baumeister's face had taken on an arrogant expression, the effect of which was dampened by the worry in his eyes.

"It relates to the Mariental convent; we've known that for a long time, so you can admit it."

"No comment."

"The fire in the annex for the homeless shelter and the smashed windows last Thursday night were supposed to motivate the nuns to leave the convent."

"I was afraid of that as well," said Baumeister. "I'm taking these warnings very seriously, and I hope you do too. I am concerned about the safety of the sisters. I see these acts of violence, in which two people have already lost their lives, as a clear sign that the enemies of the convent are rearming. It would be irresponsible of the women to remain."

"And you set the fire yourself to force them to move out."

Baumeister turned as pale as the cream-colored leather of his armchair. "That is an outrageous insinuation! How could you possibly arrive at such an absurd idea?"

"You had the opportunity, namely access to all the keys and thus to the sacristy where the oil used as the accelerant was stored and from where the stairs lead to the tower where the rope to the emergency bell had been severed. You had the means, because you are familiar with the tool that provided the crucial ignition sparks. And you have a large financial interest in the order giving up the convent because otherwise you are broke."

An awkward silence unrolled through the room. Ah, what Marlene and I would have given to be able to peer into the heads of these three parties to the case right now. Gregor and his colleague were looking at Baumeister with deadpan expressions; we couldn't read a thing from them. So we focused on Baumeister, who hadn't practiced his poker face quite as thoroughly as the two plainclothes had.

First he stared at Gregor in shock, then his shoulders drooped a notch lower. Finally his eyes looked down at the top of the coffee table and he turned pensive.

"I find your completely unfounded insinuations shameless," he said at last, forcing a faint smile, "but I recognize that you are just doing your duty and must be thorough and investigate all avenues." His smile grew slightly wider. "You sent up a trial balloon, which I admit caught me very much off guard. For a moment I really believed you thought I was the perpetrator." Now he was even laughing! "I'm sorry that I can't help you further. I hope you find the real person responsible soon so that the sisters can finally focus without worry on their charity work."

Marlene and I protested vigorously, but of course nobody heard us.

———•———

Martin was disappointed, to say the least. Birgit grabbed his hand and stroked it, although she was clearly struggling with tears herself.

"We're sure it was him, but we can't prove it."

"But—" Martin began.

Gregor interrupted. "The sleepwalker who presumably ran into him the night of the fire couldn't recognize him, even under hypnosis."

Martin's head sagged a little lower.

"Baumeister is in fact a customer of the Turkish bath, including 'additional services,' but since prostitution is legal we can't use that against him. We arrested that Kuri guy who kidnapped the women, but he isn't telling where he got the tip-off from. We've even reviewed how those Germania Ahead folks came up with the idea of holding their campaign event in the allotment garden clubhouse, but the connection is with the club's treasurer, not with Baumeister. We'll probably never know who threw the stone into the convent window. Baumeister doesn't have an alibi for the night of the fire. But that's better than if he had one, since at two thirty in the morning a normal person is lying at home in his bed asleep."

"What about DNA evidence from Baumeister in the annex or in the tower where the rope to the emergency bell was cut?" Birgit asked.

"There is DNA," Gregor sighed. "Tons of it. But that's to be expected, since the man's been spending eight hours a day at the convent for the past few weeks."

"So there's nothing . . ." Martin said.

"The DA won't file charges against Baumeister because he knows that he doesn't have anything to show in court. Not even the slightest bit of circumstantial evidence."

"Baumeister has to answer for the lives of two human beings," said Martin, "and he's getting off free."

Gregor nodded grimly. "Makes me want to puke. On days like this I really can't stand my job."

"And we can't do anything at all?" Birgit asked.

Gregor shook his head. "Nothing, apart from praying. There may be a higher justice that will step up for the nuns and force Baumeister to confess the crime. Otherwise he'll probably get his way, the nuns will abandon the convent, and he'll build his luxury hotel inside the old convent walls and be out of the red again."

"And the sickest thing is that everyone will presumably be better off after all this," Martin muttered. "The order can put its bequest into its charity work instead of investing in new masonry, the neighbors will be happy about having a fancy hotel in their neighborhood, and their houses will increase in value."

"Everyone will be better off except for those who died," Gregor sighed.

"Did you talk to the mother superior?" Birgit asked. "Does she really want to leave this place?"

"I couldn't reach her; she was at the motherhouse in Belgium yesterday and today. But if she's smart, she'll lie low. The police are too stupid to arrest the murderer, and so she has further attacks to worry about."

Gregor left Martin's apartment a short time later to seek solace from Katrin. Birgit had to go as well; she had arranged to meet a friend at the gym. Martin fell back on his couch, disappointed and sad. Marlene also wanted to clear her head and go pray, but I asked her to stay for another moment. Something Gregor said had given me an idea.

"Martin, Marlene: I know how we can still nail Baumeister."

Their response was subdued. Neither of them said anything.

"Gregor actually said it himself: Baumeister has to confess, himself, otherwise it won't work."

"Great idea," Martin said. "But he doesn't seem to be suffering from a bad conscience."

"No," I said. "Not yet."

I explained my plan to them. And we decided to spend the evening not exactly whooping it up, admittedly, but still kindling a spark of hope.

Before implementing our plan, Marlene insisted on some proper praying, so she fluttered off to the convent church, spent the night with the Holy Ghost, and in the morning joined in matins with her sisters. Because of this, I was not expecting to see her so early when she excitedly came to me around eight.

"The mother superior has apparently reached a decision; she has an appointment with Baumeister in half an hour. We should be there to hear what she says and see how he reacts." She didn't have to tell me twice.

We were already on location when Baumeister entered the mother superior's office.

"Mr. Baumeister, as you know, this has been a very difficult time for our convent."

Baumeister nodded with appropriate solemnity.

"You are not the only one who has advised us to give up the property and find a new site that better meets our current needs and causes less anger and disapproval among our neighbors."

"It is a matter of safety," Baumeister said.

"Yes," the mother superior confirmed. "That is one way to look at it. But our order has stood by the poorest of the poor for many centuries, and during this long time we have been subject to frequent hostility because of that commitment."

Baumeister took a breath, but the mother superior forced him to be quiet with a subtle gesture.

"To yield to hate and disapproval sends the wrong message. We have always trusted in God, and we shall continue to do so."

"But two dead—"

"It's very sad that Marlene and Martha were taken from our midst," she continued, "but they now dwell with God.

And we who are left behind and continue to fulfill the purpose of our order have learned from the attacks. Our trust in God does not mean that we want to leave the responsibility for our own safety to Him alone."

Baumeister stared at her uncomprehendingly.

"We shall therefore immediately secure all access points to the convent with proper doors and an alarm system. We shall also engage a security service that will patrol the neighborhood as well. And we shall install an intercom system at all the gates and entries so that no one need open a door before knowing who wants to be admitted."

Stunned, Baumeister stared at the mother superior as if she'd just announced that she and her sisters were planning a new crusade to Jerusalem. "But . . ." he stammered, "but that will undoubtedly be quite expensive."

"To cover the costs we will redo the roof without turrets and dormers, and in a few other places we will forgo some beautiful but unnecessary details."

Baumeister slumped back into his chair.

"I wanted to tell you this myself before I announce it to the press next week."

"The press?"

"We have decided that we want to publicly testify to our determination to put an end to any and all further speculation and make clear that we are serious about our commitment to the poorest in society. Out of piety we are going to wait until after Martha's interment, which at the request of her family is taking place on Monday morning in her hometown."

Baumeister left the mother superior's office slowly, dragging his feet as Marlene and I flanked him to the right and left. Once he reached the steps his strides became more resolute, and once he made it to the cloister he was standing tall with shoulders thrust back again. "Just wait," he muttered through gritted teeth. "Living at a construction site can be dangerous."

Marlene and I winced.

"He's going to attack them again," Marlene whispered at me.

"That smirk will be wiped off his face soon enough," I whispered back. "As of now, Operation Higher Justice is in effect."

We followed Baumeister to his SUV. He fished his key out of his pocket and pressed the remote button to unlock it. The power locks all popped up. A moment before he had his hand on the handle the locks all automatically popped back down again. Well, technically not entirely automatically, of course, but Baumeister had no way of knowing that. He did a double-take. Pressed the button again. Door unlocked, hand on the handle, door locked. The third time we let him get in. He tossed his cell phone into the cubby in front of the gearshift, switched on the wireless headset, stuck the thing over his left ear, jammed the key into the ignition, and exhaled when the engine started humming.

His radio immediately started blaring, which was actually perfect for my purposes. You see, I had spent the better part of the night surfing the web after Martin set up a wireless headset for me. Over the course of several hard hours, I had completed my own self-guided degree program in electrical engineering—at least with regard to the inner workings of the electronics system in Baumeister's vehicle. (In doing so I also determined that it's easier to find plans to build various bombs on the Internet than it is to find a decent textbook with an introduction to electrical engineering. In the end, however, I did strike gold.) Even though I understood only a fraction of the tech geeks' online documentation, I still had gotten my brain around enough of it to find a starting point for Operation Higher Justice. And that's all I needed.

Baumeister's radio was piping some completely schlocky one-hit wonder through his sound system—where, as I had learned last night, the radio receiver or amplifier, or whatever super-geeky component, changes the voltage signal u back into the sound pressure signal p. Such voltage signals are easily influenced by electromagnetic vortices. That's where I came in.

I tried my luck.

To start, I'd been planning to moan, "Baumeister!" deeply in the background of the radio program, then switching to a menacing, "Murderer!" Instead, all I managed to do was produce a lot of interference and white noise. No idea if that was due to fluctuations in the electric potential or if the trigger level wasn't right or if I was thinking at a frequency not suited for high-fidelity sound reproduction. Maybe the car radio was set to digital radio, and I was having a translation problem with the ones and zeros. All the super-theoretical crap hadn't totally clicked yet. OK, in all honesty, I hadn't even tried to read *that* stuff. Still, I was able to muzzle the cheerful DJ, who was now reciting the various locations and lengths of traffic bottlenecks on the autobahns around Cologne, and produce genuinely nails-on-chalkboard-style interference.

Not bad for starters.

Marlene thought so too. She was giggling like a school-girl after two glasses of Asti Spumante.

"What's wrong with you?" I asked, suspicious. I needed a serious partner, not a teenybopper on a bubble high.

"I was surfing on the signal from his headset to his cell phone, and I made it into his contact list and did a little, uh, reorganization there," she said.

She was all hot and bothered, and her nerves were vibrating. I was scared to death. Not because my sweet little Leni was losing her innocence as a ghost nun. But it was a little freaky that she found cell phone surfing to be a suit-able substitute for cruising the strip or something.

"Don't worry," she corrected me, still giggling. "I'm well past that age."

I let the radio program keep going normally, but every time Baumeister upped the volume because he wanted to hear the news, traffic reports, or an interesting piece, I'd add the white noise back in over it again. After half an hour we had him pretty much parboiled, so he switched the radio off.

In our excitement about our mission we hadn't been paying any attention at all to where Baumeister was driv-ing, but after he switched the radio off I took a curious look around. He turned two more times, and then parked in front of the bank where Birgit works. Coincidence? Divine providence? Or was it just logical to stop at the bank that is the first choice for midsize organizations—including both general contractors as well as convents?

Baumeister asked for an urgent appointment with his financial adviser, would not take no for an answer, and nerv-ously fidgeted in his chair until the man finally had time for him.

"A delay has cropped up in my project."

The adviser's face drained of all emotion for a moment. "Another delay? Mr. Baumeister, you know that the agreed term of the loan has already been extended twice . . ."

"Yes, but . . ."

"Please let me finish," the adviser interjected politely. "At the start of the year there was a bridge loan for a maximum of two months, for which we offered quite favorable terms, as you are a very good, long-time client."

Baumeister nodded.

"But even for the first extension I had to muster all my influence to continue the loan under those favorable terms, and for the second extension my manager and I had to defend our decision together and in person with the regional director."

"And I really do appreciate—"

"I'm afraid that for a third extension at this extraordinarily low interest rate—"

"But you surely don't want the project to fall through, and along with it a hundred fifty or even two hundred jobs? It wouldn't be good advertising for your bank if such a high-profile construction project were to fail merely because of a couple of extra weeks' grace period."

The adviser bit his lip. He obviously didn't take kindly to this veiled threat. "A couple of weeks, you say?"

Baumeister nodded.

"I'll see what I can do," he promised and then walked him out to Baumeister's SUV.

Marlene said she would stay with Baumeister while I zoomed to Martin. I found him in the slaughterhouse, er, autopsy room. He was just sawing open the skull of a hairless corpse.

"Martin, you've got to call Birgit. Right now."

The saw slipped and, presto, the left ear was gone.

The fidgety guy at the foot end of the autopsy table, likely someone from the district attorney's office or an insurance company investigator who wanted to verify the legitimacy of a claim, stared in dismay at the ear, which landed on the floor with a moist splat.

"What is wrong with you?" asked Martin's colleague, who had switched off the dictation device he was holding in his left hand. Because of all the noise from the electric bone saw, he couldn't document the progress of the autopsy during the sawing.

"Cramp in my middle finger," Martin growled.

Whoa! He got that from me. Martin had never yet displayed the one-finger salute, and he would certainly never do so, which is why he would never, ever get a cramp in that finger. But it still made me proud that he was learning.

His colleague's eyes narrowed. Now he was grinning. "I think I've got some superglue in my desk."

"Could you please refrain from your inappropriate jokes and complete the autopsy?" the fidgety figure asked from the foot end of the corpse.

"Certainly," Martin said. "Right away."

He stooped down, picked up the ear, wiped it off superficially, and laid it next to the corpse on the stainless steel table. Then he jimmied open the skull. The guy at the end of the table couldn't see into the skull from where he was standing, and it was probably better that way. I've gotten somewhat used to the sight of an opened abdominal cavity with its various organs and a ribcage full of lungs, but I still find a human brain in a sawed-off skull pretty nasty. It always reminds me of that Indiana Jones movie where Indy's supposed to eat some monkey brain soup with an eyeball in it. Re-volt-ing.

Martin lifted the brain out of the corpse's cranial cavity, asking me, "What's wrong?" in his thoughts.

I explained the connection between Baumeister and Birgit's employer, and I was quick to tattle on the contractor for apparently planning some final assault on the mother superior.

Martin turned pale. "And what should I do now?" He was still holding the brain in his hand. His colleague was already sending impatient signals with his eyes. Jittery Joe at the foot end wiped the beads of sweat off his snow-white forehead with the arm of his sleeve.

"Birgit has to tip off the financial adviser that Baumeister is under criminal investigation so that they don't approve the loan."

Martin agreed to call her right away and pass on the request; at the same time, he remembered the brain in his hands and slid it onto the scale. At the moment the gray matter adhered to the scale's tray with a squishy sound, the observer fled from the room with his hands pressed to his mouth.

"What's wrong with him?" asked Martin.

"Envy, probably," said his colleague, shrugging. "One and a half kilos is Nobel Prize–winner size."

THIRTEEN

I found Baumeister and Marlene at the convent. If Marlene had had cheeks or circulation, the former would have been flushed from exertion and the latter would have been surging at full power. By contrast, Baumeister was struggling not only with a laser distance meter but also with his blood pressure.

"Give me that thing again," his assistant said.

With unnecessary force, Baumeister slapped the device into his assistant's hand; the assistant placed it against the wall in the library and pressed a button. A laser beam appeared from the front of the device, and a digital display showed the distance to the opposite wall. Accurate to the millimeter. The lazy man's tape measure.

Baumeister tore the instrument out of his assistant's hand, banged it onto the wall, pressed the button, and stared at the digital display, which showed two hundred twenty centimeters, then eighteen meters, then all possible measurements in between. The numbers raced up and down.

"Oh please," Marlene groaned. "How long do I have to keep playing this game until he figures out it won't work?"

"What are you up to?" I asked, grinning.

"I'm just whooshing back and forth in front of the laser beam." She sounded breathless.

"Does it tickle?" I wanted to know.

"Try it yourself," she gasped, leaving the field to me.

It didn't tickle, but it did make you pretty limp and floppy. I admired Marlene, who had obviously been laser-surfing for quite a while.

Baumeister had finally had enough. He lobbed the gizmo at his assistant, who barely managed to catch it, and stomped off in a rage. He dug his cell phone out of his pocket as he walked.

"Ah! He wants to make a phone call!" Marlene shouted. "Oh, I'm so excited!"

Baumeister selected a name from his contact list, pressed the call button, and held the phone to his ear. We nestled between the phone and his not-quite-clean auricle (a term I learned from Martin's last autopsy).

A friendly voice almost sang: "Catholic Confession Hotline, hello. Confess whatever is weighing on your conscience. Our next available priest will be ready to hear your confession soon." This was followed by organ music.

Baumeister stared at his cell phone, mouth agape and eyes bugging out.

"May the Lord be in your heart and help you to confess your sins with true sorrow."

In his panic Baumeister had to try three times before he managed to hang up on the call. He leaned against the convent wall and tried to bring his breathing and pulse back down to normal.

"Is that hotline for real?" I asked, stunned.

"It's a pilot project at a theological seminary I heard about recently," said Marlene.

"And at the time, you immediately decided to memorize the phone number in case you were murdered and had to take out your own murderer through poltergeistery?"

"I remembered the number only because it's easy. The toll-free area code of zero eight hundred is obvious. And then the number starts with three, for the third gospel, Saint Luke. Then comes fifteen for the chapter and ten for the verse about the repentant sinner, and eleven through thirty-two for the parable of the prodigal son."

Hats off. While I was alive I could hardly even remember my own phone number.

Baumeister had calmed down by now. He carefully picked his cell phone back up and pressed a few buttons, deliberately and emphatically. Then he held the phone up, about thirty centimeters away from his ear.

"Catholic Confession Hotline—"

He nearly crushed the red button. Then he selected another name from his contact list.

"Catholic Confession Hotline, hel—"

Now Baumeister selected each individual contact, from top to bottom, starting with Abel, Jochen, head of the Department of Planning and Development, to Zilgreis, Marianne, home phone. Every time he ended up getting the Catholic Confession Hotline.

Marlene seemed quite pleased with herself.

Leni, you never cease to amaze me.

Marlene beamed.

We were a pretty damn cool team.

We kept irritating Baumeister for the rest of the day with our new little games; there weren't any other opportunities for action. At some point it occurred to Baumeister to stop using his contact list and instead dial the numbers by hand. Since Marlene could only fiddle with the contact list data, she couldn't prevent the manually dialed calls from going through successfully. Still, Baumeister knew only a couple by heart, and he wasn't carrying a little phone book around with him. So he quickly became a premier customer of directory assistance.

After a while, I left Marlene on her own so I could take a look around in Baumeister's stylish home. I wanted to be prepared for the evening, so I investigated his pad for almost an hour, searching for potential sabotage targets. And I struck the mother lode. Although professionally the man specialized in medieval buildings, in his personal life he'd already beamed himself into the future, with tons and tons of household gizmos. I inspected everything really closely, and I wondered more than once how to operate the lamps in his place. I couldn't find any light switches anywhere. I was super curious about that.

Around six, Baumeister finally left the convent, after his usual problem with the remote-control locks on his vehicle. He left the radio off, and his cell phone too. He drove aggressively and distractedly. I made myself comfortable in the back seat while Marlene pursued her newfound love of silly games.

"Aren't there sensors in these things that blink if you're not buckled in?" she asked.

I explained the connection between the pressure sensor in the seat and the locking sensor in the restraint system, and she tried to trigger the alarm, but it didn't work.

"And how do the parking sensors work?"

After a little practice she managed to trigger a brief hazard warning on the front sensor, which caused Baumeister to instinctively slam on the brakes. The car behind him hit him, and both drivers got out and started shouting at each other.

That is until Baumeister suddenly slumped onto the hood of his car and started to sob.

His opponent stopped talking, embarrassed. The cops came, took pictures of the damage, and with great reluctance let Baumeister drive himself home even though his left taillight was broken—and he wasn't in much better shape himself.

"I almost feel bad," Marlene whispered at me when Baumeister slid his key into the ignition with fingers trembling.

"He killed you and Martha and wants to screw your order out of the convent," I reminded her, as a friend.

Marlene sighed. She was truly a good-natured person, even though she'd been spending the past few hours acting like a video-game junkie unleashed.

A few minutes later, Baumeister turned into the driveway to his house. He fumbled a remote control out of a compartment.

"The garage door," I yelled to Marlene. "Interference!"

We formed as dense a shield as possible in front of the garage door opener and deflected the pulses of radiation. The garage door stayed closed. Baumeister pressed the button two more times and then sighed, emasculated, and parked his SUV in front of the single-panel garage door. He was on his way to the front entry when the garage door slowly started to rise. He didn't have any energy left to react when the bottom of the door, with its wide swing radius, thwacked into the front bumper of his car, screeching loudly as the door and bumper wedged into each other, leaving the door stuck half-open. Baumeister stared at the disaster scene for a solid half minute and then simply turned and walked to the front door.

In front of the door, Baumeister looked into a lens that I'd taken to be a security camera, but apparently it was a retina scanner, and after a couple of seconds the door automatically swung open. He stepped inside, pressed a couple of numbers on a control panel that was presumably part of the alarm system, and closed the door behind him. He left his jacket and shoes on the floor where he took them off, and then hotfooted it directly to his liquor cabinet, where he poured at least a triple grappa into a tumbler and downed the stuff in one gulp. Right on, I thought. He didn't even cough once. But the reaction was only a bit delayed: he started snorting, and his eyes teared up so much he spilled half of his refill because he could hardly see anything. He chugged this one too. If the guy kept on like this, he wasn't going to have to turn himself in to the police at all; he was going to end up snuffing it from alcohol poisoning tonight. Cowardly exit.

The puzzle about the light switches was soon solved; it turned out the lamps were controlled by sound. Baumeister clapped his hands once, lamp on. Another clap meant dim by one level, and after cycling through all the levels, the last clap turned the lamps off. I didn't understand how the lamp knew the sounds were meant for it until I noticed that apparently there was also a motion detector or some other such sensor, because the clapping activated the lamps only in the room where Baumeister was currently hanging out.

Marlene and I tried our luck with all the lamps, but we couldn't affect them. The radio and TV were also impervious to our efforts. They must have had wired connections.

We withdrew, slightly frustrated, to review the situation along the long wall of the gigantic living room where we had a decent overview of things, when suddenly an alarm went off. We winced, frightened to death. All three of us.

Baumeister came running in, stared directly at us, and started moaning with a slight slur: "This can't be happening, it's not possible, there's no way."

Marlene and I froze.

"Can he see us somehow?" Marlene asked softly.

I couldn't answer her. It was unthinkable. But with the way Baumeister was staring right into our eyes, suddenly I wasn't sure about anything anymore.

Baumeister had since taken another step forward and was now carefully touching the frame of the giant oil painting we were floating in front of. If you were close enough, behind the oil painting you could make out a metal plate.

Now I understood what was going on. The metal plate used the exact same kind of field sensor that Martin had put up in his apartment, a technology used in alarm systems protecting individual objects—I had read about it last night on the Internet. Marlene and I must have triggered the alarm with our presence; Baumeister was actually staring at the ginormous, overblobbed finger-painting—not at us.

I quickly clued Marlene in, and we breathed easier. Then we grinned at each other. He had probably secured other paintings in his pad the same way. It was going to be a long night.

And it was. Every alarm on a painting set off an automatic alarm directly with the security company, whose gorillas came racing to the rescue twice. After that they called ahead to see if it was another phantom alarm.

Around three in the morning, a neighbor called the cops because the constant wail of alarms was disturbing him. Baumeister stood in front of the cops, bleary-eyed in his sweaty and rumpled clothes and stinking of booze, and assured them that there was an unfortunate failure in the alarm system and that the security firm was already working on it.

The patrol officers turned out to be the same ones who had handled his car accident before.

"It's really not your day, huh?" said one.

"Maybe you've fallen out of the Lord's good graces," the other joked.

Baumeister turned pale as ash but said nothing.

With a doubtful sideways glance at the SUV wedged into the half-open garage door, the patrollers finally took off, but they drove past the house at regular intervals all night. Baumeister watched them several times through his half-closed curtains.

He didn't get much sleep that night.

At first we'd triggered the burglar alarms just to hound Baumeister a bit, but when the security gorillas called a third time, Marlene had an idea. Our telephony specialist sent me over to trigger the alarm while she hung out next to the base of the cordless landline phone and waited for the security guys to call again. She practiced and practiced, and by six in the morning she was sure she had the trick down. She made the phone ring.

Baumeister awoke from his troubled, repeatedly inter-rupted sleep on the couch in the living room, opened his swollen, red eyes, had trouble getting his bearings, but finally made it up onto his legs. He picked up the receiver, only to hear the dial tone, no one on the line. Not even us, unfor-tunately, because speaking messages through the receiver is something we had no clue how to do. But we *could* make it ring. And ring it we did. If Baumeister didn't pick it up, it kept on ringing. If he picked up, no one was there. He made no move to mute the phone or pull the plug. He just sat next to the device, staring into space with glassy, vacant eyes. Whenever the thing rang, he'd pick the receiver up, listen to the dial tone, and then hang it back up. The bags around his eyes had since grown to the size of beer coasters and turned the color of old engine oil. His hands were trembling, and from every pore he reeked of alcohol, sweat, and fear.

After two hours, Marlene had finally had enough.

"Let's zoom over to Martin's and the convent and see what's new," I suggested, just as the phone rang again.

"Come on, Leni," I griped. "Enough is enough."

"That wasn't me," she whispered.

We froze. This time we found the ringing eerie.

But nothing was eerie to Baumeister anymore. Like a remote-controlled zombie, he picked up the receiver, held it to his ear, and listened.

"Hello?" pierced out of it. "Mr. Baumeister?"

Baumeister held the phone in front of him, stared at it, moved it back to his ear, cleared his throat, and in a scratchy voice said, "Yes?"

"Mr. Baumeister, my apologies for bothering you at eight in the morning, but you told me that this would be a very good time to get hold of you. This is Jürgen Gehlen calling, from Nüselebank."

"Uh, yes?" Baumeister muttered.

"So, I'm calling about the loan extension."

Marlene and I looked at each other excitedly.

"I spoke with my manager. If you stop by within ten days and produce a signed, notarized, and legally executed sales contract to purchase the building, we will continue to finance the project. Otherwise, we will have to invoke the acceleration clause in your bridge loan, which will then be due immediately."

Baumeister hung up.

"Let's go and see what he does now," Marlene whispered.

We didn't have to wait long. Baumeister staggered up, took a shower, got dressed, and drank four double espressos out of his luxury turbo coffee jet. He kept grumbling "ten days, ten days" between his clenched teeth. Then he called a taxi and had it take him to . . . the convent. We were alarmed.

Marlene wanted to have a look at what was happening in all parts of the convent, so I stayed with Baumeister. He went into the room that the mother superior had made available to him for an office, sat down at the desk, and stared at the master site plan of the convent hanging on the opposite wall. He didn't move for half an hour. I got bored. Until Marlene came rushing over and warned me. We had company.

The mother superior entered the construction office along with a man who looked like Cologne's clone of Clint

Eastwood (even my editor is familiar with *him*). That's how he moved (i.e., very sparingly), that's how he squinted (i.e., his eyes were almost shut), and that's how he talked (i.e., not a hell of a lot). The mother superior introduced him as Gernot Schwegler. "He is going to be seeing to the security of our facility," she said.

Baumeister wearily got up from his chair, shook the hand he was offered, and sat back down.

"Mr. Baumeister, are you not feeling well? You look exhausted."

"I had a minor fender bender last night and I didn't sleep well," Baumeister muttered. "Nothing to worry about."

"But . . ."

"Mr. Baumeister, would you mind if we made use of your master site plan to discuss the scope of the work?" Schwegler asked. Totally Eastwood. Except dubbed. In Cologne dialect.

"Of course."

The mother superior showed Schwegler over to the large plan and explained what she wanted. Complete video surveillance over the entire exterior, with special emphasis on the gates, the gatehouse, and the main entrance to the church. Installation of an intercom system with an automatic release for the gate. Motion detector for nightly surveillance of the inner courtyard of the convent. Glass-break detectors on all windows on the ground floor. Electronic access control at all gates and doors on the ground floor, including the access door from the church into the convent yard.

Schwegler followed every gesture of the mother superior's finger on the master plan and listened carefully to her words as though he wanted to learn them by heart, which he apparently was doing since he didn't write a single thing down. Once she had finished, he repeated what she wanted back to her verbatim.

"When can you start?" the mother superior asked.

"Electronic access control at the doors and gates can be installed immediately. The procurement and installation of the cameras and motion detectors will take a few days. Today is Thursday . . ." He closed his eyes and didn't say anything for about four seconds. "We should have the equipment by Tuesday. Then everything will be done by the end of next week."

The man scared me. Marlene was also disturbed. And the mother superior seemed, well, at least surprised.

"That is delightfully fast," she said, but the hesitation in her voice clearly showed her doubt.

"You are under threat. Every day counts. A week may be too long," Schwegler said in his rough but soft Eastwood voice. I got an icy chill up my spine.

"I'm sure you'll need a written contract," the mother superior said.

"I'll prepare the contract. My coworker will arrive in an hour to secure the doors; he'll bring the contract and everything else we need. Then you need only sign."

The mother superior and her sacred security specialist left Baumeister's office. I hadn't been paying attention to him at all, but Marlene alerted me that Baumeister had been following the conversation very closely. Now he stepped up to the site plan and traced his fingers along individual sections. A nasty smile appeared on his face. Baumeister wasn't out of the running yet.

We split up again. Baumeister required uninterrupted monitoring, but we also needed to get at least some perspective on other activities going on in the convent. Marlene took over the first Baumeister shift while I circled over the grounds. The construction workers were busy with their construction work. They were raking out mortar joints, replacing porous sandstone blocks, and sealing foundations to keep moisture from seeping in. Nuns were cooking in the kitchen. The old radio was back in its place playing some talk show. The mother superior was making phone calls in her office; moles were playing in the dirt in the spring planting bed, and the novices, who were no such thing, were collaborating on a thank-you letter to their unknown hero. At least someone was doing something sensible!

I met Marlene, who was following Baumeister on a tour of the site.

"What's he been doing?" I asked.

"He's reprogrammed his cell phone, dropped off his SUV at a shop for repairs, and he appears to be feeling fairly upbeat again."

That was not good news. She promised not to let him out of her sight for a second.

Meanwhile, the employees of Gernot Eastwood had arrived. He had the mother superior sign the contract, and then he got to work installing his gizmos at the doors. I found it dizzying to watch the electricians at work. They crocheted all kinds of colored bands together, stuck wires into tiny clipped connection modules that reminded me of Legos, fiddled around with little power-testing dildos in outlets and other jacks, and—this really drove me crazy—they actually seemed to know what they were doing! I peered over the head electrician's shoulder once in a while, but otherwise I maintained my view of everything. The chief wiring guy repeated the wiring work for all the doors and gates, one after the other, except the gatehouse passage, where the kidnappers had come through. It was getting only a temporary security solution. Over the long term they were going to need a sturdy gate mounted at the outer opening of the passage, which was well worth securing.

Baumeister approached the wiring guy, said a few meaningless words, and made himself scarce again. Marlene, who'd been following Baumeister scrupulously, could sense that he was planning something, but she had no idea what she should be paying attention to. She asked if we could switch, so I spent the rest of the day with Baumeister, and she followed the electrician.

Baumeister remained a puzzle to me. Our sortie yesterday had left its mark on him, but he was slowly recovering. Plus, he definitely was up to something; you could just tell. What it was, however, I could not for the life of me figure out. This was not good. I had to terrorize him some more, but I wasn't encountering much in the way of opportunities. He wasn't driving a car, he was hardly making any phone calls, and when he did they were either on the landline or with his cell—but never with his headset. I was starting to get nervous.

Around five the construction workers and electrical assistants headed home; at five thirty the chief electrician started packing up his things, according to Marlene's update. The only other non-nun remaining was Baumeister, who was still sitting in his office sketching something out on some plans. The mother superior stopped in to see him.

"Mr. Baumeister, aren't you calling it quits for today yet?" she asked warmly.

"I'm revising the plans, which aren't totally up to date anymore since your decision," he explained with a strained smile.

"Won't you please come with me so the electrician can explain the access controls at the doors to both of us at once."

Baumeister jumped up and followed her.

The electrician told Baumeister and the mother superior how the access controls worked and then showed them how to arm the sensors for the individual doors using the security pads now mounted next to each door. Then the three of them headed to the main entry, which now had not only access control but also an automatic release with an intercom unit next to it.

"The doorbell is integrated with the intercom system, which has been mounted here in the gatekeeper's office. Tomorrow we'll run a connection to the administrative office, but we're out of time for today. For now I'll leave the box mounted on the wall like this, but tomorrow I'll recess it into the wall so it's flush. So whenever someone rings the bell, you can activate the intercom here. This button controls the door lock."

"And how does that work?" the mother superior asked.

The electrician looked at her, surprised.

"My apologies," the mother superior said with a smile. "I'm actually a bit of a technology geek, to many people's surprise, but I'm sure you're eager to head home for the evening . . ."

The electrician beamed. "It's not a bother at all. The opening of the door is now controlled by a magnet, which is recessed in the doorframe. If you press on the door opener here, it receives an electric pulse and releases the lock."

He explained and demonstrated its operation about five times until the mother superior was sure she'd understood everything. Baumeister also confirmed he could manage the system; after all, he had to come in and out several times a day, and he didn't want to bother the sister on door duty every time. With a satisfied smile, the mother superior said good-bye to the electrician, who left his toolbox in the gate-keeper's lodge, and she turned to Baumeister.

"Now I feel safer. After compline I'll do rounds and make sure all of the doors are locked tight, and then I can sleep reassured."

Baumeister nodded. "That's great."

"Is there anything else I can do for you?"

"No, thank you. I'm just going to finish one more little thing and then head home." The evil smile Baumeister had been holding back all day now reappeared, uncensored.

It scared us.

"Are you going to go pray?" I asked Marlene, since I assumed in her worry she would want to seek refuge among the sisters and the Holy Ghost.

"I'd love to . . ."

"But you want to be on standby."

"Yes, indeed."

I followed Baumeister back to his office and watched him wait motionless for seven minutes, and then he pulled on his jacket and clutched a few rolls of drawings and a cardboard box under his arm. He walked at a resolute pace toward the main entry. With two flicks of the wrist he could have unlocked the door and gone outside. The access control would then automatically kick in.

Baumeister did not go to the door. He set down his things and stepped over to the control box that the electrician was going to install properly the next day so it would be flush with the wall. He opened the box. Went to the electrician's toolbox. Used a screwdriver to loosen some clamps, reconnected a couple of wires in different terminals, put the screwdriver back, and closed the control box. Then he picked up his rolls and package, opened the door with his elbow, and disappeared in long strides.

I didn't follow him. Instead I slipped back into the gatekeeper's office, hovered in front of the control box, and tried to recall what I'd learned the past few days about electrical systems and electronics. It was not much, but what I did know was enough to stand my hair on end. The electrician had hooked up the door-opener magnet with a low-voltage signal. Baumeister had re-routed a hot 220-volt cable and connected the magnet to it. Now there was some serious juice running in a place that was not designed for it. But what was Baumeister getting out of it, if the magnet under the doorframe was electrified? I zoomed to the door and took a look at the antique frame with a loud question mark blinking in my head. The door was old, that much was clear at first glance. Five-centimeter-thick oak boards nailed in with iron mountings and hung on giant hinges. The original antique lock and handle on it were also made of iron, and that antique handle was as big as . . . *Oh shit!* The magnet was in direct contact with the iron lock! Iron conducts electricity. If 220 volts of juice sizzle to the magnet, then 220 volts would be coursing through the lock and handle too.

Anyone who touched the handle would get a tremendous electrical shock. And if someone like the mother superior with heart trouble touched it, she would likely pass through the threshold of the convent and proceed directly to the pearly gates.

We had to warn the mother superior. I zoomed into the church to find Marlene. They had just finished prayers. We were running out of time.

"The door handle is electrified. When the mother superior does her rounds here in a little bit, she'll get enough of a shock to finish her off," I told Marlene in a rush.

"How, what . . . huh?"

I gave her the digest version of the situation as we watched in horror while one sister after another left the church.

"What can we do?" Marlene asked in a panic. "We can't let her die too."

I thought about my options with some despair. Zoom to Martin and ask him to call the convent? That would take too long. Find someone close by using a wireless headset to make a call, like with Katrin's phone? Also too long. Trigger a short circuit in the system? Wouldn't work. We couldn't manipulate the electrical wiring.

One figure broke away from the group and walked toward the refectory. The mother superior. She started her rounds, checked the gatehouse passage and rear doors to the church, and approached the gate in quick steps.

"She's coming," Marlene shouted. "Think of something!"

"What the hell should I do?" I shouted back.

"No cursing," she yelled at me. "Better to ask for God's help."

I couldn't believe it. As if praying in a situation like this would help. I was about to toss some kind of smart-ass comeback at her when Leni in actual fact started to pray.

"Lord, we stand here before you as sinners. But we are not praying for ourselves."

"We do not stand here as sinners but as electromagnetic . . ." I began in a voice dripping with mockery, but then I experienced enlightenment.

"Electromagnetic waves" was what I was about to say. Electro*magnet*ic. The magnet in the door. Maybe I could send out a decent magnetic pulse. But how?

The mother superior had almost reached the door—only three steps separated her from death. She extended her right hand to grab the handle. *Now or never,* I thought, and bolted all the focus I had within me right into the gap between the door and the doorframe, where the magnet must be situated.

"Ooh!" the mother superior gasped in surprise.

The door popped ajar and in toward her only a fraction of a second before the nun had tried to grab the handle.

Wham! With the reflexes and force of two judo champions, the mother superior spun and pounded her shoulder into the oak door panel, slammed the door shut, and braced her back against it as she quickly sank down to the ground.

Whoa! Confronted with a door suddenly springing open, she immediately assumed it was another attack on the convent. This woman was on the ball—and in shape!

"Thank you, Lord," Marlene sobbed.

Silly cow. Actually I was the one who had saved the mother superior.

"Help!" the mother superior roared at such a volume it swirled Marlene's and my electrons up around our ears. The whole pack of sisters came running out of the refectory to the gate. One was holding something to her ear. Upon my soul: a cell phone!

"Yes, the Mariental convent." It was our trusty Mao frau who had the cops on the line, cool as ice like that one Charlie's Angel. The looks of a porcelain doll and the grit of Iron Man. "Probably an intruder," she said. "No, I don't know any more details. Our new access control system set off the alarm. Yes, please. Quickly. Thanks so much."

"We should all proceed to a room in the rear of the convent," Johanna said. "Mother Superior? Are you all right?"

The mother superior nodded, struggling back up onto her feet. Marlene and I had a scare for a second when she reached for the door handle to steady herself, but two other sisters moved in fast enough to help her to her feet. She rubbed her shoulder. The bruise was going to be impressive.

Marlene accompanied her sisters to the refectory while I flashed through the door and waited for the cops outside. However, outside the door I ran into none other than Siegfried Baumeister.

"Hello?" he called through the wood door. "Is there a problem? I heard someone yell for help!"

What was he doing here? Had he been waiting outside to make sure the mother superior was dead? Or did he have a guilty conscience and wanted to see if he could still salvage anything? Maybe put the wiring back the way it was before the cops showed up? Doubtful, but I couldn't be sure because I couldn't read his thoughts, and there was no answer to be found in his face.

"Please step away from the door," said a friendly voice from behind Baumeister. We both jumped. The cops had apparently arrived without their sirens because we hadn't heard them.

"I, uh . . ."

Now Baumeister had a problem. He had to assume that the first cop to touch the door handle would get toasted. And I suspected killing a cop would be going too far, even for him.

With bug eyes, quivering nostrils, and lips snapping open and shut, he looked both desperate and dimwitted at the same time. Seeming to make some internal decision, Baumeister closed his eyes and laid his hand on the handle.

— • —

It was Friday afternoon, shortly past one, when Martin's boss walked over to his desk holding his latest autopsy report. Martin removed his headset and looked calmly into his boss's face.

"This report is all in order, Dr. Gänsewein."

"Thank you."

"The issue of the ear . . ."

The colleague whose desk was across from Martin, who had assisted at the aforementioned autopsy, hid his wide grin before bending down low over his keyboard. He scratched his head with his crooked middle finger.

Martin continued looking at his boss innocently. "It was a spontaneous sneezing fit. I've never before experienced anything like it. I was truly relieved not to have injured either myself or my colleague."

"Yes, yes," the boss mumbled. "Certainly, I just mean that, well, it doesn't make a good impression in the report."

Martin looked guilty and lowered his head.

"Just delete that item," the boss said, tossing the pages of the report onto the desk.

"But Mr. Jansen was present . . ."

"Well, your report also makes no mention of the fact that Mr. Jansen spewed vomit down a full twelve meters of the hallway," the boss said warmly.

Martin nodded.

"So then we understand each other," the boss said.

As he was leaving the office, the boss practically crashed into Birgit, who only just managed to veer out of his way. They politely said hello to each other, and then Birgit rushed over to Martin's desk. "Have you heard? It's been playing on the radio for two hours. Baumeister is in jail."

Martin jumped up and hugged Birgit. "How did it happen?"

"They're reporting that a metal door handle at the convent had been electrified to kill the mother superior, who has a heart condition, but then at the last moment he grabbed the handle himself."

"Bullshit!" I yelled. "*We* saved the mother superior. Marlene and me."

Martin waved me off, mentally. He already knew the whole story; I had painted out every detail of my heroic mission the previous night in iridescent colors. But of course he didn't want to clue Birgit in on any of it.

"Baumeister suffered a serious electric shock, but since the police officer was able to tear him away, his injuries are not at all life-threatening."

"And the confession?" Martin asked.

"He had to spend the night in the hospital for observation, and all of the equipment in there was going totally crazy the whole time. There were constant alarms; at one point the nurse thought he must be dead. Around two in the morning he asked for the police to come, and he confessed. Apparently he was at the end of his wits."

Honestly, he didn't stand a ghost of a chance.

"Do you think the rejection of his loan extension made him confess?" Birgit asked excitedly.

Martin beamed at his sweetheart. "Without a doubt."

"Brownnoser," I mumbled.

"I've already left the office for the day," Birgit gushed. "I couldn't have concentrated anymore after all the great news. What about you? Do you have much more work to do?"

Martin blinked at his screen indecisively, but his colleague answered for him: "Martin's off for the weekend now too. I'll quickly proofread the report, and there'll be time to finish the rest on Monday. Ciao, you two."

He grinned at Martin, scratching his nose with his middle finger.

"That's right," Martin confirmed, also grinning. "Let's get going."

He tried to power down his computer, but I stopped him just in the nick of time.

"I want to write a report," I said.

"What kind of report?" he asked suspiciously.

"The final report about the case."

"What for?" Martin thought, now at maximum alert. He definitely was not interested in even more people knowing about the existence of the not-quite-dead Pascha

Lerchenberg, who had spent some time a few months back in Morgue Drawer Four.

"Just because," I said. "Have fun."

In fact, I soon learned, it feels fucking awesome to properly set out your achievements in solving a crime. It has nothing to do with showing off. That's just how it is.

Plus, I'd had this brilliant idea: I was going to publish my report as something made up. "Fiction," as my editor calls it.

For another moment Martin entertained his fear that I somehow was pulling a fast one on him, maybe planning to cramp his style with my scribblings or convince the boss once and for all that Martin was totally bonkers. But I really didn't have anything like that in mind. And he apparently believed me. He left his computer on.

And I proceeded to write everything down, eventually using Martin's software to e-mail the book to a publisher, which will publish it as a murder mystery. With the names changed so Martin doesn't get in trouble with the boss. We'll have to see how it works. Just in case, I didn't mention any of this to Martin.

Anyway, that night I spent hours dictating, and I didn't notice how much time had passed until it'd gotten dark out. I was in the zone. Sometimes that's how it is with us writers. Since I was bothered by neither hunger nor thirst, I just wanted to keep working through the night, but it occurred to me that I hadn't heard anything from Marlene since that morning. So I left the Institute for Forensic Medicine and made my way to Mariental.

Evening prayers had just finished when I arrived. The chapel emptied out, and then I was alone. Weird. Where was Marlene?

I waited half an hour. For nothing. I was super irritated. Evening prayers were usually Marlene's most reliable appointment of the day. Where should I look for her now? Maybe she was looking for me at the Institute for Forensic Medicine? Or maybe she was downtown in the cathedral again . . .

"Hello, Pascha."

"Leni! What have you been out haunting? You missed evening prayers."

"Time doesn't matter for me anymore."

She seemed somehow . . . different. Even more spiritualized than before. Kind, gentle, full of love. No silly giggling to swirl up her harmonious energy. Somehow . . . heavenly.

I was breathless.

"Yes," she confirmed. "I came to say good-bye to you."

"But where are you going?" I asked, even though I had an inkling of the bad news already.

"Into the light," she murmured.

"Have you been there already?"

"Oh yes."

"And? How is it?"

"Peaceful."

"How did you find your way?"

She didn't answer.

I was in turmoil. One soul after another was disappearing from this earth; I was the only one still moldering around here. Was I stupid? Or unwanted?

"Neither," Marlene murmured. "I'll take you with me if you'd like."

Boy, that was some offer. I kind of wanted to know in advance a bit more detail about what was in store for me there. It was supposed to be peaceful. I mean, peace is a great thing. But what did "peaceful" mean in this case? That all the souls spend their whole time sitting on a cloud singing kumbaya? Sounded kind of boring.

Plus, I would miss Martin. And Birgit.

"Could I come back to visit them sometimes?" I asked.

"No," Marlene whispered. "Honestly? I don't think you're quite ready to let go of this place."

Damn it. She was probably right. I liked it here on earth, even though I couldn't take part as actively in life as I used to. Bantering with Martin, watching Birgit shower, going to movies, hanging out right in front of the speakers at rock concerts and getting my head really and truly blown through—to say nothing of solving crimes that would otherwise remain unsolved. Not to mention that I was about to start my career as an author.

"I'm sorry, Leni, but I'm staying."

"I know," Marlene said.

Know-it-all.

"Farewell."

I felt a soft breath of wind, and then I was alone. On a Friday night in May. In Cologne. In Germany. I sighed. Maybe I could . . . ?

No! I pulled myself together. Just two more chapters to write and then—party time! Movies, whorehouse, emergency room.

In the end, I was still needed here.

ACKNOWLEDGMENTS

This time again, of course, a big, fat thank-you must go to my trusted forensic pathologist, Dr. Frank Glenewinkel. He pointed out to me that an electric bone saw will not saw off ears. I take full responsibility for the intentional disregard of this fact. Thanks also to all the people at my publisher, Deutscher Taschenbuch Verlag, and above all to my editor, Karoline Adler. She still believes this book is fiction.

Jutta Profijt

ABOUT THE AUTHOR

Jutta Profijt was born in 1967 in Ratingen, Germany. After finishing school, she lived abroad working as an au pair, an importer/exporter, a coach to executives and students, and a business English instructor. She published her first novel in 2003 and today works as a freelance writer and translator. Her first novel featuring coroner Martin Gänsewein, *Morgue Drawer Four,* was shortlisted for Germany's 2010 Friedrich Glauser Prize for best crime novel.

ABOUT THE TRANSLATOR

Erik J. Macki worked as a cherry orchard tour guide, copy editor, Web developer, and German and French teacher before settling into his translation career—probably an inevitable choice, as he has collected foreign language grammars, dictionaries, and language-learning books since childhood and to this day is not above diagramming sentences when duty so calls. A former resident of Cologne and Münster, Germany, and of Tours, France, he did his graduate work in Germanics and comparative syntax. He now translates books for adults and children as well as nonfiction material from his home in Seattle, where he lives with his family and their black Lab, Zephyr.